THE EXILES

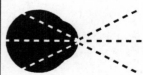

This Large Print Book carries the
Seal of Approval of N.A.V.H.

THE EXILES

GREG HUNT

THORNDIKE PRESS
A part of Gale, a Cengage Company

Farmington Hills, Mich • San Francisco • New York • Waterville, Maine
Meriden, Conn • Mason, Ohio • Chicago

Copyright © 1988 by Greg Hunt.
Thorndike Press, a part of Gale, a Cengage Company.

ALL RIGHTS RESERVED
This is a work of fiction in its entirety. Any resemblance to actual
people, places or events is purely coincidental.
Thorndike Press® Large Print Western.
The text of this Large Print edition is unabridged.
Other aspects of the book may vary from the original edition.
Set in 16 pt. Plantin.

**LIBRARY OF CONGRESS CIP DATA ON FILE.
CATALOGUING IN PUBLICATION FOR THIS BOOK
IS AVAILABLE FROM THE LIBRARY OF CONGRESS**

ISBN-13: 978-1-4328-6332-6 (hardcover alk. paper)

Published in 2019 by arrangement with Cherry Weiner Literary Agency

Printed in Mexico
1 2 3 4 5 6 7 23 22 21 20 19

To My Father and Mother
Will and Bernice Hunt
With Love and Gratitude

CHAPTER ONE

A low fog blanketed the ground, giving the camp an eerie, almost dreamlike quality. The rain had passed and the sky was clear, but the trampled ground between the long rows of tents and other makeshift shelters was still a muddy bog. In the distance a sentry occasionally called out a routine challenge, and here and there around the sleeping camp a chorus of muffled snorts and snores could be heard. Otherwise the place was still fairly quiet at this early hour of the morning.

Kneeling on the ground outside his tent, Jason Hartman heaped up a small pile of damp leaves and twigs, sprinkled a measure of precious gunpowder on top, and struck a spark to the lot. At first the gunpowder sputtered and threatened to go out, but then a weak flame appeared among the leaves and Jason carefully nourished it into a decent blaze. He continued to feed kindling to the fire until it was ready to accept a few larger sticks, and finally he laid a couple of decent-sized chunks of wood across the top.

Hard living and sparse military rations had trimmed every ounce of excess flesh from Jason Hartman's husky thirty-four-year-old frame. His thick dark hair and full beard bore a peppering of gray, a testament to the severity of frontier life, and beneath his tanned, weathered features was a distant expression of fatigue that seemed to tell of more than just the physically exhausting demands of a soldier's life. Uniforms were nonexistent in the militia unit to which he belonged, and the ragged garments he now wore had seen more than sixteen weeks of service without replacement. His trousers, supported by a length of hemp rope tied at the waist, were out at the knees and ragged at the cuffs, and his faded woolen shirt hung on his broad shoulders like a tattered, filthy rag.

Jason repositioned a chunk of wood at the edge of the fire with the toe of one scarred, decaying boot, then went back into the tent and retrieved the small pack containing his mess gear. After carrying his coffeepot to a barrel nearby and filling it with water, he added a miserly measure of coffee and set the pot in the fire to boil.

It was going to be a long day, with only the prospect of fighting and bloodshed at the end of it, and the least any sensible man could do was start it out with a cup or two of hot coffee, Jason thought. God knows it might be the only thing he had to fill his belly until they marched out of this desolate countryside and reached a more populous area where foraging parties could scatter out and seize the rations the twelve-thousand-man army so desperately needed to survive.

The camps of the various units that comprised the army were scattered north and south along a three-mile valley which bordered a small waterway named Wilson's Creek. Steep hills covered with trees and dense, almost impenetrable, brush loomed above the camp on both the east and west, and a narrow dirt pathway which scarcely deserved the designation of "road" snaked through the hills and across the valley from the southwest to the northeast. It was typical terrain for southwestern Missouri, remote, demanding, and splendid in its intolerance of all things weak and overly civilized.

Catching his first encouraging whiff of the bubbling coffee, Jason could not help but think of the sumptuous breakfast his wife Arethia was probably preparing right about now. There would be thick slabs of ham piled high on a long platter alongside at least a dozen fried eggs, and the three-inch biscuits, fresh from the oven, would be so hot that a man could scarcely stand to hold one of them long enough to slice it open and sandwich in a dollop of freshly churned butter. On the table there would be honey for the coffee, sorghum molasses for the biscuits, redeye gravy, a pitcher of fresh milk, and enough thick black coffee for a man to drink cup after cup until he sloshed like a water skin when he stood up. Arethia would call the kids at least twice before she began warning them of their fates if they didn't get up, and finally they would start stumbling into the kitchen one by one, still half asleep, mumbling routine complaints about the early hour.

He was supposed to be there, not here. In the back of his mind, that thought had been constantly nagging at him for over a month now.

Things had been very difficult four months before, in April 1861, when he signed up with the company of Home Guards which was being formed near his Clay County farm in western Missouri.

Their cause had been a simple and sensible one then, the kind of thing a man could easily understand and believe in. With the Union freshly split down the middle and armies massing all over America in preparation for open warfare, Jason Hartman, like the majority of Missourians at the time, only hoped his state could stay out of it and be left alone until the mess was settled.

The outfit he joined wasn't intended to be either a Northern or a Southern army. On the contrary, they had been told that their objective would be to prevent either side from dominating Missouri until the greater issues were decided somewhere on the distant battlefields to the east. By organizing the Home Guards, the Missourians could defend their property and their families from all interlopers, and then when the civil strife was ended, Missouri would be at liberty to decide her own position in the new order of things.

That had been the plan — but it didn't take long for the whole thing to go haywire.

In May a detachment of Union troops captured another Home Guard unit which was in training at Camp Jackson outside St. Louis. As the prisoners were being marched through the city, trouble broke out between the Union soldiers and the angry crowd of civilians that gathered to watch the procession. A Union soldier was shot and killed by someone in the crowd, and in the ensuing fight, twenty-eight civilians were massacred by the Federal troops.

In the aftermath of the "Camp Jackson Affair," Missouri Governor Claiborne Jackson, for whom the camp had been named and under whose auspices the Home Guard unit had been training, issued the call for men all over the state to rally to his banner. His message was simple — Missouri must defend herself against all such outrages in the future, no matter who the perpetrators might be.

Jason didn't mind going with his Home Guard outfit to back the governor's stand in Jefferson City. An almost festive atmosphere prevailed when they left their homes for the trip to the state capital, and the common belief was that they would probably be gone no more than a fortnight. It would be a display to show the Federal garrison in St. Louis how quickly the men of the state would rise up in defense of their own, and when the point was made, they would all be permitted to go home again.

As it turned out, Jason and his companions reached Jefferson City just in time to participate in a massive retreat from the capital. The call to arms had yielded far fewer men than the 50,000 the governor had hoped to raise, and the troops who did support him, by then under the leadership of the well-respected General Sterling Price, were pushed deep into the southern regions of the state by superior Federal forces.

For a while things just kept getting worse and worse. Price's poorly trained and ill-equipped command was ravaged by desertions, and for men like Jason who had no desire to make an open stand for either the Union or the Confederacy, it was alarming to see how quickly the army was aligning itself with the Southern cause. Suddenly they were rebels whose leaders now openly advocated Missouri's secession from the United States.

In July, when Price's army was joined by a force of Confederate Army regulars from Arkansas under the leadership of Brigadier General Ben McCulloch, it became abundantly clear to Jason Hartman that he was now involved in something far more political and dangerous than he had bargained for. He considered desertion. A number of his Clay County neighbors had already slipped away and started home, and he had no true compunctions about doing the same.

In the end, what kept him from leaving was the responsibility he felt toward those of his friends who had remained with Price. Some, like Frank James and George Todd, were so young that they had no real business being mixed up in a mess like this in the first place, and others, like Cole Younger and Bill Witherow, were as close to Jason as members of his own family.

In less than a month all of their short-term enlistments would expire, and if remaining until then meant that he might prevent the death of even one of his friends, it would be worth the effort.

But it wasn't easy. The situation in the state was so confused and the Home Guards had stayed on the move so much that not a single letter from home had reached him. He missed his wife and family so badly that at times the feeling threatened to make him physically ill. On numerous occasions, Price's army had run completely out of rations, and even such battle necessities as rifles, powder, and shot were constantly in short supply. Morale was pathetic, and it was rumored that their own highly regarded leader, General Price, was held in quite low esteem by the very Confederate leaders that he now chose to support openly. In general, McCulloch's regulars considered the Missourians to be nothing but a ragtag rabble whose value on the battlefield would be minimal at best.

But at least they now seemed to be on the offensive once more. They had been marching steadily northward for the past few days, ever since McCulloch's army joined them, and it was rumored around camp that a Union army led by General Nathaniel Lyon was moving southwest into the middle of the state to confront them. If they defeated Lyon, the entire north central part of the state would be open to them, and Price would almost certainly take advantage of the situation by marching his army back north to the Missouri River. From there, it would be easy for Jason and his remaining friends to make their way back home to Clay County after their enlistments expired.

The previous day they had been told to prepare to march all night toward Springfield, where it was said Lyon's army awaited them, but instead, heavy rains had kept them bivouacked here at Wilson's Creek about a dozen miles southwest of the city. This morning, though, with the rains past, they would almost certainly take up the march, and it seemed likely that before another day went by, they would face the enemy.

A few men were stirring around camp by the time Jason poured his first cup of coffee. Three or four times he offered coals from his fire to men nearby so they could start their own fires with the damp kindling available, but he was less generous with the contents of his bubbling coffeepot. If he was careful, he thought, he and his five tentmates might be able to enjoy the luxury of weak coffee for two or three more mornings. After that there would be no telling when they might ever taste the stuff again.

Jason rose and waved when he saw his friend Cole Younger walking toward him down the muddy path between the rows of tents. Cole had been selected for picket duty the day before and hadn't been back at camp since dusk the previous evening.

Cole Younger was a lean, rawboned man of twenty-three. On first glance he seemed to be barely twenty, but the determined set of his jaw and the cold, almost threatening directness of his gaze belied his boyish features. He was an easy person to be around, quick to laugh and always ready for any sort of adventurous diversion, but Jason also knew him as a man who could be fearless, deadly, and absolutely without mercy when the need arose. Despite the eleven-year difference in their ages, Jason Hartman and Cole Younger had forged a solid and lasting friendship during the period of savage warfare that had raged unchecked for the past seven years along the Kansas-Missouri border. In fact, Jason owed his very life to Cole's deadly accuracy with a gun, and it was a debt he would gladly repay at any time.

In addition to his field pack and rifle on one shoulder, Cole carried a bundle of wood under one arm and had a stuffed cotton sack slung over the other shoulder. Jason was glad to see the wood because it was always in short supply at every camp, but he was sure the contents of the sack would be even more welcome. It was undoubtedly some sort of food.

"We're in luck," Cole announced triumphantly as he dropped the wood to the ground and laid the sack down beside it. "I found some roasting ears in a field I passed on the way back from picket duty. The field was nearly stripped by the time I got there, but I got my hands on at least enough for breakfast for the six of us."

"Good work, Cole," Jason said with a grin. "When I got up, I figured we'd be marching all day again with our backbones rubbing against our ribs."

Jason got a bucket and filled it with water

from the barrel, then soaked some of the unshucked ears of corn in it and laid them in the fire to roast. While he was busy doing that, Cole gave directions to the cornfield to men from several neighboring tents, and encouraged them to get there as soon as possible if they hoped to find anything left. Several hurried away immediately, anxious for even such simple fare to ease the gnawing in their empty stomachs.

"How does it look out there?" Jason asked as he took a cup out of the mess gear and poured coffee for Cole.

"It was quiet all night," Cole said. "Some young kid from that Ozark outfit that joined us a few days ago got jittery during the night and popped a cap, but it turned out to be nothing. His sergeant came over later and bashed the kid in the jaw for causing a ruckus."

"Well it wouldn't bother me if we went all day without seeing a single Federal," Jason admitted. He reached out and gingerly turned some of the ears of corn in the fire.

"There's just no telling where we might run up on them," Cole said. "I heard that Ryan's cavalry was supposed to be out scouting ahead so we wouldn't be marching blind this morning, but when I passed by their bivouac a little while ago, it looked like the whole outfit was in camp. I just wish we had us some horses so we could show them what real scouting is."

"I could go for that idea myself," Jason said. "This being afoot does get mighty tiresome."

As they were talking, a sergeant came by and told them that they should be prepared to break camp and take up the march within the hour. Cole accepted the news without complaint, although it meant that after staying up all night on picket duty, he still had to face at least another twelve to fourteen hours on his feet before he had a chance to rest. But they had all been in the same position before. It was just another unpleasant part of military life.

"Well, I guess I'd better wake the others," Jason said. "If you want to, Cole, you could find someplace and stretch out while we pull down the tent and get it to a wagon."

"I don't see much use in it," Cole said. "If I got any sleep at all, it would only whet my appetite for more, so I might as well just stay up. If I'm really fagged later on, I'll catch me a nap at the noon break."

Just as Jason was about to step into the tent, a distant rumble to the south made him pause and gaze in that direction. Cole and most of the other men around had stopped what they were doing and were looking the same way.

"What do think, Jason?" Cole asked quietly. "Another storm?"

A bank of clouds hovered over the hills to the south, but they didn't look like storm clouds to Jason. A knot of tension tightened in his chest as he realized that the faraway sound they had heard was almost certainly man-made.

"Cannons, I'd say," Jason replied.

"Hellfire, what are they shooting at way down there?" Cole exclaimed.

"Probably us."

A moment later, two more distant roars sounded in close succession, followed by yet another. Jason guessed that the artillery fire was at least a mile and a half or two miles away, but in these hills it was hard to tell.

"Whose camp is south of here?" Jason asked Cole.

"McCulloch's regulars," Cole answered. "I guess the time has come to find out if they're as tough as they've been wanting us to believe."

"I'd say we're about to find out a thing or two about ourselves as well," Jason replied guardedly. He ducked into the tent to find that his companions inside were already awake and hastily pulling on their clothes.

"What is it, Jason?" one of the young men asked. His name was Frank James, a slim, smooth-cheeked youth whose boyish features and quiet ways made him seem entirely out of place in such a rough environment.

"Nobody's come around with any news yet," Jason said, "but my guess is the Federals have flanked our camp and are attacking from the south. All we know for sure right now is that some big guns have opened up down that way, and I doubt if all of them are ours."

In addition to Frank James, the other men in the tent were George Todd, Bill Witherow, and Sam Cash. Frank and George were by far the youngest members of the group, both being about eighteen years old, and Bill and Sam were in their mid-twenties.

George Todd was a native of Kentucky but had moved to Clay County the year before to live with an uncle. He and Frank James had become fast friends during his stay in Missouri and had joined the Home Guards together, almost as a lark, on the first day enlistments were allowed. Bill Witherow and his young wife, Eileen, owned a farm in Jackson County, south of where Jason's family lived, and he and Jason had been good friends for a number of years. Sam Cash, Witherow's brother-in-law, was a lazy, loutish sort of fellow who had lived with Bill and his wife before the war and apparently joined the outfit when Bill did only because he thought it might provide an easier life than dawn-to-dusk farm work. He had gotten more than he bargained for in Price's army, however, and only stayed on now because Bill threatened to turn him out if he deserted and went home before his enlistment was finished.

Jason Hartman had become the nominal leader of this small group, primarily because, at thirty-four, he was the oldest among them, and because he did have a semblance of military experience, having participated in the border fighting against the Kansas abolitionists several years before. While with Price, the six of them, including Cole, had participated in a few small skirmishes against the Federals, but Jason had an idea that today's action would try them as never before, and he wanted to make sure they were ready.

"Listen, fellows," he told the others as they continued pulling on their clothes, "if we get ordered out to fight, we have to stay together. As soon as you get dressed, the first thing I want you to do is make sure your canteen is full and that your spare powder and caps are wrapped tight in a piece of oilcloth in case we get another rain. Cole has some chow outside, and if you don't have time to eat your share, put it in your pack and take it along.

"Now, when the fighting starts, I don't want to see any of you trying to win the battle alone. A dead hero is no use to anybody. Stay back from the very front ranks if you can, advance when everybody else does, and fall back when everybody else does, too. It's going to be pretty damn confusing trying to fight in the brush and gullies around here, so we've got to take care of each other if we're going to get through this thing."

"We'll be all right, Jason," George Todd announced with bravado. "We've scrapped with the Federals before and we came out of it fine. Hell, I aim to capture me one of those new Spencer rifles they say the Dutchmen out of St. Louis carry so I can throw away this piece of shit they gave me to shoot with."

"Look, George," Jason replied tolerantly, "this isn't going to be like pot-shooting through the trees at a Federal patrol. We'll be going up against regiments of regulars this time, and I doubt that anything you've ever seen will have prepared you for what you'll face today. Just don't get too cocky, because I don't want to be writing any letter to your uncle to tell him how bravely you died."

By the time the five of them finished their discussion and got back outside, the artillery fire was thundering with increasing regularity. The whole camp had become a beehive of activity as the men took down their tents and prepared to leave, but as yet no one in charge had arrived to tell them what was happening or what they were supposed to do.

Jason and his companions folded their tent and placed it on a nearby wagon, then ate some of the roasted corn and packed the rest of their gear. Still no officer arrived to give them orders.

When a second artillery barrage opened up northwest of the camp, the men became visibly nervous and anxious to go. There was talk that they had been surrounded and that their generals had fled, leaving the army to its own devices, but nobody took such idle rumors very seriously. The Missourians had been following "Old Pap" Price too long to believe that he would commit such a craven act. Still, they were anxious to be on the move in some direction.

Finally a young lieutenant came riding furiously into the middle of the camp, and a host of men gathered eagerly around him as soon as he stopped his horse.

"The Federals have slipped up on us during the night. They've split their forces and are hitting us from two sides," the young man told them excitedly. "McCulloch's regulars are holding to the south, but Ryan's cavalry has been routed north of here and the Federals are starting to take up positions on Oak Hill."

"Where in the devil's Oak Hill, Lieutenant?" one tobacco-chewing sergeant asked.

The young officer turned in his saddle and pointed northwest to a hill which rose steeply above the surrounding countryside. "*That's Oak Hill,* goddammit!" he shouted. "And if Lyon gets his artillery in place up there before we can counterattack, you men will be eating cannon balls and canister for breakfast!

"General Price is bringing all his units on line to take the high ground away from them before they cut us to pieces," the officer continued. "This outfit is ordered to make a wide sweep west, until you're in place south of Oak Hill, and then to await the order to attack."

"But where in the hell's our officers?"

another man shouted out from the ranks. "Why aren't they here to give us our orders?"

"They're getting their instructions from Old Pap right now," the lieutenant answered. "They'll catch up to you before you reach the base of the hill, but right now the most important thing is for you men to get away from this open camp before the barrage starts. Now move out!"

A few of the sergeants tried to bring some semblance of order as the confused crowd of men started to trek westward to the base of Oak Hill, but on the whole the Home Guards still bore more resemblance to a mob than an army as they plunged into the underbrush on the west side of the camp. Cursing and sweating in the muggy August heat, they moved blindly forward, the brambles and scrub oak tugging almost constantly at their clothes and weapons, filled with that strange mix of fear and anticipation that precedes entry into battle.

The sounds of artillery fire both to the north and south continued unabated for the next quarter hour, and soon yet another battery opened up atop the hill to the west. None of the big guns had yet got their range on Jason's outfit, and he decided that the devilish underbrush they were passing through was probably a blessing in disguise because it concealed their movements from the enemy above. Instead, as the lieutenant had predicted, the shells were falling back behind them on the open camp which they had just evacuated. If they had remained there only ten or fifteen minutes longer, scores of them would already be dead or wounded.

A gruff, burly sergeant who had assumed command of the group until their officers arrived led them due west for more than a quarter of an hour before finally beginning to scatter the men out in various locations at the base of Oak Hill. By now a few random rifle shots were beginning to sing through the trees around them, but it was obvious that the enemy above still had no visible targets to shoot at and were merely firing randomly through the trees.

When the order came to disperse and wait, Jason and his companions slid down into a shallow gully and sat with their backs against a bank so the gunfire could not reach them. Their faces and arms were covered with small scratches and cuts from wading through the underbrush, but otherwise everyone seemed okay.

"I'd say Old Pap's crazy as hell if he expects us to charge up that hill right into the mouths of those cannons," Sam Cash commented nervously. "Those big guns will cut through us like a knife through butter before we make it halfway to the top. I say it can't be done."

"Why don't you shut up, Sam!" his brother-in-law, Bill Witherow, snapped impatiently. "Hell, you've got us losing the battle before it's even started good, and you don't know any more than the rest of us what's up there."

"I got ears, ain't I?" Cash protested. "I can hear that goddamn artillery up there. And besides that, with them coming at us from both sides, we won't have anyplace to run to if things go sour and we have to skedaddle. What'll we do then, Bill? Just answer me that."

"In that case, I guess we just won't run, Sam," Witherow replied. "Now why don't you just quit your bellyaching and stop trying to stir everybody up before we even start to fight."

"I'll second that idea," Cole said sharply. "If you don't feel like going up the hill, why don't you just sit here in this ditch until the rest of us are finished with what has to be done?"

Cash started to mouth off again, but then seemed to realize from the look in Cole

Younger's eyes that it might not be such a good idea. Instead, he picked his gun up off the ground, rose to his feet, and moved a few yards away from the others to grumble to himself.

The bullet that killed him entered his head at an angle behind his right ear, then tore the left side of his face off as it exited his skull on the other side. He fell so smoothly and silently that at first the others thought he had simply tripped. Frank James and George Todd even chuckled to themselves at his clumsiness. But then when he didn't move and made no attempt to rise, Witherow got up and started over to him. Half way there, his rifle dropped from his grasp and he bounded forward, ending up on his knees at the fallen man's side.

"He's shot, Jason!" Witherow exclaimed in shock. "He's dead! Sam's dead!"

The others gathered quickly around Sam as Bill Witherow gently rolled his brother-in-law over. The dead man's right eye stared up at the morning sky in amazement, and his mouth was still open slightly, as if he'd been prepared to mutter yet another complaint at the moment of death.

"Dammit, Sam! Why'd you stand up?" Witherow raged. "Why'd you have to get so mouthy and make us run you off like that?"

Jason stooped beside his friend and placed a hand on his shoulder, and the others, realizing they were just as exposed as Cash had been when he was shot, lowered themselves to the ground once more.

"I'm sorry, Bill," Jason said. "It's a hell of a way to go, getting it from a stray round like that."

"What do we do, Jason?" Witherow asked, his eyes still glassy with disbelief. "What do we do with him?"

"There's not much we can do right now," Jason admitted. "But when this is over, we'll come back for his body. As soon as we can, we'll get him buried right."

"But what if we can't? I mean, what if . . . ?"

Jason reached in his pack and took out a sliver of a pencil and a half sheet of crumpled paper that he had been saving for his next letter home. As Bill Witherow watched, he wrote:

Name — Sam Cash
Please inform Eileen Witherow
Jackson County, Missouri

Then he folded the paper once and put it in the front pocket of the dead man's shirt.

"That should do it," he said. "Now even if

we don't make it back, whoever finds him will get word to Eileen. So at least she'll know. And I'm sure a graves detail will find his body and take care of the rest. It's all we can do right now, Bill. It's all any of us can do for him."

A rustling in the brush above the gully pulled their attention away from their fallen companion and back to the battle at hand. In a moment a captain from their unit, followed by a lieutenant and two sergeants, came into view. Glancing down into the ditch at the five men gathered in a clump, the captain asked, "What's going on down there?"

"We lost a man, Cap'n," Cole Younger responded. "Sam Cash caught a Federal ball in the head."

"That's too bad," the officer said hurriedly, "but he won't be the last before this day's business is over, and we can't stop to worry about him now. The orders have just been dispatched to recapture Oak Hill from the Federals. We'll attack as soon as we can get the word to all the men in our regiment."

"How will we know when to go?" Jason asked the officer. "In this damn brush it's hard to see more than a few feet in any direction, and we won't know if everybody

31

else has started up at the same time or not."

"We've got a small, six-pound cannon in place off to your left," the captain explained. "When it's fired, you'll know to start up the hill. The brush thins about a hundred yards up the hillside, and when you get there you'll be able to tell whether or not you're in line with everybody else.

"It's vital that we take this hill, men," the officer continued urgently. "Colonel Blankenship's regiment is pinned down off to the east of us, and Lyon's artillery is cutting them to pieces. Their only hope is for the rest of us to knock out some of those Federal batteries as quickly as possible."

"We'll be ready when the signal sounds," Jason assured him.

"That's the spirit!" the captain replied. "And after we drive Lyon off the top of Oak Hill, we'll light out after him and dust his pants all the way back to Springfield!"

After the officer was gone, Jason and the others crouched down in the ditch once more, waiting grimly for the cannon shot that would launch them forward. None of them, not even Bill Witherow, looked around at the body of Sam Cash again, not wanting to be reminded in such stark and undeniable terms of what awaited them on the top of the hill. Although no more than a few minutes passed, it seemed like hours before a muffled boom to the left heralded the beginning of the onslaught.

"I guess this is it," Jason announced as he scrambled up out of the ditch and plunged into the underbrush. Glancing around as he advanced, he was proud to see that all the others were close behind. None had lost their nerve — not yet at least.

Occasionally on the left and right Jason spotted groups such as his skulking forward through the dense scrub oak, their weapons ready, but more often than not his small squad seemed completely isolated. For the first time he began to worry about whether an attack could be properly co-ordinated when the men were as scattered as their unit was. What if they began their final charge to the summit before the entire regiment came on line, or what if a portion of the regiment actually chose to remain behind, cowering out of sight in the underbrush until the fight was over? How would they know? In this chaos, how could his small group determine whether or not they were moving forward alone, or ahead of the others, to almost certain death?

When the underbrush began to thin, as the captain had warned them that it would, Jason became even more cautious in his advance. He and the others moved forward from tree to tree, remaining in the open as little as possible, and when he reached a point where he could see the smoke from the Federal infantry rifles billowing through the woods, he stopped altogether.

"What's the matter, Jason?" Cole asked from several feet away.

"Nothing," Jason replied. "I just want to wait here for a minute or two."

"Wait, hell!" George Todd complained. "We're gonna miss the fight!"

"Dammit, boy! Do you hear any of our people firing yet?" Jason snapped. "Do you want to rush out into the open before the rest of the regiment has come on line and end up like Sam did for nothing?"

"No, sir," Todd replied, subdued by the harsh words.

"Then shut up and follow my lead. I'm ready to fight with the rest of them, but I'm a lot more concerned with us staying alive than I am with taking a few acres of land away from a bunch of men I haven't got any real grudge against anyway."

As soon as the sound of rifle and musket fire exploded through the woods around them, Jason started forward once more. The Union troops on top of the hill had not had the time to put together any formal fortifications, but they had felled a number of trees to hide behind as they fired. When Jason came in sight of the first of these makeshift barriers, he stopped and fired his rifle at a flash of blue that he glimpsed beyond. The others with him followed suit, and then all took a moment to reload before advancing again.

Around them the pace of the battle was increasing. A chorus of wild screams echoed through the woods, some from men who had already fallen wounded, others from soldiers caught up in the sheer exhilaration of the fray. Soon the entire forest seemed to come alive with furious throngs of men who hurled themselves forward against the ragged enemy line.

Jason and his companions, caught up in the momentum, began to race forward with the rest, mindless of their fates, knowing only that suddenly the objective seemed almost . . . almost . . . theirs.

Without warning a cannon roared almost directly ahead. The canister round, fired at nearly point-blank range, cut a devastating swath through the approaching Confederate ranks. Out of the corner of his eye, Jason saw the round mangle nearly a dozen of his fellows no more than thirty feet to his right. Immediately he cried out to his companions, "The cannon! We've got to take the damn cannon before they can reload!"

Veering to the right, he charged up a slight embankment which served as shelter for the field piece, and suddenly he was among the crew that serviced the big gun. The startled Federal soldiers leaped frantically to retrieve their nearby rifles, but it was already too late for them. Jason shot one of them in the chest from no more than three feet away, then turned and plunged his bayonet into the throat of another. Close behind, Cole and the others waded into the fight, quickly dispatching the remaining three soldiers in the area.

Jason placed his foot on the chest of the dead man who lay at his feet, gave his rifle a sharp tug, and pulled his bayonet free from the neck of his victim. As he spun around he saw that the Federal line was being overrun on both sides, and the Union troops were withdrawing across the hilltop in panicky disarray. Somewhere down the line an officer seemed to be trying to rally the Southern forces to pursue the fleeing enemy, but his efforts were producing few results. The regiment had suffered heavily during the charge up the hillside, and for the moment the survivors of the attack were content to stop and gather their wits amid the positions they had just overrun.

George Todd immediately began sorting through the stacked enemy rifles nearby to find a replacement for the antiquated musket he had been carrying, and Bill Witherow and Frank James fell to rummaging through the dead soldiers' packs in search of food and other necessities. Cole moved over to stand at Jason's side, grinning broadly despite a bleeding gash across the left side of his neck.

"By God, we did it!" Cole announced elatedly. "I knew all along we would, but I never had any idea it would be this easy."

"We had them outnumbered maybe three or four to one," Jason explained. "I guess they didn't count on such a heavy attack on this side because of the underbrush. But the battle's not over yet, not by a long shot."

The sound of fighting coming from the other side of the hill served to verify his statement. In fact, their regiment had only captured an outer defense position on the southern fringe of the Union perimeter. The fighting still continued with unabated ferocity along other fronts.

Jason and his men eagerly distributed the stores of gunpowder they had captured with the cannon. Some of the men in the regiment had charged up the hill with only enough powder to fire their weapons two or three times, and none had enough to last them through any sort of sustained fight.

The officers had just renewed their efforts to rally the regiment and push on across the hillside when without warning the Federals counterattacked from the north. At first glance, Jason's worst fears were realized. The Union officers were making up for their earlier blunder by throwing a much larger force of men into action along this front.

The determined Southerners raked the Federal ranks with a deadly fusillade, but the blue-clad line faltered only briefly before pushing forward once more. For a time, as more and more troops appeared over the crest of the hill, it appeared as if Lyon must be hurling his entire army at this one regiment of civilian soldiers. For a while the Southern troops held firm behind the same frail barriers they had captured earlier, but soon their ranks began to thin alarmingly.

The first few men who turned in panic and began racing back down the hillside were called cowards by their fellows, but soon the trickle of retreating men became a flood.

"It's no use, Jason," Cole called out to his friend from across the cannon pit. "We're going to have to hightail it like everybody else."

"All right, but we can't leave the cannon here like this," Jason replied. "If we do, they'll be using it against us again ten minutes from now."

"Well, we sure as hell can't take it with us, so let's spike the son of a bitch," Cole said.

"All right," Jason agreed. As the others covered them, Jason and Cole searched desperately for a suitable sliver of metal. Once they found one they began to pound it down into the fuse hole at the base of the heavy cannon. When they had driven it in as deeply as it would go, Jason gave the spike a sharp rap on the side and broke it off flush with the cannon barrel.

Despite the fact that they were among the last men in the regiment to begin the embarrassing retreat down the hillside, Jason made sure that they didn't simply flee blindly toward the shelter of the trees below. Using what cover they could, they took turns loading and firing, covering one another as they did what they could to impede the Federal advance. When they were within about thirty feet of the nearest secure cover, Jason sent them racing one by one across the last stretch of open space to the relative haven of the woods beyond.

Frank James was the first to go, followed by George Todd, then by Bill Witherow, and finally by Cole Younger. Cole was only fifteen feet from safety when a Union ball found its mark, sending him lurching forward to fall on the rocky hillside.

"Shit!" Cole roared out, his bitter oath reaching Jason even above the din of gunfire. Bill Witherow ran to help his injured friend, but a hail of bullets from above immediately drove him back to shelter. Painfully, Cole pulled himself to his feet. A look of stark terror in his eyes, he scrambled down the hillside as quickly as his wounded leg would permit, but he only got a few feet before another bullet plowed into him. This time he didn't get up.

Seeing his friend fall filled Jason with a sudden surge of panic. He knew that if Cole wasn't dead already, it would be only a matter of seconds until another Federal ball finished him off.

Without thinking, Jason leaped to his feet and started across the deadly gauntlet of open ground. After only a few steps a bullet smashed into the butt of his rifle, snatching it from his hands, but still he raced on. When he reached Cole's side, he hesitated only an instant to grab his friend by the arms, then dragged him into the shelter of

40

the nearby stand of trees.

The entire regiment fell back at least another thirty or forty yards until they were deep enough into the underbrush to be clear of the worst of the Federal fire.

The Union soldiers above, who had been seriously bloodied in their counterattack, seemed content to halt their advance at the crest of the hill, and for the next half-hour the two opposing forces paused to tend their wounds.

Jason found a depression in the hillside which afforded them some slight protection from the Federal fusillade. There he gently lowered his wounded friend to the ground. He was surprised to see that not only was Cole still alive, he was conscious.

"How bad did I get it?" Cole asked, his teeth gritted against the rising pain.

"Your leg and your side," Jason told him. "I can't tell how bad yet until I get some of these clothes out of the way." With that, he fell to work with his knife, cutting away Cole's shirt and trouser leg to expose his wounds.

The bullet that had hit Cole's leg had missed the bone and Jason didn't consider the wound all that serious, although it would be causing Cole considerable pain for some time to come. The wound on his side seemed about the same. Although the bullet had gnawed a nasty tunnel through the skin and muscle just below his ribs, the wound didn't seem deep enough to have damaged any internal organs.

"Looks like we're going to have to put up with you for a while longer, Cole," Jason announced with relief.

"I'm much obliged to you for getting me out of the open like that," Cole managed to say. "After I got hit the second time I decided just to play dead, but it seemed like I could still feel half a dozen Federals drawing a bead on my backside when you came along."

For the time being, all Jason could do was bind the wounds to stop the worst of the bleeding. Both wounds would have to be sewn up eventually, but that would be a job for somebody else. Reaching into his pack, he pulled out a fist-sized roll of white muslin that he had carefully hoarded for bandage and cut a length of it off. He was nearly finished with the job when a boyish-looking lieutenant came scrambling through the woods and rolled into the depression where Jason and his companions were holed up.

"You men prime your weapons and get ready to retake the hill," the officer ordered. "We've got some unarmed troops fanning out through the woods to gather up the wounded, and your friend here will be taken care of."

"Are you out of your goddamned mind?" Jason demanded. "Hell, they just whipped us and ran us off from up there a little while ago."

"I know, but General Price has sent up two more regiments to help us out, and his orders are that we must take and hold that position."

"Well, you and the rest of your army can do what you want," Jason announced stubbornly, "but I won't leave my friend, not when he's hurt this bad."

The young lieutenant, his temper rising, drew his revolver and pointed it at Jason. "I could shoot you for refusing a battlefield order," he growled. "That's insubordination. Hell, it might even be called desertion!"

"That's a bad idea, Lieutenant," Bill Witherow announced from the side. "An awful bad idea."

The officer glanced sharply to the side and saw that Witherow's rifle was pointed directly at his head. Nearby, both Frank James and George Todd were also covering him with their weapons. Slowly the muzzle of his pistol lowered until it was pointing at

43

the ground.

"This is mutiny!" the lieutenant stated, trying to hide his fear. "When I report this, you'll all be shot!"

"Well then, maybe we better kill you now," George Todd speculated, "so you won't have the chance to stir up any trouble for us."

"Stop them, Jason," Cole interrupted, raising up slightly onto one elbow. "I appreciate the loyalty, but I don't want this boy dying on account of me. Hell, we're all on the same side, and he says there'll be somebody along to help the wounded pretty soon."

"That's right," the lieutenant said. "The two regiments that came up on line brought a company of unarmed men to carry the wounded to the rear. The word is that they've set up a field hospital over near Old Pap's headquarters. Your friend will be all right."

"You'd better be telling us the truth, Lieutenant," Jason cautioned the young officer, "because your life might depend on it."

Seeing that things were back on the right track, the officer chose to ignore Jason's threat. "We've got two cannons on line now on the right flank," he explained, "and when you hear them open up, you'll know it's time to start the counterattack. Our boys are in bad trouble over on the east side of the hill, and it's up to us to break through and give them some relief by flanking the Federals on top of Oak Hill."

"What about McCulloch?" Bill Witherow asked. "Where's that cocky bastard and his hotshot Arkansas regulars?"

"I don't know," the lieutenant admitted. "I heard he stopped the Federals from flanking us on the south, but there's no word whether he'll be able to cut loose now and give us a hand. But we can do it on our own. Even if we aren't regulars yet, we've got the best damn troops and the best damn general in the Confederate army, and if Nathaniel Lyon thinks he can just stroll in here —"

His diatribe was interrupted by the unexpected roar of cannon fire off to the right.

"That's it! That's the signal, so move out," the young officer announced excitedly. And with that, he scrambled up out of the depression and off across the forest floor.

Turning back to his wounded friend, Jason said, "I hate leaving you like this, Cole. It seems cowardly . . . almost criminal."

"It would be even worse not to take that damn hill back after all it cost us to get it the first time," Cole muttered. "Hell, even if somebody doesn't come along to take me down, I know one of you will come back for

45

me. I'm not worried about it."

"All right, then," Jason said reluctantly, "we'll go." Then, turning to the others, he asked, "Are you boys ready?"

"We are," Frank James replied. "But you haven't got a rifle, Jason. What are you going to fight with?"

"There's plenty of weapons scattered all over. I'll find myself something to shoot with. Now come on. We might as well get this thing over with."

They started once more up the long, bloody hillside. With the concentration of Federal troops on the hilltop, the firing was even heavier than before, but they made their way steadily forward, dodging from one piece of cover to another. Along the way, Jason pulled a rifle from the fingers of a fallen comrade, then, crouched behind a rock, he quickly loaded it and checked it over to make sure it was still in working condition.

When they reached the open ground beneath the Union positions once more, a host of other men were already advancing up the hillside ahead of them. Their front ranks were being devastated by the heavy enemy fire, but the pace of the attack never slackened. Fierce hand-to-hand fighting followed as the first of the Confederates overran the Federal positions, and for a time it seemed as if neither would give an inch until one army or the other was totally annihilated.

Jason and his companions reached the crest of the hill and waded into the fray with everybody else. After firing their rifles, they charged on with fixed bayonets, slashing and battering everything in their path. Out of their small group, Frank James went down first, shot in the chest, and Bill Witherow soon followed, his right leg nearly severed from his body by a Federal saber.

Jason saw them fall, but he could not even pause for an instant to help them out. It was a matter of survival now, a fight to the death against a deadly, determined foe. He had lost sight of everyone he knew by that time, but still there was nothing he could do except fight on.

Slowly, reluctantly, the Union troops began to fall back, still contesting every inch but no longer able to hold their own against the enraged, relentless Confederates. Jason pushed on with the others across the flat, open area atop Oak Hill, knowing that if the momentum of their charge faltered for even an instant, they would have to fight off an immediate counterattack.

At one point Jason paused atop a slight

rise to kneel and reload his rifle. As he was ramming the charge home, he glanced to the right and saw that, no more than two hundred yards away, other units in Price's army were advancing with equal determination up the east slope of the hill. He realized then that the battle was won. When the two fronts converged, the Federal army would have to give up all hope of holding the hill. Their only recourse would be to try to minimize their losses as they withdrew entirely from the battle.

A canister round exploded no more than fifteen yards away from him just as Jason was rising to continue his advance. He never really even heard it. The impact of the explosion hurled his body backward several feet, then deposited it, bleeding and nearly lifeless, atop the mutilated corpse of an enemy soldier.

CHAPTER TWO

Eliza Franklin was waiting in the wings with a bundle of roses in her arms as Mollie Hartman left the stage following her second curtain call. Mollie knew who the flowers were from without even looking at the card. Major Rudolph Benjamin had been sending her roses every night for a week now, and every night during that same week he had been seated in the front row during her portrayal of Emily Jasmine in the play *Oh Thou Cruel Fate!*

"Tell the gentleman that I'm still not able to join him for dinner," Mollie instructed as she started toward her dressing room, followed closely by Eliza, her dresser and personal maid. "I'm simply too exhausted after tonight's performance to even consider going out."

"Yes ma'am," Eliza answered. "And what shall I do about the flowers?"

"The ones in my dressing room are still

fresh, so why don't you take these home with you," Mollie suggested. Then she added lightly, "And you can have the gentleman as well if he suits your fancy."

"He is a handsome fellow, Miss," Eliza admitted and smiled, "but I think my man Abe would have something to say about such carryings on."

"Well, in any case, after you've gotten rid of him, hurry on back to my dressing room. I really am tired tonight, and I'd like to get changed and go home as soon as possible."

"Yes, ma'am," Eliza answered as she turned to carry out her assignment.

Mollie entered her dressing room and locked the door, then poured herself a small glass of sherry to drink while she waited for Eliza to return. If she had to, she could have got herself out of the elaborate assemblage of petticoats, corset, and gown that she wore for her role, but it was much easier with the help of her dresser.

Her thoughts turned to Captain Benjamin, and she wondered if tonight might be the night that he finally gave up trying to court her. He was, in fact, just the most recent of a string of local businessmen and military officers who sought to woo and win her. But despite the constant attentions she received, Mollie did not delude herself into

50

thinking that any of her would-be suitors had anything approaching honorable intentions toward her.

She was an actress, the oppressed and long-suffering heroine in a continuous string of popular melodramas. As such, she was fair game for a multitude of local rogues and dandies who considered the conquest of a woman like her the ultimate sport. But she had known what she was getting into when she began her stage career, and in truth she really didn't mind the succession of slick, smiling men who seemed to be constantly waiting in the wings with flowers, gifts, and invitations.

In fact, her unearned reputation as an elusive yet highly desirable temptress was good for business at the theatre, which in turn increased her pay for each successive production.

Sipping the sherry, Mollie considered the many changes that had taken place in her life over the past three years since she'd left her brother's farm and moved to Kansas City. At first she had worked as a seamstress, producing gowns and day wear for the wealthy society ladies who lived in the fine big houses up on Quality Hill. Later a local theatre manager named Brian Kerr had contracted with her to begin producing costumes for his productions. From that point she had progressed to playing minor roles in his plays.

After that, it took Mollie only a matter of months to advance from small background parts to leading roles. She seemed at once both an innocent and a seductress, and she had a natural talent for injecting force and believability info the mundane, and often ridiculous, lines she delivered on stage. She had the power to stir her audiences to tears, anger, joy, or any other emotion required by the script; and attendance at her performances had steadily risen during the eighteen months that she had been a leading actress.

A light tapping sounded on the door and Eliza called out from the other side, "Miss, it's me." Mollie rose and let her maid in, then relocked the door behind her. Occasionally, particularly aggressive suitors had felt it was their privilege to barge into her dressing room without any invitation, and so she had learned to keep the door locked whenever she didn't want to be disturbed.

With Eliza's help, Mollie began to remove the confining costume she had worn on stage. The dress, a strapless blue silk affair which she always donned for the villain-gets-his-just-deserts finale of the play, went first. Then the dozen silk petticoats came off, and finally Eliza moved around behind Mollie and went to work on the straps of the corset which daily reduced her waist to a twenty-inch circumference.

"Lord, Miss Mollie," Eliza exclaimed, "I don't see how you stand wearing a contraption such as this, even if it is only for two hours every day. There ain't a thing in the world wrong with the middle that God gave you, and I can't understand why you need to make it any littler than it already is."

"Proper young ladies who are nearly forced to marry wicked old bankers always have tiny waists," Mollie explained and laughed, "My goodness, Eliza. Don't you know anything at all about life?"

"I know one thing," Eliza responded. "I know if the Lord had seen fit to give me the same kind of package you're wrapped up in, you wouldn't ever catch me strangling it around the middle trying to make it any better." As she said that, she finished with the last strap, peeled the corset away, and Mollie enjoyed the luxury of her first full breath in more than two hours.

Not wanting to start re-dressing immediately, Mollie went to her dressing table and refilled her small sherry glass, then poured another glass for Eliza. The maid had been with Mollie almost since the start of her acting career, and the sherry was one of the small things they often shared as friends after a long, tiring day.

Opening the front of her light silk chemise, Mollie went to her mirror and examined the red indentations that the corset had left on her skin. Then she took some lightly scented oil and rubbed it onto the marks. Since moving to the city, Mollie had made special efforts to care for her body and her skin, knowing that the careers of most actresses lasted only as long as their looks. The results of her efforts were strikingly evident.

What the maid had said about her form was entirely true. Although not petite, her body was shapely and well-proportioned. Her breasts were full but not overly large, and her naturally slim waist tapered out gracefully to meet her trim, well-defined hips. She stood five feet five inches tall, but her long, slender legs made her seem a bit taller than that.

Her hair was silken blonde, with light, natural waves which outlined her finely formed features. She was not what most men would have called strikingly pretty, but she had a calm, elusive sort of beauty which added a subtle air of mystery to her appearance. Instead of staring at her in simple appreciation of her good looks, men often seemed to study her face, as if trying to determine what specific elements of it made her so inexplicably appealing.

Eliza laid out a simple cotton dress on the couch, then selected the appropriate undergarments for Mollie to wear with it. Mollie donned her street clothes without assistance while Eliza took a seat on the couch, pulled off one shoe, and rubbed the sole of her tired foot with the heel of her hand.

"It's been a long day, hasn't it?" Mollie said, smiling at her friend. Since it was Saturday, they had done two shows instead of one, and such a schedule always exhausted both of them.

"After forty, every day seems to wear you down just a mite bit more than the one before," Eliza said. "But I'll be home soon, and then my man Abe will make me forget about being tired."

"Well good for you, Eliza," Mollie said. Although she was not married, the maid had been living with the same man for the past fifteen years, and from all indications the two of them maintained a true and lasting affection for one another. Abe was a riverboat man who was gone for weeks, and sometimes months at a time, but Eliza always waited patiently and faithfully for his return.

"You know, you need yourself a man too, Miss Mollie," Eliza said. "Sometimes you just plumb puzzle me, what with all the fine-looking gentlemen that are always chasing after you, and you not ever showing any interest in any of them."

"I'll pick one out for myself one of these days, Eliza," Mollie promised. "But you know as well as I do that most of the men who try for me just do it because they want some quick pleasure. Take that Major Benjamin, for instance. I found out a couple of days ago that he has a wife and five children back in New York. But they're there and I'm here, and he thinks that because I'm an actress, it wouldn't do any harm to enjoy himself in my bed until the time comes when he can go back home to his family. When that's all that's available, I'll take nothing at all and be satisfied with it."

When Mollie was ready to leave, she sent Eliza out ahead of her to ensure that no would-be suitor was waiting for her outside the backstage entrance. Then she went out. They walked together to the corner. There Eliza turned north toward the riverside area where she lived, and Mollie started walking west. More often than not Mollie took a carriage home after a performance, but on this cool, early-September night, she decided to walk instead.

For her living quarters, Mollie rented a second-floor sitting room and bedroom in the stately Quality Hill home of Mrs. Genevieve de Mauduis. Although the elderly widow hardly needed the small rent Mollie paid her, she liked the company and enjoyed the presence of such an active, popular young woman in her home. The two of them had become fast friends, and Mollie considered the old woman to be, perhaps, her only true confidant in the city.

When she reached her home, Mollie let herself in the front door, then closed and locked it behind her. She was ready to start up the stairs to her room when she heard her hostess call out her name from the back of the first floor where the kitchen was located. The summons surprised her because the old woman was usually in bed asleep long before Mollie arrived home.

Genevieve de Mauduis met Mollie in the long hallway which led back from the front vestibule to the rear of the house.

"Why are you up so late, Ginny? Is everything all right?" Mollie asked quickly. The old woman wore a heavy chenille robe over her nightgown, and her thinning, silver hair was primly secured beneath a hairnet and sleeping bonnet. The tired smile on her lined features showed how badly she needed the rest that she was now missing.

"I've been staying up to entertain your visitor until you got home," the old woman explained.

"I have a visitor?" Mollie asked. "Who is it?"

"Come and see for yourself," Genevieve suggested as she turned and started back toward the kitchen.

Cole Younger rose from the kitchen table as soon as Mollie walked through the door. Spotting him, Mollie sprang across the room and into his arms. She kissed him warmly, delighted to see him so unexpectedly, then stepped back to get a better look at him.

"You look like hell, Cole, but it's still wonderful to see you back," Mollie exclaimed. "Are you home on furlough?"

"Nope, I'm out," Cole explained. "The war's over for me and Jason and the others that went with us."

"My God, you mean Jason's home, too? My brother's back home with his family again?" Mollie said excitedly.

"He's there, Mollie, but listen . . ." Cole

said hesitantly.

"Is he hurt, Cole? How bad is it?"

"It's not good, Mollie," Cole conceded. "You might have heard about the fight down at Wilson's Creek outside Springfield."

"We did, but I didn't know whether any of you were in it. The news we got was pretty confused."

"Well, we were there, and we whipped the Federals, but we got shot up pretty bad doing it. Sam Cash was killed straight out, and Bill Witherow died of a festered leg on the way home. Young Frank James got a hole shot through the side of his chest, and I got clipped in the leg and the side."

"But what about *Jason?*" Mollie demanded frantically. "Is he going to die?"

"We don't know yet," Cole admitted. "He got blown up by a canister round and he's got shrapnel all through him. They patched him up some and dug the worst of it out, but it still took us nearly a month to get back to Clay County, and most of the way we figured he might go any day. Hell, Bill Witherow didn't seem nearly as bad off as your brother, and he went in six days."

By now tears were streaming down Mollie's face. The news about Jason was devastating, and for a moment all she could do was listen in stunned silence to her friend's

59

revelations.

"I'm sorry, Mollie," Cole told her. "I'd just about as soon it be me lying up there as Jason. He saved my life at Wilson's Creek. The Federals got me with two bullets, and after I went down, he ran and pulled me out of the line of fire. But then the rest of them went on off to fight some more, and I couldn't go with them because I was shot. That's when Jason and Frank and Bill got it . . ."

His throat constricted with emotion, and for a moment he could say no more. When Genevieve de Mauduis moved over to place an arm around her young friend, Mollie turned to her and buried her face against the older woman's shoulder, crying uncontrollably. Genevieve stroked Mollie's hair with her hand, whispering gentle reassurance to her until she gained control of herself again.

"I've got to go to him," Mollie announced, turning back to Cole at last. "Will you take me?"

"Of course. That's why I came," Cole told her.

"Good. I can be ready to leave in thirty minutes," Mollie said. "Stony's in the stable out back, and I'll put on riding clothes so we won't even have to bother with a carriage. If we ride all night . . ."

"I don't think that's such a good idea, Mollie," Cole interrupted.

"What do you mean?" she asked in surprise.

"I don't think it's a good idea to start out tonight," Cole said. "The roads aren't safe at night between here and Clay County, and in the shape I'm in, I don't think I'm up for a fight with any of the Jayhawkers or owl-hoots we might come up against. This hole in my side is still giving me a lot of trouble . . ."

"Oh, Cole! I'm sorry!" Mollie exclaimed. "I wasn't thinking of you at all, was I?" She went to him and kissed his stubbled cheek in apology, then drew back slightly and examined his features once more with renewed concern. "The first thing we need to do is get some food in you, and then you need a good night's rest. There'll be plenty of time to make the trip in the daylight tomorrow, and maybe Ginny will let us use her carriage so you won't have to jolt along the whole way on horseback."

"Of course you can take it, dear," Genevieve quickly agreed.

Cole smiled to show his consent to the plans, then sat down in the chair Mollie guided him to. Within a few minutes, the two women had a feast of cold roast beef, bread, cooked vegetables, and apple pie laid out for him. Then, as he began to eat, Genevieve de Mauduis excused herself and started back to bed, knowing that the two young people would want some time alone.

"It's so good to see you again, Cole," Mollie said as she sat down across the table from her friend to watch him eat. "I thought about you and Jason every day while you were away, and I've written dozens of letters to the two of you. I don't guess you ever got any of them, though. I never really knew where to send them."

"No mail ever caught up to us," Cole replied, "but there were times when I would have traded anything I had for even a scrap of news from home."

"Are you really out of the war? For good?" Mollie asked.

"I guess I am. None of us knew what we were getting into when we joined up and headed out for Jefferson City. Your brother and I and the others thought we'd be defending our own state and our own people. None of us ever cared much about this secessionist business. I don't like the idea of not being an American anymore, or of seeing our state pull out of the Union to become a part of this new Confederate government they've started up down south. And Jason feels the same way about things. We talked about it over many a campfire."

"Jason . . ." Mollie mumbled almost to herself. The thought of her brother lying unconscious in his bed, riddled with wounds and near death, almost brought her to the point of tears again. But she controlled herself.

"Listen, Mollie," Cole said. "We've got plenty of reason to hope that he'll pull through this thing. There were signs that he was getting better just before I left to come down here. The day before yesterday he sat up in bed to eat, and the doctor said it looked like some of the worst of his wounds were beginning to heal. During the trip north from Springfield I was pretty sure we were going to lose him, but just being back with Arethia and the children has made a lot of difference."

"I just wish I was there with him already."

"You will be soon, Mollie. Before this time tomorrow, you'll be sitting by his bed talking to him." Cole paused to take a drink of the buttermilk Mollie had poured for him, then asked, "But what about your job here? What about your acting?"

"I'll leave a note for Brian Kerr before I go," Mollie said. "He's got a little girlfriend

63

named Kate Bonette who's been studying the script, and she's just been dying for something to happen to me so she could take my place in the play. She can't act, but she'll do until I get back."

"I've got to hand it to you, Mollie," Cole told her with a smile. "You've done all right for yourself here in Kansas City. You know, when you first told me you were leaving Clay County, I figured you'd just marry some fellow here in the city and have two or three brats hanging on your skirts before now. Instead, you're an actress and everybody in this part of the state knows your name. Why I'll bet you turn down a dozen proposals a week from wealthy admirers."

"I do turn down plenty of proposals," Mollie laughed, "but few of them are ever for marriage. This is what I want, though, right now. You know ever since I was a child I hoped that I could spend at least part of my life on stage." She paused reflectively for a moment, then added, "I know my family really doesn't understand all that. Right now, I guess I'm just as much of an embarrassment to them as I've always been."

"Your father probably feels that way," Cole agreed, "but I don't think Jason and Arethia do. They know you aren't . . . aren't like most actresses."

64

"I know, Cole, and I love them for that."

When he was finished eating, Mollie picked up the lamp off the kitchen table, then led him into the front part of the house and up the broad main staircase. At the second-floor landing, she turned and walked a few steps to a doorway on the right. Mollie opened the door and started in, but Cole stopped, looking uncertain.

"Come on in," she said encouragingly. "Before I left for the theatre this afternoon I asked the butler to bring a bathtub to my room and fill it, but it looks like you need a bath much worse than I do!"

"But what about the old lady?" Cole asked with concern. "She's sure to throw me out of here, and maybe you as well, if she finds out that I —"

"It's clear you don't know much about Ginny," Mollie said and laughed. "If she says anything at all about you staying with me, it will probably be because she wants to hear all about it!"

"I just don't want to cause any trouble," Cole insisted.

"It's all right," Mollie assured him, taking his hand and drawing him into the room. "I've told her all about us. That's probably why she was so nice to you tonight."

As Cole undressed and settled into the

65

tub, which was placed on a large mat in the middle of her parlor, Mollie disappeared into her bedroom. A few moments later she came back dressed in a long silken night-gown. Pouring two glasses of wine for them, she sat down on the floor beside the tub. Cole took a sip of the wine, then slid back until the warm water nearly reached his chin.

"You know, I was thinking just the other day about the first time we made love," Mollie told him. "It was only about five years ago, I guess, but it seems like twenty after all we've been through together. You were still just a tall gangly kid, and I felt positively wicked for seducing you, what with me being four years older than you and all. But even then there was something about you that excited me, something manly and strong, something that made me want to share myself with you."

Cole smiled, his eyes closed. "I thought I'd died and gone to heaven that day." He grinned. "You had a way of making me feel so special. Hell, you still do."

"You are a special man, Cole," Mollie said. "If I knew I could only have one friend for the rest of my life, it would be you."

"Well, seeing as how you feel that way," Cole said as he raised himself back up to a sitting position, "maybe you wouldn't mind scrubbing the back of such an outstanding fellow as me."

"I'd be delighted." Mollie smiled and reached for the washcloth and soap.

After Cole had bathed, Mollie got a heavy towel and helped him dry off. It was then that she got her first look at the angry red welts on his side and leg that marked the passage of the two Union bullets through his body. The leg wound was nearly healed, but the two round scars on his side, one where the bullet entered and the other where it left, were still puffy with a persistent infection and tender to the touch. Mollie could tell by the careful way that he stepped out of the tub that the injury was still causing him considerable pain.

"I don't have anything for you to sleep in, so the way you are will have to do," she told him as she led him to the bed. She turned the covers back, and Cole crawled under them with a deep moan of contentment. Before joining him, Mollie extinguished the lamp and then, on an impulse, peeled out of her nightgown.

The room was bathed in pale moonlight, and a faint breeze blowing in through an open window stirred against the lace curtains. Lying close beside Cole, Mollie put her head on his shoulder and listened to the sound of his heartbeat and his even breathing. To her they were like the voices of old friends too long unheard.

"Do you think the Union soldiers will leave you and Jason and the others alone now that you've quit the war?" Mollie asked.

"I don't know," he answered. "I hope so."

"Maybe you could try living here in Kansas City," she suggested. "I could help you find a job. You might even be able to do something in the theatre — carpentry work or something. We've always talked about being together, and this might be our chance to give it a try."

"The part about being with you would be good," Cole replied, "but I couldn't be happy here in the city. It's not for me."

Mollie started to say more, to suggest that he might change his mind if he just tried it for a while, but something stopped her. One of the things that had always kept them close was that she and Cole had never tried to change each other's lives. It would never have occurred to him to ask her to give up her life in the theatre and move away with him, so she had no right to make any similar request of him.

And yet there were times, like right now, when she thought that she must be crazy for not giving up whatever it took to be with Cole forever. Feeling the warmth of his strong young body against hers, she could recall no pleasure in life as fulfilling as that she had experienced in Cole Younger's arms.

But even more valuable to her than the physical side of their relationship was the depth and permanence of the friendship they shared. During the recent border wars with the Kansas abolitionists and Jayhawkers, there had been times when Mollie's very survival had depended on Cole's strength and courage, and he had never failed her. Nor had she him when the circumstance required it. Such shared experiences had cemented their friendship more permanently than any mere sexual attraction ever could have.

After a while Mollie realized by the evenness of his breathing that Cole had fallen asleep. Sighing in sleepy contentment, she snuggled even closer against him and did the same.

CHAPTER THREE

The darkened room where Jason Hartman lay smelled of illness and decay. He was covered with layers of quilts and blankets, defenses against the chills and fever that tormented him. Except for the ragged sound of his shallow breathing, it would have been easy to believe that he was already dead.

Arethia, Jason's wife, had come in with Mollie when she first entered the room, but then, sensing that Mollie wanted to spend a few minutes alone with her brother, she slipped out of the room and eased the door closed behind her.

For a while Mollie just stood at the bedside, a look of concern on her face as she studied Jason's ashen features in the dim light. A bandage concealed his left eye and the entire left side of his face and head. There was a deep gash, now almost healed, down his right cheek, and another puffy red scar on his right temple near the hairline. Without having to look, she knew that beneath the blankets he probably bore many other scars and festering wounds. The shrapnel from the canister round that had wounded him had peppered him from head to foot. If he had been any closer to the exploding artillery round he'd have been ripped to pieces, she thought.

The sight of her injured brother jarred her to the core of her being, disturbing her so profoundly that even tears seemed inadequate to express the depth of her sorrow. He had always been so vital and active, always the one that everyone else looked to for strength and the will to persevere through the hardest of times. She could not quite imagine what the world would be like if he was no longer in it.

At first she had thought he was asleep or unconscious, but after a moment he opened his right eye slightly and looked up at her. Jason seemed as if he was trying to smile as he whispered her name. Then a hand appeared from under the edge of the blanket and she grasped it eagerly.

"I'm glad you came, little sister," Jason whispered weakly.

"The whole Union army couldn't have kept me away," Mollie said.

"Cole tells me we won the fight, but you couldn't tell it from the looks of me, could you?" He chuckled at his own remark, then winced at the pain the slight movement caused.

"Well, I just hope it's the last one you're ever in," Mollie replied. "We need you here too much to have you going out all the time and getting yourself battered up like this."

"Arethia says the same thing, but you don't have to worry. I don't think I've got much fight left in me. Matter of fact, I don't feel like doing much of anything these days except sleeping. Just sleeping . . ."

During the long moment of silence that followed, Jason's eyes sagged closed and Mollie knew that he had faded into unconsciousness. Arethia had warned her that he drifted in and out like that. Even a minute or two of conversation exhausted him, and sleep was the only true defense he had against the pain.

She stayed with him a short time longer, then turned and went back out of the room. Now that she had seen him and he knew she was there, what he needed more than her company was rest and quiet.

She found Cole and Arethia in the kitchen. Cole was sitting at the table with a cup of coffee in front of him, and her sister-in-law was putting the finishing touches on supper. Mollie poured herself a cup of coffee from the pot on the stove, then sat down beside Cole. She was still shaken by the sight of her brother, but was hesitant to discuss her feelings with Arethia for fear of adding to her sister-in-law's worries. Instead, she brought up an entirely different topic.

"You say Dad is here today?" she asked.

"Yes, he and the boys are still out working in the fields, but they should be in any time now," Arethia answered. "It's almost night, and in another half-hour it will be too dark for them to work."

"Why is he working over here instead of at his own place?" Mollie asked.

"Your father has most of his land rented out this year," Arethia explained. "With Jason gone most of the spring and summer we decided that he and the boys couldn't keep both places going, so he leased all but forty acres of his crop land to Abe Drury. Now he and the boys go back and forth, working three days on one place and then three days on the other. They found out they can get more done when they work together, and this way John and Daniel are always there to do the heaviest jobs that Will shouldn't be taking on. For a sixty-seven-year-old man your father is in remarkable shape, but he can't do everything that he used to."

"If he weren't so bullheaded he would hire some men to help out," Mollie complained. "With a farm that size, he could afford to work the whole place with hired labor and never have to lift a finger himself except to oversee."

"He had some cash back in February, and he and Jason talked about that very thing. But then when the Home Guard was formed, your father donated the money for guns and supplies instead. He said that if he was too old to fight, the least he could do was pay for some of the powder and shot that our boys used to kill Federals. You know how he is."

"Yes, I know how he is," Mollie said.

Will Hartman, Jason and Mollie's father, was a Southerner to the core. He had lived in Virginia for most of his life and had only been persuaded to move to Missouri after his oldest son, William, had been killed and left his large holdings to his father. Prior to his death, William had worked the farm with the aid of a dozen slaves, but the slaves had been stolen at the same time that their owner had been murdered by Kansas aboli- tionists, and old Will Hartman had chosen not to replace them.

Even in the early days in Virginia when he was struggling to raise a family of eight children, Will Hartman had never opted to own black men as farmhands. It wasn't so much that he was opposed to the institution of slavery as the fact that he simply preferred that he and his family work their own land with their own hands. He believed that if a man labored to break the soil, planted the seeds with his own hands, and worked himself half to death harvesting the crop, then he understood as others couldn't what his life was all about. He knew the price to be paid for what he had, and he knew the reward.

Jason held many of the same beliefs that his father did. When he moved his family west in 1854, accompanied by Mollie and another brother, Tyson, he could have set up an operation like William's and by now would probably have been as successful as William had been before his death. Instead, Jason had done it all on his own, and over the years it had probably never even occurred to him to consider how much more he could have owned if he had followed in his brother's footsteps.

As the daylight faded and the kitchen grew dim, Mollie rose and lit the two oil lamps that hung by brackets on the wall. A few minutes later the rest of the family began to arrive for supper. The two girls in the family, seventeen-year-old Ruth and twelve-year-old Cassie, both had chores in the garden and barn to perform when they got home from school, and the boys, John, age eighteen, Daniel, age sixteen, and thirteen-year-old Benjamin, all worked until day's end in the fields with their grandfather. Harvest time was upon them now, and everything, even school for the boys, took second place to getting the crops out of the fields and into the barns and storage sheds.

All the children were delighted to see Mollie, treating her as much like a sister as an aunt, and even old Will Hartman gave her a warm hug and a smile when he trudged into the kitchen. For a while the scene in the kitchen was crowded and confused as all the children jostled one another to get washed up and the women worked to get the meal of pork, fresh vegetables, and cornbread on the table.

Finally they all took places at the table, including Cole, who planned to spend a couple of days at the farm resting up from his trip to Kansas City. He had decided that later, when he felt up to it, he would travel on to Harrisonville, about fifty miles to the south, where his father now owned a successful livery business.

Even in Jason's home Will Hartman, as leader of the family, took the seat at the head of the long wooden table. Tonight Jason's seat, which was opposite his father's, was conspicuously empty, and the old man sighed sadly as he looked at it. Throughout the meal Mollie was plagued by a single thought which almost prevented her from taking a single bite of food. *It was like he was dead already.*

The night was dark and cool. After living in the city for so long, sometimes Mollie forgot how dark it could be in the country when the moon was down and most of the lamps in the house had been extinguished.

She had walked up to the barn with Cole, carrying a pillow and a couple of quilts to make his bed for the night, and then had stayed on for a while talking about the feelings she had kept locked up inside all through the evening. Now, on her way back, it looked as if everyone in the house had gone to sleep, and the house itself seemed little more than a faint charcoal apparition outlined vaguely against the backdrop of the inky night. But she knew the path well and her steps never faltered as she headed toward the front porch.

Seeing a faint glow of red in the darkness on the porch gave Mollie her first clue that her father was still up, smoking a last bowl of tobacco as he often did before going to bed.

"Hi, Daddy," Mollie said, kissing him on the temple and then taking a seat on the edge of the porch at his feet. As he drew on the pipe to keep the fire alive, the red glow from within it briefly illuminated his face, giving his features an unnatural, wizened quality.

"Nice boy, that Cole Younger," Will commented without removing the pipe from his mouth. "I don't suppose your brother would have made it back here alive if he hadn't had a friend like that to take care of him."

"I've known Cole almost as long as I've been here," Mollie said, "and I think an awful lot of him."

"I noticed," Will told her. "Have the two of you ever thought about getting married?"

"We've never talked about it, Daddy," Mollie admitted. "I suppose it could happen someday, but not anytime soon."

"Well he sure beats the hell out of that Rakestraw fellow that you used to go with back in Virginia. There was a time back then that I thought that worthless rambler was going to completely ruin you even before you got fully grown, and I still wonder sometimes if it wasn't just by the grace of God that he got itchy feet and decided to move on again."

"That was a long time ago, Daddy," Mollie said. "All that happened years ago. Do we have to bring it up now?"

"No, honey, we don't," Will told her. "You and me haven't agreed on hardly anything since you were about eight years old, but I'm not fishing for a fight like the ones we used to have. I'm too tired, and I've got too much on my mind to want to fight with you about things that don't matter much to anybody anymore."

Mollie put her arm across her father's knees, then laid her head on it. "I love you, Daddy," she whispered. In response, Will reached out to stroke her soft blonde hair.

Mollie was the youngest of Will's eight children, and in many ways she was also the most rebellious of the lot. Since her early teen-age years, she had felt stifled and frustrated by her father's stern authority and rigid opinions of the way a woman was supposed to act. Looking back now, she thought that the two of them had probably never understood one another, but at least in recent years, since Will's move to Missouri, they had begun to accept each other and even to like each other.

"How's the harvesting going?" Mollie asked at last.

"Not bad, I guess," Will told her. "You never get as much done as you think you should, but you always seem to do enough to get by. If the rains will hold off another week, we'll have most of it in."

"I worry about you sometimes, though, Daddy. That's such hard work for a man your age."

"It's always been hard, but I've never known any different," Will said. "I wouldn't know how to stop working if I had to, and if the truth were told, I guess I'd rather go on to my reward walking behind a mule in the middle of a fresh-plowed field than I would sitting in a rocking chair."

Somewhere along the way his pipe had gone out and so he paused to give it the attention it needed. He took a match from his shirt pocket, used it to rearrange the contents of the bowl, then struck it and relit the remaining tobacco.

"You know the worst thing about growing old is outliving the people you love," Will said. "I lost my first wife way back in 'twenty-four, and then your mama in 'fifty-one. Both times I thought it had to be about the sorest trial the Lord ever gave a man to face.

"But then three years ago I found out what it was like to start outliving your own children. First William, and then Charles . . . I tell you, girl, there's something devilishly unnatural about it. It makes a man begin to wonder if he hasn't been on this old earth entirely too long. And then there was the way they died, all full of hate for each other, not caring any longer that they shared the same family and the same blood."

"It was a terrible, terrible time for everybody," Mollie agreed. "If there was even a single blessing about it, it was that you were still back in Virginia and didn't have to be here and see how bad things got toward the last."

Both William and Charles had perished within a week of one another during the worst of the Kansas-Missouri border warfare in 1858. But beyond their deaths, what made the losses even more tragic was the fact that the two brothers had been on opposite sides of the conflict that raged in the area throughout most of the 1850s. Charles, an ardent abolitionist, lived in Kansas Territory and actively supported the antislavery movement there, while William was in the forefront of the Missouri pro-slavery faction.

Mollie fell silent as she considered that brutal era, remembering suddenly the tragic secret that she, Jason, and Cole had kept carefully guarded for these past three years, a secret that each of them knew they must carry to their graves without revealing.

The times being what they were, all of them had been caught up in the savage struggle for survival along the border, and when their brother Charles had fallen in a battle at John Brown's prairie stronghold at Osawatomie River, the shot that claimed his life had been fired by none other than his brother Jason. He had done it to save Mollie's life, as well as his own and Cole's, and afterward the three of them had made a solemn pact never to tell another living soul the awful truth.

"I was in to see Jason after supper," Will Hartman said, breaking the long reflective silence at last, "and he told me how much it meant to him to have you here."

"There's no other place I could stand to be right now," Mollie answered.

"You know it's a funny thing about that son of mine," Will continued. "He's always thought and acted as much from the heart as from the head, and it's something I never quite understood about him. I remember when he was eleven years old he took on all three of those rotten little Parson kids because one of them had shoved Tyson down in the schoolyard. And then no more than a week later, damned if he didn't jump into Cane Creek when it was flooding and overrunning its banks, just to save the life of a little sooner puppy that belonged to the same three boys.

"I never could make anything out of it," Will admitted. "I couldn't figure out whether I was supposed to punish him for the one thing or the other, so finally I just told myself that that was the kind of person he was going to be and let it all drop."

"What's going to happen to him, Daddy?" Mollie asked impulsively, desperately. "I love Jason so much that I just can't stand the idea that he might . . . might die, but I still know that all of us loving him as much as we can won't help him now."

"Maybe love is all that *can* help him now," Will said thoughtfully. "It's like I've been saying: That son of mine fights from his heart, and if he's going to win this one, it'll be his heart that pulls him through. It'll be not wanting to give up all of us, and all of the life that he should still have left to live."

■ ■ ■ ■

In the morning Mollie rose early, borrowed an old dress from Arethia, and went out to work in the fields with the men. She had always hated farm work passionately, but she knew how much difference another set of hands could make in getting the crop in, and at the moment she had an even greater aversion to the idea of sitting around the house, idle and unhappy, while everyone else was occupied with their daily routines.

They put her to work driving a wagon past the rows of corn while John and Daniel walked alongside stripping the ears from the stalks and tossing them into the bed. In a nearby field Will and his youngest grandson, Benjamin, were digging potatoes and collecting them in large burlap bags to be loaded later on the wagon.

It had been quite a while since Mollie had spent any length of time alone with her two nephews, and she enjoyed talking with them as they strode along performing the tedious work.

John, the oldest, had grown remarkably over the past couple of years. He stood only an inch or two under six feet now and was already beginning to exhibit the broad shoulders and husky frame which was typical of the Hartman men. The deepness in his voice and his often serious expression reminded Mollie in many ways of her brother William, and the beginnings of a dark beard across the lower half of his face only served to enhance the youth's resemblance to his dead uncle.

Daniel, on the other hand, seemed to Mollie to be much more like his father. Although still a slender youth with plenty of growing ahead of him, he shared Jason's quick grin, casual manner, and steadfast dependability.

Unlike many brothers their age, John and Daniel got along well together, working efficiently as a team and seldom showing any desire to bicker or fight. It occurred to Mollie that these past few months while their father was away had probably required many sacrifices on the part of the two boys, but there was no sign that they resented any of the increased demands that had been made of them. In fact, Jason's absence and his participation in the war seemed only to have heightened their respect and admiration for him.

For a while Mollie's conversation with her nephews centered primarily on mundane matters such as news of the family, farm work, and events of the community. But eventually, of course, their talk turned to the most exciting and cataclysmic topic of the day, the fledgling war between the Northern and Southern states.

"I still wish Daddy had let me go with him when he went off to join General Price's army," John complained. "I can fight and I can shoot as well as practically any man in Clay County, and they took my friend Frank James quick enough when the call went out for men."

"I'm sure it all seems pretty exciting to you, John, but you can't ignore what happened to the ones who did go," Mollie reminded him. "I've seen men in situations where they had to fight for their lives, and I promise you that all the glory disappears when the shooting starts."

"That's what Daddy said," Daniel agreed. "He told us that a dead man doesn't have any way of knowing whether he died a hero or a scoundrel. He's just dead."

"Well, that's just the chance you take," John replied doggedly. "Frank and George and Cole and Daddy and all of the rest of them knew that when they signed on, and so do I. Shootfire! I whipped Frank James in a fair fight not six months ago, and that's not a thing many boys or grown men in this county can say they did. I'm not afraid to face what comes just like they did!"

Mollie knew it would be pointless to try to dissuade her nephew from his vision of glory and conquest on the battlefield. Even the sight of his own father lying maimed and near death seemed not to have done that. In these dangerous and uncertain times, fighting had almost become a way of life, and it was natural for a youth like John to want to prove his manhood with feats of courage. Still, she hated to see him in such a hurry to go to war.

They moved along down the rows of corn for another few feet, each lost in thought.

"When they brought Daddy home and I saw what the Federals had done to him," John said, breaking the silence at last, "I swore I'd make them pay. They've got no right to come into our state and try to run roughshod over us like this."

"But they're trying to hold the Union together, John," Mollie pointed out, "and I can't really find it in me to fault them for that. I don't like to see blue uniforms everywhere I go any more than you do, but I don't like the idea of the South trying to draw us into their squabbles either."

"I don't know about that," John admitted. "I don't really understand all those things.

But I know it's not right for a bunch of outsiders to come in here and try to run our lives for us. Grandpa says we'd be all right if they'd just leave us alone. We know how to run our own lives and make our own decisions."

"Ah yes, your grandfather . . ." Mollie said. She had suspected that she was beginning to hear the old man's words spoken in her nephew's voice.

"The only thing is," John continued, hardly noticing the interruption, "I don't know where to go or what to do to join up. The Federals are the only ones doing any recruiting around here now, and the Home Guards that Daddy was with are way off down in Arkansas."

"Well, you'll have your chance, I'm sure, if your mind is made up," Mollie said.

"I'll have my chance," John agreed.

They worked along in silence for another minute, then Daniel spoke up. "You know, Aunt Mollie, John hasn't said anything to Mama about leaving. We don't talk about it around her. What with taking care of Daddy and all, she has enough to worry about already."

"I understand," Mollie said, nodding her willingness not to mention this conversation. It was kind of them to want to protect

88

their mother, Mollie thought, but it was also pointless. Arethia had seen her husband go off to fight too many times not to understand the angry emotions that trying times stirred in the hearts of men. Now, as this ugly mess just began to gather its momentum and exact its toll, Arethia, perhaps more than anyone else in the family, would know the price that she and the people she loved would soon be required to pay. John's leaving might not be discussed aloud like the weather or the price of corn, but Mollie felt certain that it still haunted Arethia's thoughts like a nightmare that refused to end when the morning came. First Jason, then John . . . and then, if the war should drag on, how many of her sons after that . . . ?

They worked throughout the day, gathering the bounty that the land had yielded, then headed to the house only after it became too dark to continue. After supper Mollie checked in on her brother briefly, but he did not open his eyes when she stood by the edge of the bed gazing down at him, so she did not disturb him. Arethia reported that he had had a mixed day. In the morning he had been able to sit up in bed and had even eaten a few bites of solid food, but later his fever had flared up again and the long, hot afternoon had been a difficult one for him. After all the days and weeks of suffering, still he teetered on the edge of the chasm.

Mollie slept soundly that night, craving the rest like some exhausted animal and grateful for the escape the few hours of deep sleep provided her. In the morning she stayed at the house to see Cole off and wish him safety during his trip to Harrisonville, then she returned again to the fields to spend the remainder of the day working alongside her father and nephews.

CHAPTER FOUR

April 1862

A dozen men rode in the vanguard, tall, dusty, determined-looking horsemen, men that no sensible person would dare delay for even a moment by inquiring about their destination or their intentions. Each carried a Sharps rifle, either in a scabbard on his saddle or lying across his lap, and the variety of their additional armaments covered the spectrum of lethal weapons: pistols, sabers, long bowie knives, even a second rifle or shotgun for some. Their mission was primarily to serve as scouts, to ensure that the main body of men behind them was not caught off guard by any sort of trap or ambush.

About a quarter mile behind them rode a force of more than one hundred mounted men. They could scarcely be described as soldiers. None wore anything resembling a uniform, and none had ever bothered to enlist in any formal military organization. Their authority was derived solely from their numbers, their multitude of weapons, and the fearsome reputation of the man who rode proudly at the head of the column.

James H. Lane's career on the western frontier had been varied and violent. When he first came west in the early 1850s, his apparent intentions had been to serve as a champion of the pro-slavery cause. The reception he had received from the slavery advocates along the Kansas-Missouri border must have been something less than he expected, however, because he soon began to appear at abolitionist meetings and rallies, violently damning the same cause he had so recently supported.

During the worst of the trouble between pro- and antislavery forces in the late 1850s, Lane exhibited an amazing ability to be where the fighting was *not* taking place. Despite that, his natural ability to gather a following behind him, and then to incite those followers to a deadly pitch of righteous anger, thrust him frequently into the limelight during those sad, chaotic years.

To some, the mere mention of Jim Lane's name stirred images of hordes of angry abolitionists charging fearlessly against their enemies, giving no quarter and expecting none in the battle to free all black men and women from oppression and servitude. Whether or not that image was heroic or nightmarish eventually came to depend on which side of the border you lived on.

Lane was a tall, angular man with a frame that looked to be forged of nothing more than lean meat and bones. His voice was deep and confident, automatically capturing the attention of anyone who listened to him, and his power with words had over the years earned him the grudging respect of many a rival politician and orator. He seemed to look angry most of the time, an expression he carefully cultivated, and it was said that his heart turned to pure stone whenever his eyes fell on any man who continued to support the subjugation of other human beings.

The war had come at an opportune time for Lane. After Kansas achieved statehood he was easily elected as one of its first U.S. senators, but his popularity immediately began to diminish when he left the state for Washington D.C. His strength lay in having a cause to champion and in being among the people so he could be perceived as leading them personally against the foe.

The expedition he was now leading into Missouri, in early April 1862, was not sanctioned by any Union commander or government leader, but such was his influence in the area that none dared oppose it either. Over the past three days, he and his men had arrested more than a dozen men who were known to support the Southern cause, and a handful of others had died for having the audacity to challenge his authority. A trail of burned houses, barns, fences, and outbuildings marked his meandering progress through the western Missouri countryside, and numerous wagons had already been sent back across the state line into Kansas bearing furniture, clothing, household goods, and, in a couple of cases, the entire inventories of small rural stores encountered along the way.

This was just the most recent of Lane's excursions into the territories of his enemies. The previous fall he had led an even larger band of men to the town of Osceola, Missouri. There they had taken a number of rebels into custody, killed a few others, and generally brutalized the entire community. When they rode away toward home a few hours later, practically every building in town was in flames.

Lane believed it was the only way to treat this rebellious border trash. They were a die-hard lot, unchangeable by any powers of reason or compromise. The only things they understood were bullets, brutality, and blood, and in most cases the only way to stop them was to kill them, which he and his men were more than willing to do.

When Jim Lane saw one of his outriders approaching, he knew that either there was trouble ahead or that they were close to their destination. He stopped the column and waited for the man to reach him.

"Yes, Higgins. What is it?" Lane asked.

"We've found it, sir," the man reported. "It's just up the road a piece."

"Are you sure it's the right place?" Lane asked.

"Yes sir, it's the right place. Toby remembers it from a raid he made over here with John Brown a few years back. The others have spread out to watch until you get there and take over."

"Good. Good!" Jim Lane grinned. "For the life of me I can't see why somebody hasn't killed this Jason Hartman long before now, but perhaps we can take care of that little detail today. Just remember your standing orders. If he puts up any sort of fight . . ."

Jason saw the men in the trees through the front parlor window. The fact that they were making no serious efforts to conceal themselves worried him even more than if they had approached by stealth and tried to hide their presence until the time for action arrived. In that case he might have mistaken them for mere outlaws, or even for a small band of Confederates trying to carry out some covert misson in the area.

But the way they simply sat there amidst the scattered trees, waiting and watching like wolves around their cornered prey, left no doubt in Jason's mind about who they were and why they were here.

When a man like Jim Lane led a band of more than a hundred men into Missouri, nobody had to wait to read about it in a newspaper. Word of his presence and the outrages his men were committing had spread across the west central portion of the state like a prairie fire. Lane's destruction of Osceola had left few doubts in anybody's mind about his intentions toward his Missouri rivals, and Jason quickly accepted the fact that if he was indeed about to face the deadly Kansas abolitionist, he could expect little mercy.

Leaning heavily on his cane to keep most of the weight off his crippled right leg, Jason hobbled to the kitchen door to warn his wife about the impending intrusion. That proved unnecessary, though. Arethia stood at the window along the back wall, a paring knife in one hand and a half-peeled potato in the other, staring out silently. She noticed Jason out of the corner of her eye and looked at him, her face a mask of dread and uncertainty.

"Lane?" she asked.

"It's bound to be," Jason answered quietly.

"Well, whatever happens," Arethia said, "at least the children aren't here. Thank God for that."

"Listen, Arethia," Jason told her quickly. "There's not much doubt about what they've come for. I'm sure I've been on Lane's list for a long time now, and if those are his men out there, I'm in for a rough time. But whatever he plans, I don't want you here to see it."

"My place is with you," Arethia replied, throwing her arms around Jason. "Do you think I'm not able to face up to this kind of trouble as well as you?"

"I know you are," Jason said. "You've done it too many times for me to think otherwise. But we have the rest of the family to think about, too. I can't imagine what it would be like for the children to come home from school this afternoon and see . . . and find us . . ." He knew he didn't have to finish the description for her. They both re-alized that whatever was about to happen here today, it wouldn't be pleasant.

"I want you to go out through the tun-nel," he continued, "and when you get in the clear, head straight for my father's. Tell John to take to the brush for a few days, just in case they start looking for him as well, and then go to the school and get the children. Take them to Dad's and make them stay there until you can find out what happened here. And tell Dad and John that I don't want either of them to come over here for any reason until at least tomorrrow morning. That'll give Lane and his bunch a chance to get completely out of the area."

"We can both go, Jason!" his wife pleaded. "We can leave through the tunnel together and just let them do whatever they want with this place. I don't care what happens to it as long as you're alive and we're to-gether."

"It wouldn't work," Jason said. "If they don't find me here they'll just start search-ing the area, and if that happened we'd both be caught. And besides, they probably know about Dad's place too. They might go there next looking for me."

Arethia wanted to continue her argu-ments. He could see it in her eyes. But instead she simply held her husband more tightly as her tears moistened the coarse material of his shirt.

"I'll do what you say, but in return you must promise me that you won't fight them, Jason," Arethia said. "No matter what they do, you have to promise me that you won't lose your temper and do something foolish and reckless. I know you have more than the usual share of pride, but in this case, the price you'll have to pay for pride will just be too high. If there's even a chance that they'll let you live . . ."

"I know," Jason answered softly, "and I promise I won't do anything stupid. Considering the shape I'm in, whatever I tried to do would probably look pretty feeble and ridiculous anyway."

Together they rushed to the back bedroom of the house where the tunnel entrance was hidden beneath a large cedar chest. With some effort, Jason slid the chest aside, rolled back the rug beneath it, and opened a trapdoor in the floor. Beneath it was a ladder which led downward to a dark passageway below.

Some years ago, Jason had recognized the possibility that his family might someday be trapped in the house by marauders such as these, and so he had painstakingly constructed a tunnel that would give them at least a chance at escape. It was a crude affair, only about three feet square, unlit, and usually filled with several inches of seepage. It led across the side yard at an angle for about forty yards to a dense thicket east of the house which Jason had purposely left uncleared in order to conceal the opposite end of the tunnel.

Whether Arethia could make it from the thicket to the woods beyond would depend on how many men Lane had in the area, but because they had not already approached the house, either to talk or fight, he guessed that their numbers were few. She had a chance. Perhaps it was not such a good one, but right now it was the only one available.

"I'm with you," Arethia said as she kissed him one last time before descending into the dark hole in the floor.

"I know," Jason answered. "I can hardly ever remember a time when you weren't."

He heard her feet sink in the muck as she reached the bottom of the passageway, and he waited a moment longer until she leaned down and started forward into the tunnel. Then he closed the trapdoor, replaced the rug, and slid the chest back in place. If Lane's men searched the house thoroughly they would find the tunnel entrance, but by that time it wouldn't make any difference. In five minutes, Arethia would be out the other end and on her way to Will Hartman's.

Jason felt surprisingly calm as he went back through the house and opened the front door. Just knowing that his wife and children were safe removed much of the burden from his shoulders, and he felt ready now to deal with whatever was to come.

The men in the woods south of the house didn't move when Jason stepped out on the front porch and closed the door behind him. He stood staring at them for a moment, making it clear that he knew they were there, then took a seat in a cane-bottomed chair on the porch.

Scattered memories began to drift through his mind as he waited for his enemies to come: the family gathered around the dinner table the previous evening, laughing and happy, together; lying in bed for weeks after his return from the war, not knowing whether he would live or die and sometimes hardly caring; working the land and watching the fruits of his labor grow and ripen to maturity; waking in the middle of the night and reaching out in drowsy desire for the loving woman who lay beside him; coming here eight years ago and building his new home on the ashes of another family's dream . . .

It was nearly gone now. He could feel it like a sharp stab in his chest, more painful in its own way than any physical wound he had ever suffered. All that had been would soon disappear, and as for the future . . . In these deadly, uncertain times, what man could even hope to predict what lay ahead?

Jason didn't bother to rise from his chair even when the main column arrived. He had watched their dust cloud rising on the horizon and knew that Lane had many men with him, more than enough to capture another town like Osceola. A place like this and a man like Jason would hardly be a challenge to a force so large. Ten minutes' work, he guessed. Fifteen at the outside, and his home would be totally destroyed.

They paused a few dozen yards from the house, ignoring Jason entirely for the moment, while a man who was obviously the leader gave some orders to several of his subordinates. Jason had never seen Jim Lane before but had no trouble recognizing him from the descriptions he had heard over the years. In response to Lane's instructions, a score or more of men scattered in all directions to begin the destruction.

Finally Lane turned his horse and rode to

the house to confront Jason alone. They eyed one another curiously for a moment, then Lane said, "So this is what the notorious Jason Hartman looks like! You know, on the way here, I half expected to find some frothing monster with a gun in either hand and a bowie knife in his teeth. Hell, you look like something my kid sister could whip with one hand on her worst day."

"It wouldn't surprise me a bit, Lane," Jason admitted. "I've had a lot of the fight taken out of me these last few months." As he spoke, several men passed by him on the porch and stormed into the house. He hardly glanced at them.

"Yeah, I heard you got worked over pretty good last year down at Wilson's Creek," Lane said. "But I was still hoping for a little more interesting reception than this from you. You aren't going to give me any reason at all to put a bullet in you, are you, Hartman?"

"Nope. I promised my wife I wouldn't. But since when have you and your bunch started needing a reason for that sort of business?" Jason asked. "From the minute I saw your men out there in the trees, I've figured I was about to die. I don't even know whether I'll be alive five minutes from now, but you already do, don't you, Lane?"

"I do," Lane answered calmly.

Up in the barn, four men were hitching horses up to Jason's two large field wagons, and three more were rounding up the remaining horse and cows. Meanwhile, the men who had entered the house began to carry out the best of the furniture and other property such as weapons, bedding, and clothing.

"Who else is here, Hartman?" Lane demanded. "Where's your wife and children? Where's that oldest boy of yours? From what I've heard, he's just about the right age to make another rebel out of himself."

"They're all gone. When I heard you had crossed over the line, I sent them away to Booneville to stay with friends, just in case you decided to make my place a stop along your way."

"You're a lying bastard, Hartman," Lane growled.

Jason didn't respond. Glancing to one side, he saw the first tongues of flame begin to lap out one side window of the barn. The chicken house was in flames as well, and a man carrying a burning brand was making his way around the barn lot, putting the torch to even the fences. A little beyond him another man raised his rifle to his shoulder and drew a bead on Jason's brood sow. The shot rang out and the two-hundred-pound pig squealed out in painful surprise as she tumbled clumsily to the ground.

"So what's it going to be, Lane?" Jason asked at last. "Do you just want to enjoy making me watch all this before you kill me, or do you have something else in mind? Am I going to die today or not?"

"You sound almost like you want me to kill you," Lane commented.

"No, it's not that," Jason said. "Nobody wants to die, but I guess after a while a man just gets tired of worrying about it. You've probably felt that same way."

Lane stared curiously at him for a moment without answering. His entire encounter with this notorious enemy had not been at all what he expected. He had, in fact, arrived here eager to end Jason Hartman's life, but not this way, not with Hartman just sitting there in his chair, accepting the whole thing as calmly as a man accepts the weather and the changes in the seasons. It wasn't natural, somehow.

"As of now you're under arrest for rebellion against the government," Lane found himself saying. "We'll turn you over to the military authorities in Kansas City and let them decide what to do with you."

Jason knew that at this point he could not

afford to let Lane see what a relief the announcement was to him. Throughout the encounter he had not permitted himself to read any sign of hope into anything Lane said or did, but of course hope had always been there, even if Jason had not acknowledged it. Hope could never fully die until the man did.

When Lane went off to supervise the final looting and destruction of the Hartman farm, Jason rose wearily from his seat and walked out into the yard. Curiously, nobody even bothered to stand guard over him, but in fact there was probably no real reason to do so, he thought. Without a weapon, crippled by his wounds, and confronted with the presence of more than a hundred armed opponents, how could he even consider making any sort of desperate attempt to escape? He was their prisoner as surely as if he had been bound hand and foot and guarded by a dozen of the Jayhawkers.

Lane's men worked with a proficiency gained through much recent practice. The wagons were brought down from the barn and quickly loaded, then several ropes were used to secure the loads for the long trip back to Kansas. By then the dead hog had been bled, quartered and tied atop a spare horse, and all of Jason's remaining stock had been herded up near the road. The cattle would probably be slaughtered one by one over the next few days to feed the band, and the horses would either be sold or sent back to Kansas with Jason's other belongings.

The way Lane and his men went about it, this soldiering business seemed to be quite a lucrative undertaking, Jason thought.

Jason was standing under a big elm tree watching the flames destroy his family's home when Lane rode back over to him again.

"This is the price of being a rebel," Lane commented, "and if you ask me, you've been long overdue in paying it, Hartman." Jason said nothing. He didn't trust himself to speak at the moment because if he opened his mouth, he had no idea of what words might come spilling out.

"You'll go with the wagons down to Kansas City," Lane continued, "and my men will turn you over to the military authorities there. From the looks of you, I don't think you'll be a threat to the good people of Kansas ever again, and that's the only reason why you're alive this minute. But if there does come a time when you get any crazy notions in your head, just remember this day, and remember that we can always come back again. We can, and probably will, come back again, and again, and again . . ."

CHAPTER FIVE

Major Benjamin was waiting with a carriage and driver outside the stage door when Mollie came out after her evening performance. He stepped to the ground when he saw her and, with an exaggerated bow, helped her up to the seat. Then, after stepping up to join her, he leaned forward and told the driver, "Take us to the Jefferson Hotel."

When Benjamin turned his face to Mollie again, his smile was filled with pleasure and no small trace of desire. She could smell the brandy on his breath, and his eyes were already beginning to take on that vague sheen of intoxication.

"You look absolutely stunning tonight, Miss Hartman," the major told her. His gaze swept down across her bare shoulders and briefly beyond before returning again to her face. "I don't believe I have the words at my command to tell you what that gown does for you."

"You don't think it's too daring, then?" Mollie asked with a smile. "I wasn't absolutely sure what to wear to a formal military soiree. I've never been to one before."

"It's perfect," Benjamin assured her. "It's the one you wore in *Desperate Fortunes,* isn't it?"

"Yes! In the second act!" Mollie laughed. "I'm surprised you remember."

"I saw the play eight times," he explained. "Twice while you were away and that silly little piece of no-talent fluff was taking your place, and then six more times after you returned. I could never forget that gown."

"Well I just hope you don't mind my wearing a 'costume,' so to speak," Mollie said. "I must admit that my personal wardrobe cannot compare with the clothes I wear on stage."

Benjamin's eyes roamed down Mollie's body again for a moment, surveying the smooth skin of her exposed breasts and the delicate curve of her cleavage. "I hardly mind," he assured her. "If there's a man there tonight who doesn't envy me, it will because God has made him blind."

The dress she wore was quite striking. It was made of white satin which molded itself smoothly to the contours of her slender figure. The skirts were full, and the strapless bodice was cut to a *V* in front. The entire garment was trimmed in an abundance of delicate lace, and she wore white satin gloves trimmed in lace to match.

Mollie was neither surprised nor particularly bothered by her companion's ardent praise and attention. By accepting the major's invitation to this party, and by dressing as she did, she knew she was practically guaranteeing herself an evening of shallow, worshipful attention, leering smiles, and indecent proposals cloaked in the guise of humor and good fun. But she had her reasons for everything she was doing, and she was determined to play her role to the fullest. Tonight she would be the belle of the ball.

The night was warm, and the sound of the horse's hooves clattered sharply on the cobblestones of the nearly empty street. Before they had gone more than a couple of blocks, the major produced a contoured silver flask from his back pocket and offered Mollie a drink.

"It's an excellent French brandy," Benjamin explained. "I brought two cases of it with me when I was assigned out here last summer, and this is nearly the last of it. But I'm not complaining, mind you. We all have to make our sacrifices for the war effort." Smiling, Mollie accepted the flask, tipped it to her lips as if taking a drink, then passed it back to its owner. Her role demanded that she seem to be enjoying every pleasure available, but in fact she did not want to let her wits become clouded even in the slightest by strong drink. Too much was at stake.

"I have to confess to you, Miss Hartman," Benjamin said, taking a stiff pull on the flask and then putting it away, "that I'm still wondering why you accepted my invitation to this affair. Last fall, despite all my efforts, I could scarcely get a smile from you, and you seldom even bothered to respond to any of my gifts or invitations. What made you decide to say yes this time?"

"I insist upon my right to change my mind at any time about anything I choose," Mollie told him lightly. "It's a woman's prerogative, you know. It's one of the tools we use to keep you men slightly off balance all the time."

"I thought perhaps it was because of my, uh, marital situation," Benjamin suggested uncomfortably.

"I must admit it's not exactly a point in your favor, Major."

"Over the past few years, my marriage has become one in name only," the major assured her. "Even when I am home, we hardly even speak to one another, and the only reason we don't end the whole thing is because of families and business and all that nonsense. She doesn't understand me, nor I her, so we just go our separate ways and do as we please. But all that doesn't have to affect whatever happens between you and me, Mollie. I have an idea that things could work out very well between us despite the fact that a piece of paper somewhere says I'm a married man."

"I suppose we'll just have to see about that, Major Benjamin," Mollie told him. "But I am here with you, aren't I? That must mean that the situation is not without hope." She was doing her best to walk a fine line with Benjamin, to keep him attentive but not too close, encouraged but not overconfident. She wasn't quite sure yet that he was the man she needed to do the job she had in mind, and yet she had to keep him available until she found another who would be better suited for her purposes. But before the night was ended, Mollie thought, she would know in which direction she should turn.

The major drew the flask out and took another swallow, then settled back more comfortably in the seat to enjoy the remainder of the ride. If the situation had been different, Mollie thought, she might actually have become interested in this man, for he was in fact quite a handsome fellow. His dark blond hair was combed back in natural waves across the top of his head, and his well-kept beard complemented his tanned, rugged features. He had probably passed his fortieth year already, but his body was trim and muscular, and he wore his dress-blue uniform with a distinctive military bearing.

As the carriage turned onto the block where the Jefferson Hotel was located, Mollie began to hear the music and commotion of the party they were going to. The event was being held to honor the arrival of a new military commander to the area, Brigadier General Thomas Ewing, and from all indications, good times were being had by all. Major Benjamin explained that he had already been at the party earlier, which accounted for his present semi-intoxicated condition, but had left in time to pick Mollie up at the theatre.

In a moment the driver steered the carriage to the curb in front of the hotel and stopped. The major paid the fare, then he and Mollie stepped down to the sidewalk.

The Jefferson Hotel was a four-story stone

building, one of the newest and finest structures in the young, burgeoning metropolis of Kansas City. Since the beginning of the war, it had become a favorite spot for the scores of Union officers stationed in the area, and there was even talk that soon a portion of the hotel might be commandeered to serve as the district headquarters for the Union army. Until tonight, Mollie had always avoided going to the Jefferson, preferring not to have to cope with the shallow attentions of the many young officers who considered the place to be theirs. But tonight was different. Tonight she would be throwing herself into the fray willingly, even eagerly.

About fifty officers, along with their wives or female companions, were gathered in the large ballroom on the ground floor of the hotel when Mollie and Major Benjamin entered. A band at the far end of the room was pounding out a lively, popular tune, and a number of couples were dancing on the hardwood dance floor in front of the stage. Others were filling plates from the buffet set up along one wall, waiting their turn at the bar to purchase drinks, or simply standing around talking, laughing and enjoying the music.

Admiring eyes began to follow Mollie as

soon as she entered and started with her escort across the room. When they reached the bar, which was Benjamin's first objective, his friends and fellow officers began to assemble nearby in hopes of being introduced to his lovely young companion. None was disappointed.

The major took great pleasure in introducing Mollie all around, and she did her best to charm and dazzle everyone she met. In particular, Mollie made an effort to show an interest in the duties of as many of the officers as possible. As man after man took her off to glide and twirl around the dance floor, she interrogated each about his work as if he were the most fascinating individual she had ever met.

It was surprisingly easy making them talk. Her interest seemed genuine, and few could resist trying to impress such a lovely and alluring young woman. For the first hour or so that they were there Major Benjamin seemed content to share her attentions with her growing number of admirers. He remained at or near the bar most of the time, drinking steadily, laughing and talking with his cronies, and waiting patiently for her return each time another dance was finished.

Mollie was glad the major was not proving to be the possessive, jealous type, but she had a pretty good idea why he was permitting his fellow officers to enjoy so much of her time and attention. Finally, during a break in the music, and at a time when nobody else was within earshot, Benjamin began to reveal his plans for later in the evening.

"I'm sorry if my friends are tiring you out," he said. "You aren't obligated to dance with every man who asks you if you don't want to." He held a half-filled glass of wine in his hand, and from the look of his bloodshot eyes and flushed features, the effects of the drink and the countless others he had already consumed were beginning to take their toll. Without realizing it, he weaved slightly as he stood talking to her.

"No, I'm having a wonderful time!" Mollie assured him. "I haven't danced this much in years, and what woman wouldn't enjoy the kind of attention I'm getting here tonight? But I suppose I will be exhausted by the end of the night."

"I thought you might." Benjamin grinned. "These things sometimes go on until dawn, and often the people who attend them don't want to bother going all the way back to their homes to get some rest. Quite a few of the people here have taken rooms in the hotel for the night, and I took the liberty of reserving one for you, just in case you decided to use it." He reached into the side pocket of his jacket and produced a key, which he let Mollie glimpse for an instant before putting it away again. "I just thought I'd let you know it's in there and available to you."

"I see," Mollie said, still trying to keep her tone light and noncommittal. "And should I assume that you have not taken a second room for yourself, that I would not be spending the night alone if I stayed here?"

"A man can only hope," Benjamin said, grinning foolishly. As his eyes fondled her once more, Mollie found herself thinking that at this point his caresses would probably be as clumsy and annoying as his stares were beginning to be, but she tried to hide her distaste at the idea of giving into his proposition.

"Yes, a man can hope," Mollie agreed lightly, "and you strike me as a very hopeful fellow indeed. But I don't know yet. I'm not sure whether I'll be wanting to go home when the party is over or not."

"Well it's there, Mollie. It's there if you want it."

As the evening progressed a few of the

people, primarily the older officers and married couples, began to leave, but most of the others seemed intent on making a night of it, just as Benjamin had predicted. Finally, more than an hour later, Mollie found herself suddenly, almost unexpectedly, on the dance floor in the arms of precisely the man she had come here to meet.

His name was Cory Winstead and he was a young infantry officer from Des Moines. Apparently out of shyness, he was one of the last available men at the party to ask her to dance, and he seemed almost surprised when she accepted his invitation, although she had yet to turn anyone down all night.

He was clumsy and obviously uncomfortable on the dance floor at first, holding Mollie as if she were some sort of delicate treasure that might shatter in this arms at any mintue. But soon Mollie got him talking freely about himself and his life in the service, and he began to waltz her around the floor with increasing ease and style.

He was several years younger than Mollie, no more than twenty-one or twenty-two, she guessed, and he explained that he owed his rank of lieutenant to the fact that his father had been one of the organizers of the military unit that he had joined when the war began. All that was of very little interest to Mollie, but what did interest her was the duty he performed here in the western Missouri military district.

Young Lieutenant Winstead was in charge of the compound on the edge of town where Confederate prisoners of war and rebel sympathizers were held, the same compound where Mollie's brother Jason had been held prisoner for the past four weeks.

"I must tell you, Lieutenant," Mollie said as they glided across the floor, "that it's quite a pleasure to meet someone as courteous and respectful as you. I'm afraid my companion is in his cups, and the evening is turning into something more than what I bargained for."

"Is the major being offensive, ma'am?" Winstead asked in alarm. She could see his chivalrous tendencies rising to the surface, which is exactly what she had hoped would happen. "If he is, Miss Hartman, I will be glad to remind him of his obligation to conduct himself as a gentleman and an officer in the United States Army."

"No, please don't do that," Mollie said. "As drunk as he is, that kind of thing would certainly stir up more trouble than it's worth, and it would probably bring repercussions on you as well."

"But still, Miss Hartman, you are a lady and you are our guest here tonight," the lieutenant protested. "You have a right to be treated with respect. Excuse me for saying it, miss, but damn the repercussions!"

"No, I don't want you to say anything to him," Mollie insisted, "but . . ." She paused, as if an idea had just occurred to her. "But perhaps there is something you could do for me. I hate to ask, but it would be a great favor. An important favor."

"Anything, Miss Hartman," Winstead told her eagerly. "Anything you need."

"Well I was thinking of telling Major Benjamin that I wasn't feeling well and wanted to leave. I thought that if he saw that tonight wasn't going to end as he had planned, he would probably agree to let me leave alone and I could take a carriage home. But the streets are so empty at this time of night, and I don't relish the idea of making the ride with only an unarmed carriage driver to stand between me and any danger that might come along. It's frightening, and I wasn't sure what I should do . . ."

"It will be my honor to escort you home," the lieutenant volunteered. "You're right about the dangers, and I think you're smart not to want to make the ride alone."

As the music ended and they started back

toward Major Benjamin, Mollie quickly concocted her plan of escape.

"After you leave us, wait a few minutes for appearance's sake, and then act as if you've decided to leave for the night," she said. "When I see you go out, I'll begin making my excuses to the major. While I'm doing that, you can get a carriage ready, and I'll meet you outside the front entrance as soon as I get away from him."

"That's fine, but if you have any trouble, you let me know. He might outrank me, but that's no excuse for being disrespectful to a lady, and I won't stand for it."

"It'll be fine," Mollie assured him. "You just have the carriage waiting, and I'll take care of the major."

"Yes, ma'am, I will," Winstead promised.

After he had returned Mollie to the major, the lieutenant thanked her for the dance and drifted away into the crowd. Mollie kept track of him out of the corner of her eye, and soon she saw him leave the ballroom alone.

Gazing into the bleary eyes of her companion, Mollie said, "You know you're beginning to look very tired. Don't you think it's about time to think about putting that room you have upstairs to good use?"

The major's expression brightened immediately at the suggestion. "I think it's an excellent idea, Mollie," he said. "We can —"

"I haven't made up my mind yet whether I'll be joining you. I think I need to step outside to get some fresh air and think about this thing alone for a minute. And in any event, I don't want everybody seeing us going upstairs to your room together. I may be an actress, but I still value my reputation."

"There are ways to handle these matters discreetly," Benjamin suggested.

"Yes, we must be discreet," Mollie agreed. "That's why I think you should go up to the room by yourself, and if I decide to join you there, I'll use the back stairway. What is the room number?"

"Three-fourteen," the major said.

"Room 314," Mollie repeated. "I'll remember."

"All right then, I'll see you there," the major said, suddenly eager now that his moment of conquest seemed so close at hand.

"Perhaps," Mollie said, kissing him lightly on the cheek before sending him away. She waited until he was out of earshot, then muttered quietly to herself, "Perhaps you'll see me in your dreams, but no place else, you bastard!"

She gave Major Benjamin a few minutes to get past the lobby, then she too left the ballroom. She paused at the front desk of the hotel long enough to jot down a note filled with apology and regret for the major to read in the morning. When she got outside, Lieutenant Winstead was waiting near the door with a carriage and driver. They both got in and Mollie gave the driver the address of Genevieve de Mauduis's home on Quality Hill.

"No problems with the major?" Winstead asked.

"No problems," Mollie replied. "He was so tired and drunk that the news probably came as something of a relief to him. He has a room in the hotel and said he planned to stay there tonight."

It was nearly three in the morning now, and a damp fog had drifted up from the nearby Missouri River to settle over the town. When Mollie felt a chill on her bare arms and shoulders, she recognized an opportunity to use even the cool night air to her advantage.

Sliding a little closer to the lieutenant, she said, "You've been so gallent tonight, I wonder if I could ask you one more small favor. I'm getting a little cold, and I thought you might be willing to put your arm around me to warm my shoulders."

"I'll give you my jacket," Winstead volunteered, reaching immediately for the gold buttons on the front of his uniform tunic.

"No thank you," Mollie told him. "Your arm will do nicely." And with that, she raised his arm and lifted it over her head, then snuggled close against his side as his hand settled across her shoulder.

They talked very little on the way to Mollie's home. For his part, the young lieutenant was enjoying the situation too much to think of anything else, and Mollie was simply waiting for what she knew her new friend must inevitably do before they parted company tonight. Finally, as they turned up a broad quiet street west of town, Mollie leaned forward on the seat and pointed out the house to the driver. He stopped in front of it, and Winstead got down, helped Mollie from the carriage, and walked her to the door.

"I've enjoyed being with you very much this evening, Miss Hartman," he told her, "and you've seemed to enjoy my company as well. Would it be possible for me to call on you next week?"

"I'm sorry, but I'm afraid not, Lieutenant Winstead," Mollie told him. "You've been very kind, but I think tonight is probably the last time we will ever see one another."

Winstead was obviously struck by the abruptness and finality of her words, but at last he managed to stammer out, "Please accept my apology. I suppose it was very rude of me to try to take advantage of the trust you placed in me tonight."

"No, no! It's not that!" Mollie protested. "You're very nice and I wasn't offended at all by your suggestion. I like you, and if the situation were different, I think you and I . . ." She paused, as if considering her next words before going on. "But you see, I have to leave Kansas City in a few days. Perhaps for a long time. Perhaps forever."

They had stopped at the front door to face one another, and even in the moonlight, Mollie could see how disappointed Winstead was. To heighten the effect of the moment, she leaned forward unexpectedly and kissed him softly on the lips. "Yes, I can imagine that it would be very enjoyable having you come to call on me," she whispered. "But I must go. I have no choice."

Caught completely by surprise, the lieutenant's first reaction was to glance back down the walk toward the carriage, as if he and Mollie were a couple of youngsters in danger of being caught in some mischief. But the driver sat waiting with his head turned slightly away from them.

"Is it your career?" he asked. "Is it your acting that is taking you away?"

"No, it's not that. It's a family matter," Mollie said with some reluctance, appearing very troubled. Then she looked deeply into Lieutenant Winstead's eyes, and after what seemed a few seconds of hesitation, she said, "My father lives on a farm up in Clay County, and until recently my brother and his family lived on another farm nearby. But about a month ago Lane's Jayhawkers rode through and burned my brother and his family out. They took my brother Jason away, and —"

"Jason?" Winstead interrupted. "Jason Hartman? Yes, I know that name. We're holding him as a prisoner in the camp where I work."

"I knew he was being held somewhere close by," Mollie replied, "but I haven't been able to see him and I haven't been able to find out anything about what's to happen to him. My father's a feeble old man and he can't take care of everything by himself, nor can my sister-in-law Arethia, with her husband locked up and her home destroyed. She's not the strongest woman in the world, and she's always leaned heavily on her husband for support. Now she has five children to take care of, and everything they owned was burned up by Lane's men. With Jason away, they need me there, so I have no choice but to give up everything I have here and try to help them."

"If I remember your brother's case correctly," Winstead said, "I believe he was one of the rebels who fought at Wilson's Creek, and he then refused to turn himself in for parole after he returned home."

"Yes, he was there," Mollie admitted. "In fact, he almost died there. But those poor men didn't believe they were joining the Confederate army when they signed up with the Home Guards. They were duped. After Wilson's Creek, my brother and all his friends who survived the battle decided to stay out of the rest of the war. Some of them did turn themselves in for parole, but when the word came around about what they were supposed to do, Jason was still so sick that he couldn't even stand up alone. And now look what's happened to him! It's a terrible, terrible injustice!"

Winstead was silent for a moment, and Mollie hoped he was beginning to make the connection she was trying to suggest to him. The two of them were attracted to each other, but they could not be together. Mollie had to go away and help her family because her brother had been unjustly imprisoned. But if that injustice were corrected, and if her brother were freed . . .

Of course she had no real intentions of quitting the theatre and moving back to Clay County. Arethia would have laughed at Mollie's description of her, and Will Hartman would certainly have chaffed at being referred to as "feeble." But the script Mollie had devised in her mind required these deceptions, and they added a definite impact to the self-sacrificing act she claimed to be ready to commit.

"I really don't know much about your brother's case," the lieutenant admitted at last, "but I do know that there are things that can be done in certain situations. I know of some provisions in the regulations for special cases."

Mollie acted almost shocked at his implied offer. "I hope you don't think I was trying to suggest . . ." she stammered, ". . . that I had any idea of asking you to . . ." This was, of course, her precise objective, but she certainly didn't want him to *think* it was! "But if there is something you could do, someone you could talk to . . ." She threw her arms around his neck and gave him a sudden, excited kiss. "Oh, Cory! It would mean so much to me. So very much. I wouldn't have to give up my career or anything else here. I wouldn't have to move away!"

"I can't make you any promises, Mollie," Winstead told her. "I don't know if there's anything I can do to help. But for you . . ."

During their next embrace, Winstead finally began to respond with enthusiasm instead of shock. He held her tightly against him, savoring her kisses with a hot-blooded youthful enthusiasm that reminded Mollie suddenly of . . .

Just thinking of Cole made Mollie stiffen in the lieutenant's arms and involuntarily draw away from him.

"I'm sorry," Winstead muttered hurriedly, thinking that his own eagerness must have caused her to pull back. "It's just that I've never met anyone like you . . . and I've never kissed anyone quite like that."

"No, it's not you," Mollie assured him. "You haven't done anything. I've just been so upset lately about Jason. I thought this party tonight might take my mind off things, but still I can't forget him. I keep thinking of him losing his home and farm, of being torn away from his family by those awful men, and then being locked up some-where through no fault of his own . . ."

"I'll find some way to help you, Mollie,"

Winstead promised.

"I'll be so grateful to you if you do, Cory," Mollie said. "But you must be careful about how you go about things, you know. It wouldn't look good for you if people knew you were involved with the sister of a man whose release you were responsible for. They wouldn't understand. They might think you did it simply because you wanted something from me in return."

"No, no. It's not that way at all!" Winstead protested.

"Of course it's not," she agreed. "I can see that you're doing this because you're the kind of person who dislikes injustice, and that's something that I find very attractive about you, Cory." She paused a moment, thinking, then told him, "On Sundays the woman I live with always has her cook prepare a massive dinner which the two of us can seldom do justice to alone. I'd love to have you come, and perhaps we could take a ride in the country later. And when you come you can bring me whatever news you have about my brother."

CHAPTER SIX

September 1962

John Hartman knelt by the tiny fire, feeding it just enough twigs and leaves to heat the charred metal pan which sat amidst the flames. Supper on this particular night consisted of about a cupful of beans and the remnants of a pone of cornbread that he had baked the night before. It was all the food he had left, which meant that tomorrow he would have to go out for more. He both dreaded and looked forward to the prospect.

Tonight's camp was on a small hummock of high ground in the edge of a large marshy area just north of the Missouri River in Clay County. He had used the spot before, but not too often, and liked its location because of the acres of muck and stagnant water which surrounded him on all sides. There was enough grass available for his horse, and anyone approaching him could certainly be heard wading or riding toward him through the water. He felt safe here, able to sleep soundly through the night without having to reach for his rifle every time an acorn fell or a possum passed nearby in the darkness.

Now, after nearly five weeks of being a fugitive, John had started to settle into a regular, though seldom comfortable, routine. He moved his camp almost every day, normally preferring to travel before daybreak or after nightfall, and most of his waking hours were spent in the deepest woods he could find, usually looking for food. He had become adept at snaring rabbits, squirrels, and other small game, and by trial and error, he had discovered a wide variety of edible woodland plants and roots. As much as half of the food he ate came from the wilds, but he still felt the need for such civilized staples as salt, corn meal, coffee, vegetables, and occasional sweets.

At first, John Hartman had thought that he would have to hide out only a week or two at most. After the Jayhawkers returned to Kansas and the furor of their passing died down, he was sure that he could go back to his grandfather's farm undisturbed. After all, he had not been with his father at Wilson's Creek, and he had yet to fulfill his ambition of joining the military forces who were fighting in defense of Missouri and the South.

He returned home twice at night that first week, once to get more food, and again to get some calamine for a severe case of poison ivy he had contracted. Although there had been no word from his father and his family was still in a state of shock over their devastating losses, things were quiet. He and his grandfather had even discussed a possible trip into Kansas City to try to discover if Jason had made it safely into Union hands, and if so, to learn where he was being held.

Another week passed before he returned a third time, and on the way he told himself that if things seemed all right he probably wouldn't bother to leave again.

It was only by chance that he had spotted the men in the brush near his grandfather's farm before they saw him. There were three of them, hidden in a strategic spot in the woods north of the house where they could watch all the comings and goings on the farm. Two of the men were strangers to John, but he recognized the third as a man named Isaac Paul, a part-time deputy of the county sheriff and full-time troublemaker.

The presence of the men simply confused

John at first, but still, for safety's sake, he stayed away from the house until nightfall when he was finally able to slip in undetected. His mother was not there, but his grandfather had plenty of news to convey. The good news was that John's father was still alive and was being held in a Union prison compound outside of Kansas City. Arethia had gone there the day before to try to see him, but there had been no word yet about whether she was successful.

John's pleasure at learning that his father had not been killed by Lane was tempered, however, by the rest of what his grandfather had to say. Before leaving the area, James Lane had apparently left a list of names with the local civilian authorities, names of men that he had been unable to capture but still wanted. The county sheriff had been to the farm twice in the past week snooping around and asking about John, and Isaac Paul had also come by to deliver an assortment of loutish threats.

For the sake of his family's safety, John left almost immediately, and he had only been back once since then to visit briefly with his mother and pick up some badly needed supplies.

It was a lonely life for a youth of nineteen who had never been away from his family for more than a night or two at a time. During the entire ordeal, he had never roamed farther than twenty miles from home, but at times it seemed as if such a great distance separated him from his loved ones that he might never see any of them again.

Sometimes he thought about simply getting on his horse and riding south until he reached Confederate territory, but the notion was so foreign and uncertain to him that he could never quite bring himself to do it. Eventually, his grandfather had predicted, General Price would march back northward again and run all the Federals out of the state. And when that happened, John vowed, he would be one of the first to enlist so he could personally see to it that men like James Lane and Isaac Paul never held sway over his and his family's lives again. Many a night as he sat in his lonely camp, he imagined the eloquent speech about treachery and oppression he would deliver to Paul before finally putting a bullet in his chest.

John suddenly heard the sound of some living thing splashing through the swamp water, and he reached automatically for the ancient muzzle-loading rifle which he now kept close at hand at all times. He wasn't too alarmed at first. There were a lot of deer, and even a few wild boars and small black bears in this region, and he had long ago learned how pointless it was to get excited about every noise he heard in the night.

But the splashing continued to get louder, drawing ever closer as the moments passed. Finally John took a stick and scattered his small fire, then checked the load in his rifle and rose to his feet. The sound he was hearing, he realized, was the same one he had heard earlier in the evening when he himself had approached this campsite. It was the sound of a horse making its way carefully through the muck and mire of the knee-deep swamp water.

When the noise drew close, John backed away into the brush at the south edge of the clearing and hid behind the thick roots of a cypress tree, his rifle ready. With the fire out, the darkness would work in his favor now. He knew the lay of the land quite well, and he knew the precise direction of approach of his adversary, while whoever it was out there would probably have only a vague notion that someone was somewhere up ahead.

With any luck, John thought, the intruder might miss the clearing entirely and pass on by without ever realizing that there was a spot of dry land anywhere around. But if not, if he did find the camp . . . well, there was moonlight enough to see everything in the clearing quite plainly, and he was still so close that he could hardly miss anything he aimed the rifle at.

In a minute a lone rider entered the clearing from the north, riding a fine husky roan, which made him appear huge and ominous in the dim forest light. He stopped near the spot where John had built his fire, dismounted, and dropped his mount's reins casually to the ground. As near as John could tell the man had no weapon in his hand, nor did he seem particularly alarmed by the deserted camp he had just come across.

From several feet away Ned, John's mount, raised his head from grazing and snorted at the new arrival. The intruder looked in Ned's direction for a moment and shook his head, then knelt to pick up John's cook pot and sniff at its contents.

"Looks like I caught you right in the middle of supper," he commented. The fact that he spoke so casually, and that he seemed to know that John was someplace close by, only served to set John's nerves on edge all the more. The rifle was aimed and his finger was on the trigger, but a rising curiosity kept him from firing.

"You are John Hartman, aren't you?" the stranger asked. "If you are, you're the fellow we've been looking for. It was just by a stroke of luck that a friend of ours saw you ride into the swamp 'long about dusk. Otherwise we might never have found you."

John didn't like the way the man used the words "we" and "our," but he realized that it might be just a ruse to make John believe he was not alone. He decided not to speak up and reveal his location, not just yet.

"I have to tell you, John," the man continued. "This is really a pretty sloppy way to go about things. You left your horse here, and your bedroll, and all your supplies. If it came to a chase in these marshes, what with you being on foot and without any food, you'd be in a hell of a predicament." He glanced down at the ground nearby, then added, "Look! Look here! You even left your powder and shot behind. It's a careless way to go about things, boy. Mighty sloppy work!"

"I've got my rifle aimed at you," John announced at last, unable to remain quiet any longer.

"Well I should hope so," the man replied. "I'd hope you have sense enough to do at least that."

"Put your hands straight up in the air, and step away from that horse," John ordered. "If you do anything to make me think you're going for a gun, I'll shoot you."

"Sure, I'll do that," the man said. He raised his arms up at his sides and walked a couple of paces away from his mount. "And now will you come out of the bushes? I need to talk to you."

John considered the request for a moment. He knew he had heard the sound of only one horse approaching earlier, and now the woods were silent on all sides. Anyone who had come into the swamp with this fellow would be quite a distance away right now, too far away to be any threat for the time being. Finally he stepped out from behind the cypress and moved forward into the clearing.

After getting his first good look at John, the man said, "Let's see. You're about the right age and size. You are John Hartman, aren't you?"

"That's right. I am," John said. "But unless you're a Federal, I don't see how that's any of your business. And if you are a Federal —"

"My name's Wiliam Gregg and I've come to take you out of here," the stranger interrupted.

"The hell you have," John told him "The way things are shaping up right now, you'll be pretty damn lucky to get out of here yourself."

"I came in here with Cole Younger and George Todd," Gregg announced. "Right now Cole and George and two other fellows are riding around somewhere out in this swamp just like I was, looking for where you hid yourself. We figured it was about time you quit hiding out in the bush like a coyote and started riding with us."

The announcement caught John completely by surprise. Until that instant, he had simply assumed that this man must be an enemy. Of course, he still might be. Everything he said could be a lie . . . but what if it was true? The idea of having some companionship, of being among friends again after so many weeks of solitude, stirred a feeling of excitement he found difficult to hide.

"If that proves to be true," John said, "then I'll owe you a long apology later, but right now I'll have to disarm you. What kind of weapons are you carrying?"

"I've got two revolvers in my belt, one front and one back," Gregg announced, "and there's another in my left coat pocket. I've also got a small pistol in a shoulder holster, and a knife in my boot. That's about it, I guess, unless you want my folding knife as well. Do you want to get them, or shall I?"

"You can do it," John said. "But be real careful. I'd hate to have to shoot you at this point, just in case you are who you say you are."

As Gregg began to disarm himself, removing each piece slowly and placing it on the ground in front of him, John was amazed at the number of weapons the other man was carrying. Including the rifle and the shotgun that he had left in the scabbards on his horse, the man rode around with a total of six firearms and a bowie knife that looked to have at least a twelve-inch blade.

When Gregg was finished at last, John said, "All right, now turn around and let me pat you down. I want to make sure you didn't forget anything." Gregg did as he was told, and after the search was over, John said, "All right, you said you came looking for me, so what now? How do I find out whether or not you've been telling me the truth?"

"I figure it's about ten now," Gregg told him, "and at midnight we're supposed to meet back at that little natural spring over on the west side of this marsh. Do you know the place?"

"I do," John answered.

"Well, I suggest we go there. You're going to feel a whole lot better about this business once you see your friends and find out I've been dealing straight with you."

"That's God's own truth!" John said.

When they came to within a quarter mile of the spring where Gregg said the rendezvous was to be, John stopped to bind and gag his prisoner. He left Gregg tied to a tree, tethered the horses, and proceeded on foot. They had left the swamp behind them by this time, and now John was finally able to make his way on dry land.

During the past hour they had spent together, John found himself becoming more and more convinced that the man with him was telling the truth.

Until about three months before, Gregg had explained during their ride through the swamp, he had been in a situation similar to John's own. After learning that the Union troops had slated him for arrest, he had gone into hiding in the brushy hills near Blue Springs. He had spent nearly two months in the wilds, coming out only rarely for news and supplies.

"Then one day I got myself in a hell of a

mess while I was leaving town after a visit with my folks," Gregg had told him. "A Federal patrol on the road outside town tried to stop me, and when I wouldn't stop, they lit out after me. I was riding an old plow horse, which was the best I could get my hands on back then, and the only gun I had with me was a single-shot shotgun that I used in the bush for squirrels and rabbits. I figured my fat was in the fire for sure, because there was five of them, and they had me outhorsed and outgunned seven ways from Sunday.

"Well, we scooted along for a mile or two, and all the time they were gaining ground on me fast. When I heard the first shots, I thought it was them shooting at me, but when I looked back, I saw two empty saddles, and the three Federals who hadn't gone down yet were shooting into the trees off to their left. Then, in a minute, out from those same trees comes six men, all whooping and cussing and shooting like mad with a pistol in each hand. In another minute, all five of those Union soldiers were dead on the road, and the men that took them out never suffered even a scratch.

"That was the first time I ever laid eyes on Bill Quantrill and his bunch," Gregg had explained, "but I joined up on the spot, and

I've been with them ever since."

It had been a pretty convincing story, John thought as he made his way cautiously through the brush toward the spring. He had never heard of anyone named Bill Quantrill, but for the past few months there had been occasional talk of the scattered groups of men who were banding together to resist what they considered the Union occupation of their state.

John had asked some pointed questions about Cole Younger, hoping to determine if Gregg knew him as he claimed, but Gregg readily admitted that he didn't know Cole very well. He said Cole had only joined their group a couple of weeks before, and this was the first time the two of them had actually been out on any sort of operation together.

"But he seems like a straight fellow, all right," Gregg had said. "Him and George Todd both. When I found out they had fought at Wilson's Creek, that was enough for me. I wish I'd been there with them, but my daddy wouldn't let me join up. Said I was too young."

Gregg, it turned out, was only twenty, just a year older than John. It surprised John to find that out, because he seemed so much older. But then, John thought, the kind of life Bill Gregg had been leading that spring and summer would tend to age a young man pretty fast.

As he drew closer to where he knew the spring was located, John moved forward with ever-increasing stealth. He began to use some of the hunting tricks his father had taught him years ago, taking only a silent step or two at a time before pausing to look and listen intently. Soon he began to smell smoke, and finally he moved close enough to see three or four shadowy figures moving around a small fire.

"I don't like this," he heard one of the men ahead saying, "riding around a damned swamp all night, fighting the skeeters and snakes trying to find a needle in a haystack. I lost my hat out there somewhere, and I damn near got bit by a water moccasin as big around as my leg. And beside that, we need to be clean out of Clay County before the sun comes up. Everybody knows the sheriff here don't like our kind."

"What are you saying we should do, Trace?" another man asked. "Just ride out even before Bill shows up to go with us?"

"He knows where we're headed," the other man said.

"Yeah, but I bet you wouldn't want to ride alone all the way to Lee's Summit in day-

146

light, so why make him do it? We can afford to wait just a little while longer."

"Well, you fellows do what you want, but I'm not leaving here until I've found this boy. George and I are staying, aren't we, George?" a third man said. John's heart surged. He knew that voice! "This boy's daddy is the best friend I ever had," the man went on. "He saved my life at Wilson's Creek, and I'm not about to ride away now when we're so close and leave his son behind —"

"Cole! Cole, I'm here!" John said, fairly shouting out the announcement in his eagerness to let his friend know he was close by.

John felt happier than he had in weeks as he rushed through the tangle of brush and toward the fire. It was almost like coming home.

"I can't believe old Ned's still around," Cole commented as they rode down the back country road on their way to Lee's Summit. The sun had risen more than an hour before, but despite the daylight these men rode bravely and confidently in the open, and John was proud to be with them. "That horse must live some sort of charmed life to still be plugging along after all he's been through. But we'll still have to get you something better if you're going to keep up with this bunch."

"I don't mind that, but I'll have to find a way to get Ned back home," John said. "You know, when Lane raided our place and took everything we had, the only reason he didn't get his hands on Ned was that I just happened to ride him over to my grandfather's that morning. Of all our livestock, this is the only animal we didn't lose. Daddy'd never forgive me if I sold or traded him away now. And besides that, old as he is, he's still done all right by me all the time that I've been hiding out."

"We'll take care of him, John," Cole told him. "Don't worry. And with any luck, your daddy will be there to give Ned his first brushing once you get him back."

The best part about joining up with Cole last night, John had discovered, was the good news that his father's friend had delivered. Cole had just been to Kansas City a few days before to visit Mollie and learned from her that a parole for Jason was in the works. From Kansas City, Cole had ridden to Clay County to deliver the good news to Jason's family, and during that visit he had learned about John being on the run.

"Bill Quantrill's gathering up men like you

and me from all over this part of the state," Cole explained to John. "Men that have had enough of what the Jayhawkers and the Federals are doing to our people but haven't known what they could do about it until now. He started out last spring with just a handful, only enough to wipe out a small patrol occasionally or to cut down a few telegraph wires. But now he can sometimes bring together as many as fifty men with only a day or two's notice, and there's talk going around that something big is in the works, something that will serve notice on men like James Lane that Missouri is ready to fight back."

To John, it all sounded almost too good to be true. But what was equally welcome to him was the ready acceptance he had received from the men with Cole. To them he was not simply Jason Hartman's son, a youth in need of their protection, he was John Hartman, a man in his own right, worthy and welcome among them. Even Bill Gregg seemed to hold no grudges over his treatment in the swamp. In fact, he told John he would have thought less of him if he hadn't been so cautious.

They arrived at Quantrill's camp east of Lee's Summit shortly before noon. The camp was situated in a large open pasture on the back acreage of a farm owned by a man named Rupert Bone. The site had woods on three sides, a nearby creek for water, and plenty of lush green grass for the horses. About twenty-five men were already there. A few were cooking a midday meal for the group over three open fires, others were taking care of their horses by a large makeshift corral, and the rest were simply lounging around, talking, laughing, and sipping from large earthen jugs of homemade whiskey.

What surprised John the most about the camp was that it appeared to have been there for quite some time, days at least, and perhaps weeks.

"What keeps the Federals from attacking this place?" John asked. "With all the spies they have scattered around, they're bound to know about it, and no matter how well these men might be able to fight, they couldn't hope to stand up in a battle against even a company of regulars."

"They couldn't," Cole agreed, "and I'd be surprised if there is a man here who was foolish enough to try. Instead, they'd scatter like a covey of quail if any of the sentries around camp sounded the alarm, and by the time the Federals got here, this place would be deserted. Some of these men live close by, and they would probably just go home and act like they never heard of the war. The others would simply go into hiding, and then everybody would come together in another place two or three days from now."

"But what good is all this if they can't stand and fight?" John asked.

"It's a new kind of fighting for this war," Cole said, "but actually it's a lot like the way George Washington went about things back during the Revolution. You see, it's the Federals who have to be concerned with taking territory and holding it, and all we have to concentrate on is killing Federals. Quantrill's idea is that you should hit them where they're the weakest, not where they're the strongest. They can't have scores of troops in every place at the same time, so you hit where they've only got six or ten or a dozen men, and then you scatter so there's no way any larger force can follow you. The whole scheme works pretty well in an area like this where most of the men are locals who know the lay of the land well, and most of the people are on our side and willing to support us."

John had never considered fighting the war on such terms. His notion of how the enemy should be dealt with always had more to do with open battlefields and hordes of men rushing at one another to fight face to face, man to man. There was something about running away whenever the enemy outnumbered you, of having to be content to nip at his heels like a dog, or to wait in hiding until you could shoot at his backside that was distasteful to John, perhaps even dishonorable. But if it worked . . .

When they reached the corral, all six men unsaddled their horses and turned them loose with the other animals in the large makeshift pen. While they were busy with that, a number of other men came up to greet them, and John was introduced to several more members of the group.

"Come on, John," Cole said after they were finished caring for their mounts. "Let's get something to eat, then we'll see what we can do about getting you another horse and something better to shoot with than that worthless relic you're carrying. Nobody is going to cut you any slack, and if you're going to make it in this outfit, you're going to have to be able to ride as fast and shoot as straight as any man here."

"I'll give it the best I've got, Cole," John promised, "and if that isn't enough, I guess you'll just have to send me on back to the swamp."

"You'll do fine," Cole assured him. "After all, you're Jason Hartman's son, and for any man who knows your daddy, that should be recommendation enough." John was pleased to think that his father was so highly regarded by men of this kind, but he also resolved that before long, he would deserve their respect because of his own deeds and not those of his parent.

After their meal, Cole asked around and found out that several of Quantrill's men had captured a small Union army patrol just the day before. He was able to get John one of the horses that had been seized after the fight, and he also located a brace of revolvers and a short, single-shot carbine for him. Then they started Jason's horse, Ned, back on his way to Will Hartman's farm with a man named Samson who was traveling to Clay County on some errand for Quantrill.

A trickle of reinforcements from several neighboring counties continued to arrive all during the afternoon, and by nightfall the group had nearly doubled in size. John was delighted to discover his friend Frank James among the new arrivals. When the two of them met, Frank explained proudly that he had already been riding with Quantrill for more than a month and had only left for a brief time to go home and visit his family.

After a simple evening meal of boiled beef and potatoes, they all assembled in the center of the camp on Quantrill's orders. A large bonfire had been built there, and the men gathered around it, laughing and talking with one another as they waited for the meeting to begin.

When Quantrill appeared at last, John studied him with great curiosity. He appeared to be only about twenty-five, with a slender, almost boyish, frame. His features revealed none of the ferocity John would have expected in the leader of a force such as this, and when he spoke, his voice was quiet and earnest, but hardly forceful. He was dressed in a dusty black suit, crumpled linen shirt, and expensive-looking black leather boots. Like most of his followers, he carried numerous weapons of every size and description.

Whatever reservations John might have felt quickly disappeared, however, when he saw the quiet, confident authority that Quantrill asserted over his men.

"A while ago I had Bill Gregg take a head count," Quantrill told them, "and he reported back that there's seventy of us here right now, and others are still on their way. Outside of General Price's army, this is the largest force of loyal Southern men ever assembled in this part of the state since the war began!"

The announcement brought a rousing cheer from the men. Quantrill waited patiently for the burst of enthusiasm to pass before continuing.

"As some of you probably know," he continued, "I've been out scouting for the past week, and I've selected our next target. Considering the number of brave men who answered my call and have rallied here to the banner of the South, I've decided it's high time we took on some greater mission than ambushing Federal patrols and cutting down telegraph wires. This time, boys, we're going to strike a blow that will be felt all the way to Washington. We're going to hit so hard and so fast that from this day forward, men like Jim Lane and Charles Jennison will never again be foolish enough to believe that they can come into our state and do what they want, where they want, without having to pay the price for their deeds on their own home soil."

Again the men cheered their approval of Quantrill's words. Every man among them, even the newcomers like John Hartman, understood where the target Quantrill had selected must lie. They were going to attack Kansas!

"I guess that's all that needs to be said," Quantrill continued. "Get whatever praying and letter-writing you need to do out of the way tonight, because tomorrow we're going to take the devil by the tail and give him a good kick in the backside. We ride at dawn!"

Despite his exhaustion, John found it almost impossible to sleep that night. Myriad thoughts and questions filled his head at the same time. For months now he had thought of little else but leaving home and going off to fight in the war, but this was not at all how he had expected it to happen. In the span of slightly less than twenty-four hours, he had gone from hiding in a swamp, a lonely fugitive, to preparing for battle. What would his family think if they knew where he was and what he was about to take part in? How would his mother feel if she realized that her oldest son was now a part of the war that had come so close to killing her husband? And how would he act when the bullets started flying and the time for killing came? Despite all the confident words he had heard himself speaking since joining up with Cole and the others, he wasn't sure he was brave enough, man enough, to do this thing. As yet, he still wasn't sure that he deserved the confidence that Cole and all the others seemed to automatically place in him. But tomorrow would tell.

Hardly realizing that sleep had ever come, he found himself being shaken awake in what seemed like the middle of the night.

"Come on, John. It's time to get ready." Cole knelt over him, jostling his arm. "It's going to be daylight in about thirty minutes, and we still have to get something to eat, pack our gear, and saddle up."

John raised up onto one elbow and looked around. A kerosene lamp sat on the ground in one corner of the shelter, and by its light he saw that Cole was already dressed and that George Todd was just now tugging on his trousers. A few feet away, Frank James was still a prone, sleeping lump beneath his blankets, but Cole soon remedied that.

They ate a hurried meal of cold sliced beef and last night's cornbread on their way to the corral. A number of men were already saddled up and ready to go, and most of the others were there trying to cut their mounts out of the herd. After a few minutes, John was able to get a bridle on the horse Cole had acquired for him and led the animal out of the corral to where his saddle and bedroll lay.

Soon Quantrill appeared, mounted and ready to go. The talk was that he had spent the night in Rupert Bone's farmhouse, and John even heard one lewd, lighthearted suggestion that Bone's pretty seventeen-year-old daughter, Ellen, might have made the leader's last night before battle a memorable one.

They were on their way by the time the first traces of yellow and pink began to tint the eastern sky. To John it was a stirring moment, one that etched itself into his memory in vivid detail. With Quantrill at the head, the men formed a long column as they rode across the pasture and turned down the road leading west. They rode at a gallop for the first mile or two, letting their horses stretch their legs and work off some of their initial exuberance. Then they settled back into a slower gait which would be necessary for the long trip to Kansas.

John was more than pleased with the horse Cole had got for him. After some initial negotiations about who was to be in control, the big husky bay finally accepted his new passenger and soon began to prove himself to be as strong and quick as any horse John had ever ridden. Riding down the road atop the splendid animal, with his two new revolvers thrust in the waistband of his trousers and his carbine lying across his lap, John felt very formidable indeed. The fears and apprehensions of the previous night were gone, and he now felt able and eager to take on any foe their leader led them against. The next time he visited home, he realized with a rush of pride, it would be with his head held high and his first battle behind him.

As yet no one except Quantrill himself, and perhaps a couple of his most trusted lieutenants, knew what their destination was. Cole explained that this was standard practice with the band, since there was always the possibility that spies among them would slip away and reveal their target to the enemy. But this morning the specifics mattered little to John. The fact that they continued to ride due west, straight toward Kansas, was enough for him.

About three hours into the ride they encountered their first Federal patrol. They were passing just a few miles before West-port, which lay due south of Kansas City, when they spotted the six mounted, blue-clad figures stopped in the road ahead. For a critical moment the Union soldiers seemed confused by the large mounted band approaching them, and the minute or two that they hesitated proved to be their ruin.

The instant Quantrill spotted the enemy troops ahead, he and a number of other men in the front ranks of the column opened fire. One of the Federals fell heavily to the ground and another reeled clumsily in the saddle as he attempted to pull his mount around and flee. Immediately the remaining soldiers turned their horses and began to gallop away, but just as quickly Quantrill and the others near him put the spurs to their mounts and took up the pursuit.

The chase lasted more than two miles, and though John and most of the others in Quantill's band never got a chance to fire a shot, they all still rode along. The frantic Federals were soon lined out along the road according to their riding ability and the speed of their horses, and each time one of them was unfortunate enough to fall too far behind, he was immediately felled by a hailstorm of gunfire.

A man or two from Quantrill's column stopped briefly each time a downed soldier was passed in order to strip him of his weapons and finish him off if necessary. John glimpsed each of the bodies as he galloped along, but it was hard to see much because of the speed at which he was moving. The main thought that kept running through his head during the ten-minute chase was that he really was in the war at last. Real shots were being fired, and real men were being turned into real corpses.

Quantrill finally began to slow the pace as the last Union soldier tumbled backward out of the saddle and skidded to a stop, facedown in the dusty road. When Quantrill reached the body he stopped his horse alongside it, aimed his revolver, and fired an insurance shot into the back of the man's head.

"Anybody need a good pair of boots?" Quantrill asked loudly. "This fellow's look brand-new, and I don't think he'll object to giving them up." A man nearby accepted the offer and slid to the ground to claim his prize.

Everybody was in extremely high spirits now that the skirmish was over. They waited around for a moment, discussing what had happened, mocking the Federal troops for their useless, craven flight, and basking in the seeming invulnerability of their band. Not a one of the six enemy soldiers had ever fired a shot, and no one in Quantrill's group had suffered a scratch during the chase.

"All right, the fun's over so let's get going," Quantrill announced at last. "By the time these bodies are found, we'll probably already be where we want to go."

"And where's that, Bill?" one of the men finally had the nerve to ask. "This far along, it don't look like it'll hurt to let us in on the secret."

"You're right," Quantrill agreed. "We're going to take Olathe."

"The whole damn town?" someone exclaimed.

"Why not?" Quantrill grinned. "Who's to stop us? I was over there just a few days ago, and I can promise you the whole town of Olathe is just lying there waiting for us like a ripe peach."

John was amazed by the audacity of the plan. He realized that, until that moment, he had just assumed that they would make a raid similar to those that James Lane was in the habit of making in Missouri, burning farms along the way and generally terrorizing a swath of Kansas countryside. It had never occurred to him that they might actually seize a whole town.

As they proceeded, everybody began talking about the brilliance of Quantrill's plan. Olathe was right in the midst of enemy-controlled territory, just a scant few miles southeast of Lawrence, but Quantrill had discovered that no large body of enemy soldiers — Union or Jayhawker — was permanently stationed there. If they could reach the town without being discovered, it would be hours before any band large enough to give them any problems could be dispatched from either Kansas City to the northeast or Lawrence to the northwest.

Just inside the Kansas border, Quantrill's men stopped, questioned, and then killed a man who had the great misfortune to fall into their hands. Then, a few miles farther along, a dozen or so men split off from the main column just long enough to torch the house and all the outbuildings of a large, prosperous-looking farm which they passed along the way.

Noon came and passed without any sort of stop to rest and eat. Now that they were deep into Kansas, enemy territory, a sense of urgency was beginning to overtake them. Although they had taken as many precautions as possible, including the annihilation of the Union patrol, there was still a good chance that riders were already on their way to Kansas City and Lawrence to spread the alarm. No matter how exhausted and hungry they might get, they knew they must press on steadily if they hoped to accomplish their objective and get back into safe territory alive.

About midafternoon one of the scouts came galloping back with the news that the road ahead was clear all the way into Olathe. When that news arrived, Quantrill stopped to give the group some final instructions.

"Men, we've made it this far without any problems," their leader told them, "and I don't want any of you getting careless from this point on, so stay on your toes. But remember, we're not here to hurt children, and if I hear of any of you laying a finger on a woman except to defend yourself, I'll personally put a bullet in you. Other than that, the place is yours and you can do what you want with it. Take what you want, and burn what you want. Any man you see in this town with a gun in his hand or on his hip should be considered an enemy, and you've got to deal with him appropriately. We're in Jim Lane's territory and we'll play by his rules today, which means that just about anything goes.

"I want to be in and out of this place in one hour, though," Quantrill continued. "Anybody that's not ready to leave when the rest of us are gets left behind . . . and God help you if that happens to any one of you. Now let's go in there and give them a taste of their own medicine!"

When they got in sight of Olathe, everybody put the spurs to their horses, and they thundered into town whooping and hollering and firing their guns in the air. Most of the town's fifteen or so businesses were located along one main street, with a scattering of homes, barns, and sheds situated on all four sides of the main part of town.

For the first few seconds the hundred or so startled residents of the small town were thrown into utter confusion. In general, they seemed to have no notion that these noisy, armed men could be from Missouri, but it didn't take them long to realize what a dread fate had befallen them.

Here and there a few townsmen made desperate attempts to resist the raiders, but they were quickly dispatched by Quantrill's men. By the time Cole, John, and Frank arrived in town slightly behind the first of the raiders, the main street of Olathe was already littered with several corpses. Within minutes, however, all resistance had ended.

"Look, there's a general store," Cole said, pointing off to their left. "Let's go in there. I need a couple of boxes of cartridges, and you never can tell what else we might decide to pick up."

They dismounted in front of the store and drew their revolvers before entering. All up and down the street others in the band were doing the same, bursting through the doors of stores and shops with their guns drawn, ready to take what they wanted and gun down anyone foolish enough to oppose them.

The general store was empty, and after checking behind all the counters and in the back storage room, John and his companions felt secure enough to holster their weapons again.

"Just think, John!" Frank exclaimed. "We can have anything in the place that we want. And it's not like stealing because we're taking it from some Jayhawker bastard who would be glad to do the same thing to us if he ever got the chance. Anything we want!"

Both Cole and Frank headed straight for the weapons case, where they spread a blanket out on a counter and began piling an assortment of pistols and ammunition on top of it. John, however, had something different in mind. The suit of clothes he had on were the same ones he had been wearing all during his five weeks of fugitive life, and he could not resist the rows of trousers and heavy work shirts piled neatly on the shelves behind one of the store's long counters.

When he found an outfit that looked like it would fit, he quickly peeled down to the skin, donned a fresh pair of long johns from the shelves, and then put on a new shirt, trousers, and belt. New socks and boots came next, and when he was finished, he went to a full-length mirror along one wall to examine his new outfit.

While admiring himself in the mirror, John caught sight of a movement reflected behind him. First he spotted the metal barrel of a shotgun protruding through the curtain over the doorway leading to the back room, and then he saw the man behind it. As he spun to face the stranger, he realized in a rush of panic that he had left all his weapons lying with his old clothes several feet away. The man who held the gun was in his early forties, wearing a dirty shop apron over his street clothes. His face was flushed and his eyes were large with fear, but during that first instant when they gazed at one another, John realized that the man was not going to let his fear keep him from doing what he thought he must do.

John made a desperate dive to the right, sprawling on the floor, just as the shotgun exploded. The mirror John had been using disintegrated in a shower of glass fragments, but before the man had time to shift his weapon and fire again, another shot roared out from near the front of the store. Screaming in sudden pain, the man let the shotgun slip from his grasp and staggered back against a row of shelves. Cole's shot, fired at an angle, had caught the man low on the left side of his abdomen.

John scrambled to his feet and raced over to snatch the man's shotgun off the floor, then held it pointed at his chest until Cole and Frank reached him.

"Kill the bastard, John," Frank James urged his friend. "Blow his damn head off, just like he tried to do to you!"

John's finger began to tighten on the trigger as he considered the fact that, if he hadn't glanced back in the mirror at the precise instant he did, this man would have killed him.

"Please . . ." the man begged. "Please, young man . . ." Tears were welling in his eyes, and his face was contorted with fear and pain. Low on his left side, where he held both hands protectively over his wound, blood was saturating his shirt and trickling between his fingers.

John glanced at Cole's face, wordlessly asking his friend for advice, but Cole had none to give him. "It's your call, John," Cole said. "It was you he nearly killed, not me. Nobody will blame you if you shoot him."

"I didn't mean it, young man," John's

prisoner blubbered desperately. "I'm sorry. I just lost my head when I saw you coming in here to steal everything . . ."

"Where were you?" John asked sharply. "We checked that back room. Where were you hiding?"

"Trapdoor . . ." the man replied. "Under the floor . . ." Even as they watched, the man's face grew deathly pale. John simply stepped back and watched as the man's legs failed him and his body crumpled to the floor.

"Better check it, Frank," Cole advised. "Find the trapdoor and see if there's anybody else hiding back there. Holler out if you need any help."

John stood for a moment longer staring down at the unconscious man, then laid the shotgun aside. "I can't do it, Cole," he admitted. "It's not like he was a Federal and there was some point in killing him now."

"He's not a Federal, but he could be a Jayhawker," Cole suggested.

"I doubt it," John said. "Judging by the look on his face, I doubt if he has guts enough for even that."

"It's your call, John," Cole repeated.

A sudden scuffle in the back room diverted their attention, and an instant later

169

they heard Frank call out, "Hey Cole! You'll never guess what I found back here. Look at this!" He emerged from the back room holding a furious, struggling boy of about twelve. When the boy saw the man lying unconscious on the floor, he managed to break free from Frank's grip and spring forward.

"Don't worry, boy," Cole said. "He's not dead. I just winged him. Is that your father?"

The boy looked up at the three of them. Tears were streaming down his face, but his eyes were filled with anger. "You bastards!" he cried.

"Look, boy, your old man's losing a lot of blood there," Cole answered, calmly ignoring the insult. "Instead of cussing us, if I was you, I'd be thinking about finding something to cover that hole with before he bleeds to death."

For a couple of minutes the three of them watched the boy's clumsy efforts to care for his father, and then Cole said, "Look, there's no sense in the three of us standing here gawking. John, you keep an eye on these two while Frank and I load up as much of this stuff here as we can carry. If there's time, I might even try to scare up a couple of spare horses we can load up. I bet there's a lot of things in this store that your family will be able to use when they start to set up their own place again."

Cole and Frank both left the store carrying blankets loaded down with weapons and other goods from the general store. Through the front window, John saw them tie the bundles across the backs of their horses, and then they disappeared down the street. A few shots were still being fired outside, and once in a while an exuberant raider galloped past the store. The air was beginning to fill with the scent of burning wood, and although John could not see very far in either direction down the street, he guessed that many of the buildings in town had already been put to the torch. They had been in Olathe less than thirty minutes, which meant that he still had nearly half an hour to stand guard over these prisoners.

With his first-aid work completed, the boy now sat in sullen silence beside his unconscious father, glancing up only occasionally to give John a look filled with hatred and disdain.

"Is there a doctor in this town, kid?" John asked at last.

The boy nodded silently without bothering to speak.

"Well, we'll be out of here in a little while, and then you can get him to take care of your father."

"He might die before then," the boy said at last. "Look, he's already bled through the bandage."

"Look, kid," John said. "He tried to shoot me, but he got himself shot instead. He deserves what he got. He should have just stayed there under the floor and let us take what we wanted. Right now you should be thanking me for staying here with you, because that might be the only way the both of you make it through this thing alive."

"I ain't thanking you for nothing," the boy hissed. "You just wait, you damn rebel bastard. You just wait until I get old enough . . ."

John didn't reply, nor did he take any particular offense at the outburst. From the boy's perspective, he figured, John and his friends were pretty lowdown characters, and he had a right to be angry and outraged. The insults didn't bother John, and his only hope was that the boy didn't get so filled up with hatred that he decided to try something stupid.

Hurried footsteps on the wooden sidewalk outside alerted John that someone was coming, and a moment later Frank James stuck his head in the front doorway. "Come on, John. We're leaving," Frank announced breathlessly. "Our scouts spotted a column headed this way from the north. Nobody seems to know who they are or how many of them there are, but Quantrill has spread the word that we're leaving. Some of the men have already gone, and we'll have to hurry up if we don't want to be left behind!"

"Looks like you'll be getting that doctor for your old man sooner than you thought," John said as he rose to go. He had already taken a couple of steps toward the door before some vague but undeniable apprehension made him pause and look back. The boy already had his hands on his father's shotgun but had not yet been able to swing the muzzle around so he could aim and fire.

John spun reflexively, drew his revolver and fired one quick shot which caught the boy in the center of his chest. The boy fell like a stone, not uttering a sound as he collapsed, already dead, atop the body of his father.

Frank had already left the doorway, but came hurrying back, gun in hand, when he heard the shot. He found John still standing where he had turned and fired.

"He tried to shoot me, Frank," John explained dully. "He had the shotgun."

"Stupid bastards," Frank exclaimed angrily. "They could have stayed alive. Both of them could have lived through this thing, but not now, not either of them . . ." He picked up a glass lamp from a counter nearby and dashed it to the floor almost at John's feet. "Come on, John," he said. "Back away from that stuff. We've got to get out of here."

John took a few clumsy steps backward, still not quite aware of what was going on around him. Frank waited until he was in the clear, then drew his revolver and fired at the spilled kerosene on the floor. It ignited immediately, and slowly the flames began to spread across the saturated wooden planks.

"Let's skedaddle!" Frank said, grabbing his friend's arm and jerking him toward the door. John's senses were beginning to return to him by the time they reached their horses. As they were mounting, Cole raced toward them and leaped astride his horse.

Cole cast one hurried glance at the blaze inside the store, and another at John, but there was no time for questions. Gunfire was already beginning to sound at the north end of town where Quantrill had sent a dozen of his men to fight a delaying action. The remaining raiders were scattered in a long ragged line across the prairie to the south.

The three of them leaned forward in their saddles as they goaded their horses' flanks with their heels. It was going to be a long ride home.

CHAPTER SEVEN

Cole was surprised by the intensity of Mollie's first embrace. There was something urgent, almost desperate, in the way she held herself tightly against him, clinging to him as if he were her only salvation from some terrible disaster.

"I could tell by your note that you wanted me to hurry," Cole said, "but I had no idea it would be this important."

"Oh, Cole, I'm in such a mess!" Mollie told him, her face resting against the coarse cloth of his shirt. "I don't know what I would have done if you hadn't got my message and come as quickly as you did. As it is, I've already put him off for four days, but I don't think he would have listened to any more excuses from me."

It was late at night and they were standing in the middle of the stable behind Genevieve de Mauduis' house. After arriving in the city, Cole had sent a message to Mollie

176

at the theatre informing her that he had come, and then had waited until after dark before slipping down an alley and into the stable. He had no idea what the problem was, but just to be safe he wanted to stay out of sight until they met.

"Who have you been putting off?" Cole asked. "I don't understand any of what you're saying!"

"I know, I'm just babbling," Mollie said. "It's the excitement of your being here . . . of knowing that that Walt Samson was actually able to find you and give you my message."

"I got it last night. I might have been here sooner, but we were off on a little 'errand' across the border."

"Well you got it in time, and that's the most important thing," Mollie told him. "Come on. Let's sit over here and I'll tell you all about it." She picked up the lamp she had brought into the stable with her and hung it on a peg, then led the way to a pile of hay bales which were stacked along one wall.

"You know, when you were here before," she began at last, "I explained to you how I finally managed to get Jason released from that camp."

"Yes, I remember," Cole said. "I wasn't

very fond of the idea of you playing up to that Yankee officer to do it, but I guess there was no other way."

"No there wasn't," she agreed, "and that part of things went fine. It was later, after Jason was out and on his way home, that things started getting so messed up. You see, after Jason was out, I couldn't just refuse to see Cory Winstead anymore. If I did that, he would have figured out pretty fast that I had just used him, and he would probably have had Jason arrested again. And besides, I got this idea in my head that if I could talk him into helping me once, I could probably do it again."

"But what kind of help did you need?" Cole asked. "Jason is out already, and John is with us."

"Well, it occurred to me that if Cory could help me get Jason free, he might also help me find out about others of our friends and neighbors who had been or were about to be arrested."

"My God, Mollie!" Cole exclaimed. "That's spying, woman. Don't you know you could get shot for that?"

"I could have been shot for a lot of the things I've done in my life," Mollie reminded him. "And you were there when I did most of them. But I wanted to do something. If I could prevent it, I didn't want what happened to Jason and Arethia to happen to anyone else that we know. And by then there was no problem in handling Cory. He was so crazy about me . . ."

She paused as a dark expression of disapproval crossed Cole's features, then she gathered her courage and plunged on ahead.

"But you see, there was another Union officer mixed up in this as well, a major named Rudolph Benjamin, and he wasn't quite so easy to manage as Cory was. This Major Benjamin has been interested in me for quite some time now, and he didn't take it very well when he saw that I had taken up with another officer instead of him.

"Finally last Thursday things began to come to a head. Cory visited me that evening and said that he had taken about all the harassment he would tolerate from Benjamin. It seems the major had been pulling all sorts of tricks . . . trying to get Cory reassigned, arranging surprise inspections, and spreading rumors that he was soliciting bribes from the prisoners at the camp in exchange for their release. That night Cory told me he was going to challenge Major Benjamin to a duel." Mollie stopped speaking for a moment, as if it were somehow difficult for her to go on. "They fought on

Saturday morning. The major killed Cory with one shot to the chest."

"Well he was a Federal, Mollie," Cole reminded her with some impatience. "I say let them kill each other off as much as they want. It just saves us that much trouble."

"No, that's not the problem, Cole. I was fond of Cory and I was sorry to see him die, but that's not what has me so upset. It was what happened afterward that made me decide to send for you. I just didn't know what else to do or who else to turn to. You see, a day or so after the major shot Cory Winstead, he came to me and told me he had discovered what Cory and I had been up to. He had learned about Jason's release, and somehow he had discovered that Cory was supplying me with information about the arrest list. He told me that it would probably be enough grounds to have me and Jason and Jason's entire family arrested, but that if I was willing to co-operate with him, the information need never come to light."

"I see," Cole said quietly. "And by 'co-operate,' I guess you mean . . ."

"I told you he was interested in me," Mollie said. "Major Benjamin is the kind of man who's used to having what he wants, and it goaded him that he couldn't have me. But I

180

had no idea that he would go to these extremes."

"I'll kill him for you, Mollie," Cole stated matter-of-factly. "There's no problem with that. Just tell me where to find him, and I'll kill him and be out of town before anybody can do anything about it."

"That would be the easiest way," she conceded, "but unfortunately not the safest. Before he dies, I need to be assured that he hasn't told anyone else about what he knows. And to do that, I need to talk to him."

"It sounds to me like you already have a plan in mind, Mollie."

"Yes, I do. But I'll need your help to do it right. If you and I can pull this off, everything will be fine, but if we bungle it, not only my life, but the lives of everyone in my family will be at stake."

"We can do it. We've always made a hell of a team, Mollie," Cole told her confidently.

"We have, haven't we?" Mollie said, smiling for the first time since she entered the stable. "We've always been good together . . . in more ways than one." Just having Cole here made her feel better than she had in days, and now that their course was decided, it was almost as if the matter was taken care of already. A look of anticipation on her face, she reached out once again and took Cole's hand in hers.

"I think it would be safe for you to come into the house with me, Cole," Mollie said softly. "There's no use in your spending the night in the stable when much more pleasant accommodations are available."

A broad smile was spread across Rudolph Benjamin's face as he mounted the stairs to the second floor of the Danforth Inn, carrying a bottle of wine. Things couldn't be better as far as he was concerned. He had been able to vindicate himself completely in the killing of Cory Winstead, and, during the court of inquiry, he had even managed to create the impression in the minds of some senior officers that he had done the service a favor by ridding it of a corrupt and untrustworthy officer. Hell, there might even be a promotion in this for him, he thought. A man just had to know how to handle things, how to manipulate people and circumstances to his own ends.

And what was about to happen this evening was another good example of that. He had tolerated Miss Mollie Hartman's aloofness and capricious deceits for many weeks now, far longer than any other man probably would have, but finally, through patience and skill, he had managed to place her in a position where she had no choice except to submit to him. It was a glorious day, and he intended to enjoy it to its fullest.

He paused outside a door in the empty, second-floor hallway and took a deep breath, a feeling of anticipation already pulsing through him. He raised his hand to knock, then decided not to bother and reached for the doorknob instead.

Mollie was already there, sitting on the edge of the bed, looking at him with an expression that was hard to interpret. She seemed neither hostile nor fearful, as he had half expected her to be. In fact, although she was not quite smiling, there was a gleam in her eye, as if she too had been secretly looking forward to this rendezvous.

"Good evening, Major," Mollie said quietly.

"Wouldn't you say the situation calls for a little less formality, Mollie?" he asked. "Why don't you call me Rudy?"

"All right, then. Hello, Rudy."

"That's better." Benjamin closed the door behind him and set the bottle of wine on a nearby table. Seeing her here, available to him at last, made him feel suddenly too impatient even to do any drinking. There would be time to uncork the wine afterward.

"You were outstanding in your performance tonight," the major told her. "I've seen the show three times before, but tonight during the third act I was ready to come up on stage and beat hell out of Billingsly myself."

"Maybe it was just knowing that pretty soon you would be doing to Miss Penelope what Billingsly had been trying to do all during the play," Mollie suggested. A hint of a smile crossed her features and then vanished again. She was still playing with him, Benjamin thought. But that was all right. At this point her coyness only served to heighten his anticipation.

Mollie rose from the bed and crossed the room to give the major an unexpected kiss. She caressed his cheek and then smiled at him at last, fully and openly.

"This is not going to be at all as you imagined," she said softly. "You set your trap well and drew me into it, but now that I'm here, I must confess that I'm not so unhappy about the way things have turned out. You're a handsome man, a dashing officer with style and money, and I've been thinking it's time to have a man in my life again. In fact, if you play your cards right, this could work out quite well for both of us." She kissed him warmly once again, then stepped back slightly and began opening the buttons of her blouse.

Without any apparent embarrassment, Mollie removed her blouse and floor-length skirt. She stopped undressing only when she reached the light silk camisole and short silk slip which she wore under her other clothes. Benjamin watched with delight, hardly able to believe her forwardness.

"I just have one question for you though, Rudy," Mollie told him. "Do you know the difference between a whore and a lover?"

"Yes, of course," he replied.

"Then I want you to know that I won't be your whore, not ever, no matter what you threaten me with. You've wanted me for a long time and now I'm here, but that doesn't mean you own me."

"I wouldn't want it that way either," he vowed.

"I'm glad to hear you say that, Rudy," Mollie told him. "But for things to be really good, we have to put this other business behind us, this business of threats and whatever it was that Cory Winstead was supposed to have told me."

"No one knows about all of that but me," he assured her. "And even now, after the board of inquiry, no one else has any suspicions." Unable to resist any longer, he stepped forward and took Mollie in his arms, kissing her as his hands began to explore her body hungrily.

She let him do as he wished for a moment, then drew her lips away and said, "Promise me, Rudy."

"Promise you what?" he asked.

"Promise me that no one else knows and that you won't ever again try to force me to do anything because of some list of names or any other ridiculous evidence that you think you have against me." The softness in her voice was suddenly gone, and it struck Benjamin that even now, even knowing that he could ruin her and her family with a few simple words to the right people, it was she, not he, who was still in control.

"I'm not a fool, Mollie," he said with sudden irritation. "I wouldn't risk all this by telling anybody what I knew before I saw what you were going to decide. And as for the list of names I found in Winstead's things, I returned that to the files. I knew it would always be there if I needed it again. You and your family are as safe as anyone can be in these crazy times."

"Good! That's what I wanted to hear," Mollie said.

"And me too," a calm male voice announced unexpectedly from behind the major. Even as Mollie pulled free of Benjamin's grasp and backed away, he was spinning to gaze in amazement at the man who stood in the middle of the room with a pistol in his hand.

"Where . . . who . . . ?" the major stammered, still too dumbfounded to figure out what was going on. A few feet away the open closet door provided an answer to the "Where" part of the question, and the barrel of the stranger's gun made all other questions irrelevant.

"Don't make a move, and don't say a word," the intruder commanded. "Mollie, get his gun out of his holster and give it to me, then get dressed."

As Benjamin felt his weapon being removed from behind him, he turned his head to the side and hissed, "You treacherous goddamn whore. When I'm through with you —"

The barrel of Cole's pistol smashed against the side of his head before he could say any more, and he toppled, nearly unconscious, across the bed. For a moment he lay in a daze, vaguely aware that his legs were being lifted up onto the bed and his arms were being moved around above his head. Then his arms and feet were tied to the metal bedstead, and some sort of gag was stuffed into his mouth.

Cole remained standing over Rudolph Benjamin until full consciousness returned to him. Off to the side, Mollie Hartman finished dressing, then joined her cohort beside the bed. Now, instead of the blouse and skirt she had been wearing earlier, she had on loose-fitting masculine clothes, and her hair was tucked up under a wide-brimmed felt hat.

"Now see what your philandering has done to you, Major?" she said. The look on her face approached one of compassion, but the features of her companion remained devoid of any expression. "You should have let well enough alone because you're not nearly as crafty as you thought you were."

Benjamin tried desperately to speak past the gag in his mouth, but his words were muffled beyond recognition.

"I know," Mollie said tolerantly. "You were lying before, weren't you? Others know about the list, and they know you were coming to meet me here as well. Is that it?"

Benjamin nodded eagerly. Those were almost precisely the words he had tried to utter.

"Well, I'll find out soon enough if either of those things is true," Mollie said, "but I do know that nobody saw me come here up the back stairs, and no one will see me leave. And the room is not registered in my name either. My friend here was kind enough to rent it for me in a fictitious name. So I guess I'll just take my chances. Good-bye, Major Benjamin."

After Mollie was gone, Cole turned the lamp down, then stood by the window for a moment or two, as if waiting for a signal. Finally he nodded his head, apparently in response to some sign from the alley below. By the time he returned to the bed, he had put his pistol in its holster and now held some other object in his hand instead. White-hot terror raced through Benjamin's veins as the object descended toward his throat and he saw the lamplight glitter off the long shiny blade. He began to buck and thrash desperately but Cole simply reached out and got a handful of his hair to hold his head steady.

"I want you to die knowing that you got what you deserved, and that it was Cole Younger that gave it to you!"

Major Rudolph Benjamin had only an instant to endure a flash of pain before sinking into the void.

Sitting in the tub of steaming water, Mollie

scrubbed herself until all the places Benjamin had touched were chafed and stinging, but still the eerie sensation of being filthy and defiled would not leave her. Finally she gave up, left the tub, and began drying herself off. Then, when she was finished, she put on a nightgown, savoring the cool, soft sensation of the silk against her irritated skin.

On the table beside her bed sat a brandy bottle and a nearly empty glass. She filled the glass almost to the brim, quickly drank half its contents, and put it back on the table again. She had been drinking steadily ever since she arrived home nearly an hour before, but it hadn't helped much . . . not yet at least.

A strange mix of emotions stirred in Mollie as she heard Cole walking down the hall toward her room. Much of what she felt was relief at knowing that everything had gone as planned and that she would not have to spend this dreadful night alone. They had agreed before starting out that if there were any problems or complications, Cole would simply leave the city instead of coming back here tonight.

But another sensation arose in her as well, something so closely akin to shame that it could hardly be interpreted as anything else.

Since becoming an actress, and especially since entering the arena of wartime intrigue, she had grown accustomed to using her beauty, her charm, and her sensuality to get what she wanted, but only tonight had she finally gained any real understanding of what power lay hidden beneath her abilities to appeal to the sexual side of men and what frightening levels of self-degradation lay ahead of her if she continued to use this power.

Tonight she had caused the death of a man . . . and Cole had been there. He had seen and heard everything.

For his part, Cole Younger hardly looked as if he had sorted out any such great realizations as he entered the room and closed the door behind him. He took in Mollie, the bathtub, and the brandy with a single sweeping glance, then crossed the room and emptied the remaining liquor in Mollie's glass with a single gulp.

"I never killed a man that way before," Cole said. He refilled the glass with brandy, then emptied it again. "I didn't think it would get to me, but it did, even with a bastard like that. There was this look in his eye that last second —"

"I know, Cole," Mollie said quickly. She desperately didn't want to hear this, didn't want to know what their victim had looked like or to imagine what terror he must have felt at the moment of his death. "But it had to be done."

"That's right," Cole said. "It needed doing, and now it's done." He began to peel off his clothes, pitching the garments one by one in a pile on the floor. When he settled into the bathtub, Mollie knelt on the floor beside him.

She helped him bathe and dry off, neither of them saying much, and when he was ready they both got into the bed. Cole put the lamp out and then lay back with Mollie clinging tightly to him.

"You know," Cole said at last, "there's been damn few times I've ever tried to tell you what to do, and I won't start making a habit of it now. But I will tell you that if you're going to keep on doing what you're doing, you'd better start being more careful about it. You can't count on getting into too many messes like this one without finally being caught, and from what I know about them, the Federals probably wouldn't hesitate to shoot someone for spying, man or woman."

"I know all that," Mollie answered. "The truth is, though, I haven't been thinking anything about the future lately. All that's been on my mind since I started trying to get Jason freed was what was happening at the moment. But tell me this, Cole. What would it be worth to a bunch like Quantrill's to have somebody right here in the enemy camp who could pass on information about what was going on?"

"It could count for a lot," Cole said.

"And would the risks I would be taking be any greater than the ones you and John take every day that you stay with Quantrill?"

"No, they wouldn't," Cole reluctantly admitted.

Mollie could tell that he didn't have much argument left in him, but she also knew him well enough to realize that, even if he didn't say it, he would disapprove of her getting any more involved with the Federal officers here in Kansas City than she already was. That was understandable enough, she thought. After what happened tonight he realized full well what direction that sort of involvement would almost certainly take.

After a long period of silence, Mollie raised her head to kiss the side of Cole's neck, and when he turned his face down to hers, she kissed his lips as well.

"Thank you for coming, Cole," she whispered.

"As long as there's life left in me, Mollie,

all you'll ever have to do is tell me you need me," he promised.

"I know," she murmured. "And right now is one of those times."

"You only have to say it once," Cole chuckled, shifting around in the bed until they were face to face, their bodies in full contact from shoulder to knee. The instant he touched her, Mollie could feel the desire begin to surge, flowing through her veins like some healing potion, driving away at last the dreadful memory of Rudolph Benjamin's touch.

Mollie plunged herself fully, desperately, into their lovemaking, abandoning all rational thought as she soared away into an incredible realm where, for the moment, desire alone existed.

As she neared the summit of pleasure, Mollie listened to her own moans of fulfillment as if they were coming from some other place and some other person. Imprisoned beneath the pounding weight of Cole's body, she thrashed and heaved like a wild thing entangled hopelessly, desperately, in a primal struggle for survival. They crested together, their mingled cries flooding the room, then plunged beyond the brink, still locked together in a spent, slippery embrace, into an exhausted, gasping aftermath.

After a few moments Cole rolled aside, still breathing heavily, moving his body as if it were little more than a dead weight. Mollie, feeling a chill begin to settle in after their heated lovemaking, pulled the bed sheet up to cover them. Then she settled once again against her lover, sighing contentedly as she drifted toward sleep.

CHAPTER EIGHT

It was one of those steamy August afternoons, the kind where even the leaves on the trees seem wilted and no hint of breeze stirs to relieve the tedious, sweltering heat. But despite the weather, Daniel Hartman still considered it one of the best times of year. The crops were laid by for the summer, which meant there was less farm work to do than at any other time during the growing season, and the dread prospect of school was still nearly a month away. It was a time for spending lazy afternoons on a creek bank, fishing pole in hand, for riding to town on Saturday and spending *all day* doing just as you pleased, for telling the rooster to go to hell when he crowed at the crack of dawn and then rolling over and sleeping for two or three more hours.

Everyone still had their chores to do around the farm, but Jason Hartman, remembering how much he had enjoyed the late summer when he was a youth, tried to keep the workload as light as possible for his children during the final few weeks before school and the critical fall harvesting.

On this particular afternoon, Daniel's friend Jesse had come for him shortly after lunch, all grins and secrets because of the mysterious adventure he had planned for them. Saddling the old mule that his grandfather sometimes let him use, Daniel told his mother that he was going fishing, as Jesse had suggested, and the two of them headed out.

"Couldn't you get a *real* horse, Dan?" Jesse complained as they pointed their animals toward the deep woods behind Will Hartman's farm. "We've got a long way to go, and if we don't get a move on, I'm not sure we'll get there in time."

"Ol' Buff here will have to do, Jesse," Daniel replied. "Daddy's away on Ned right now, and after Grandpa caught me racing on that bay of his this spring, he swore he wouldn't let me ride any of his stock until I proved to him I knew which horses could hold up to a race and which ones couldn't."

"Well, I guess that mule will get you there in time if you'll just push him," Jesse conceded. "But if I have to, I swear I'm going to go on without you. I don't plan to miss this, at least not because of some damned old plow mule."

"It sure would be nice if you would tell me where we're going and what we're going to see when we get there," Daniel said.

"I told you I can't, Dan. I swore an oath that wouldn't tell a soul, not even my own mama, and won't go against my word. But I didn't promise I wouldn't show up to watch, and even bring a friend with me."

"This just better be good, Jesse," Daniel said. "After all this, it better be good."

"Just shut up and come on," Jesse said, tapping his heels against the flanks of his own mount and encouraging it to an even faster gait.

They followed a series of game trails and dry creek washes which led them along a surprisingly straight path to the northeast. Daniel knew from long familiarity with the countryside that, whatever their destination might be, it must lie somewhere in the vicinity of Clark's Crossing. And he knew as well that by taking this route, Jesse was cutting at least six or seven miles off what would otherwise be a twelve-to-fifteen-mile ride on the regular roads.

It looked like Jesse was going to get him in trouble again, Daniel thought anxiously.

If they rode all the way to Clark's Crossing, it would be long past dark before he got home again, and for the next few days he would pay the price for his tardiness in additional chores and fewer privileges. But it would probably be worth it. More often than not, the kind of trouble Jesse James got his friends in was worth the punishment that came later.

Jesse's brother Frank had been home to visit just the week before, and now Jesse was all full of talk about the raid on Olathe and the other exploits of the bushwhackers in Quantrill's band. Daniel's own brother, John, had also been home recently, but he wasn't quite as caught up in the glory of what he was doing as Frank apparently was. In fact he had acted quite strange and withdrawn, unwilling to answer any of Daniel's questions about Olathe, and he had spent hours on end during the three-day stay talking privately with his father.

Later, after John was gone, Jason had tried to explain to Daniel that his brother was just having trouble getting used to some of the things a man had to do during wartime, but Daniel still felt a little hurt at being so unexpectedly shut out of his brother's life.

After a couple of hours of steady riding, Daniel and Jesse stopped for a few minutes to let their horses drink and rest.

"I want to show you something," Jesse said once the two of them had plunked down in the shade of a tree after tying up their mounts. He reached inside his shirt and pulled out a pistol, a shiny new revolver which he proudly explained was one of the new-model Colts. "Frank gave it to me," Jesse explained. "He didn't have a holster to go with it, but he said he'd bring me one the next time he came home."

"I've never seen anybody but Union officers carrying these," Daniel said, accepting the weapon from his friend and inspecting it enviously.

"Well where in the hell do you think he got it, Dan?" Jesse scoffed. "He took it off a Federal officer himself, a dead one!"

"You could get into trouble for having that, Jesse," Daniel warned as he returned the revolver. "If the Federals caught you with it, they might even shoot you!"

"Now that I've got it," Jesse said, "anybody that tried to take it away from me would have a fight on their hands. I've been practicing out in the woods behind our house, and I'm getting to be a decent shot already. I'm not afraid."

"Nobody said you were afraid, Jesse," Daniel told him. "I was just trying to warn you to be careful. That's all."

They were back on their way a few minutes later. At the pace they were going, John estimated that they would reach Clark's Crossing at about five o'clock, and Jesse said that would be plenty of time.

Clark's Crossing was situated at the point where the north-south post road between Stockdale and Chandler forded a tributary of the Fishing River. Similar to countless rural settlements that dotted this part of the state, it consisted of a wood-frame country store, a small Methodist church, a one-room school, and two private homes. Daniel had been there only twice, once three years before while on his way to Stockdale with his father to trade some livestock, and again just the previous year to attend a party being given by Rebecca Clark, the granddaughter of the man for whom the settlement was named.

It was hard for Dan to imagine what interesting occurrence at Clark's Crossing might inspire Jesse to want to ride so far on such short notice. From time to time he had heard talk that Becy Clark might be worth the long ride all by herself, for it was said that she had blossomed considerably over the past year and that a buggy ride with her on a warm summer evening could be quite an entertaining and educational experience.

But that hardly seemed to be Jesse's motive today. If that had been on his mind, certainly he would have wanted to go alone, Dan reasoned.

No, it had to be something else, he thought. But despite all his speculating, he was no closer to an answer than he had been when they started out, and it seemed certain at this point that Jesse was not going to divulge their purpose until they were actually there.

After another hour of steady riding they reached a real road, and Jessed followed it for more than a mile before cutting back into the woods again. John guessed that they were within about half a mile of Clark's Crossing by then, and Jesse's only explanation for the unexpected maneuver was that they "couldn't afford to be seen."

They stopped at last in the edge of the woods with the settlement in view about a hundred yards away across an open field. The river, which at this time of the year was only a narrow, knee-deep channel, was to their right. Daniel looked up the road, which was directly in front of them. The store building was the closest structure to them, he noticed. Two white frame houses were situated side by side a few dozen yards south of the store, and both the church and school buildings were on the opposite side of the road.

They tied their horses several yards back into the woods where they could not be seen, then moved forward stealthily to crouch behind a row of bushes. A portion of the field, the part nearest the houses, was fenced to keep in the cattle and livestock that grazed there, but the area nearest to them was not fenced.

"So now what?" Daniel asked.

"Seems like we must have got here early," Jesse told him, "so I guess now we have to wait."

"But damn it, Jesse, what are we waiting for?" Daniel demanded with irritation. The late-afternoon sun was shining into their faces, and sweat was already beginning to pour off of them now that they had left the shade and relative coolness of the woods. "Surely you can tell me now that we're here!"

"I promised, Dan," Jesse replied resolutely. "But you'll see soon enough. When this is all over with, you'll thank me for rounding you up and bringing you along."

"Well, I'll save my thanks until I can make up my mind for myself," Dan grumbled. He settled down with his back against a tree, closing his eyes against the glaring afternoon sun, but Jesse remained crouched and alert behind the bushes, as if the tranquil, deserted settlement required his constant surveillance.

Without realizing it, Daniel fell into a deep sleep. Suddenly he felt Jesse's hand on his arm and heard his friend announce excitedly, "Wake up, Dan. This is it. It's about to start!"

Instantly awake, Daniel scrambled over to the bushes with Jesse. The scene in and around Clark's Crossing seemed not to have changed, but off to the left he spotted a single horse-drawn vehicle, a caisson of some sort with the letters U.S. painted boldly on the side. Accompanying it was a squad of a dozen mounted soldiers, two in front and ten behind, and the entire procession was making its way north up the road toward the settlement and the river.

"Is that it? Is that what we've been waiting for?" Daniel asked. "A pack of Federals?"

"It's the mail detail heading north to Cameron," Jesse explained.

"Well let's just ride over and see if they've got anything for us," Daniel said sarcastically. "A letter from President Lincoln, maybe, or a —"

"Look over there, Dan," Jesse interrupted urgently, his voice lowering automatically, as if the Union detail might accidentally hear them even from this distance. "Look at the window of the schoolhouse."

Daniel looked but at first noticed nothing. Then he saw what his friend was talking about. Someone was inside the school, moving around in the shadowy interior beyond the open window. Then, even as they watched, the door to the building began to ease slowly open.

"They're in the church and the store too," Jesse explained, unable to keep his secret to himself any longer.

"Who is?" Daniel demanded.

"Quantrill's men are, you dope!" Jesse said. "Haven't you figured it out yet? This is an ambush! A trap set for the north bound mail detail! Frank told me about it a week ago, and I guarantee you I've been busting my buttons to talk to somebody else about it ever since. But I promised him I wouldn't breathe a word about it to anyone. Not even you."

Daniel couldn't figure out whether the feeling that suddenly surged through him was one of excitement or fear. Probably it was both, he decided. It was just like Jesse to get him involved in something like this without even giving him the chance to say no, but then he wondered what his response would have been if he had been given a choice.

He would have come anyway, he knew. A chance to see something like this, to actually see Quantrill's men at work against the enemy, would have just been too good to miss. He would have come.

During the seemingly endless two or three minutes that it took the soldiers to approach the center of the settlement, Daniel was able to spot three more of the waiting bushwhackers. Two were inside the church, and one was crouching on top of the flat roof of the store.

"I wonder if John's out there," Daniel said. "Did Frank say anything about whether John would be in on this?" The idea of his own brother waiting out there in hiding, waiting to actually kill somebody, was utterly astonishing to him, but he knew it was a real possibility.

"I don't even know if Frank's there, but probably both of them are," Jesse answered. "It makes sense that Quantrill would send them on this because they both know the territory hereabouts as well as anybody in the county."

The first shot fired sounded surprisingly

close despite the distance that separated the two young men from the road. One of the two men on the seat of the caisson grabbed at his chest and slumped sideways, his body lodging precariously between the seat and the footboard.

That first shot seemed to be the signal, because a furious volley of shots followed almost immediately. Quantrill's men had not waited for the soldiers to get directly in front of them because that would have caused the bushwhackers to be firing straight across the road at one another. Instead, they opened up when the procession was still about twenty yards away from the front of the store and church.

Four of the Union soldiers went down during the first minute of the fight, and the rest quickly dismounted and scrambled for any cover available, firing their weapons as they ran. Within moments, the entire settlement was so enshrouded in a fog of black powder smoke and dust that it was difficult for Daniel and Jesse to make out much of what was going on. The gunfire continued unabated for the next few minutes, indicating that the victory had not been as quick and complete as many of Quantrill's were said to be.

"I bet they didn't bring enough men to

do the job," Jesse announced worriedly. "Frank told me that only three or four guards usually rode along on these mail runs, and I bet they weren't expecting to have to take on a dozen."

"Well they've already cut the odds back some," Daniel reasoned. "Counting the driver, I've seen four Federals go down myself, and I bet there's more than that who've been shot that we didn't see."

For the next few minutes, the sound of gunfire came and went in bursts. Once in a while, the two observers caught a glimpse of a distant figure darting from one bit of cover to another, but beyond that it was impossible to see what was happening. As more time passed the pair of them became increasingly nervous, wondering if perhaps the skirmish might have already been fought to a stalemate, or, even more unthinkable, that Quantrill's men were about to be beaten.

"I just wish we could do something," Jesse complained, fondling his new revolver anxiously. "I wonder if I could make it over there without being seen and give them a hand."

"If you're honestly thinking about doing that," Daniel told him, "I'd say you might as well just shoot yourself here and now and save yourself a lot of trouble. Even if the Federals didn't get you, our fellows wouldn't know who you were and one of them would probably put a bullet in you."

"I guess you're right, but . . ." Jesse's voice trailed off as he noticed a flurry of movement on the south side of one of the houses. "Look! Look there. A couple of damn Federals are hightailing it!"

Daniel and Jesse watched in surprise as two mounted Union soldiers burst from around the side of the house and galloped straight across the field behind. They leaned forward against the necks of their mounts, making no attempts even to fire a parting shot as they drove their horses on frantically.

"They're coming right at us, Jesse!" Daniel shouted, feeling a rush of panic race through him. "We've got to get out of here!"

"We're better off where we're at," Jesse said, his voice surprisingly calm. "The fight's gone out of those two, and even if they do see us when they get close, they're not going to do anything. All they've got on their minds is running."

Every instinct told Daniel to get away, to sprint back into the woods to his mule and then to ride as fast and as far away from this place as he possibly could. But instead he crouched down lower behind the brush, trying not to let his terror show.

When the two soldiers had made it about halfway across the field, Daniel came to a startling realization. "I know those two, Jesse," he announced. "The one on the left is Joe Ford from down near Liberty. My grandfather bought a bull from his father at the stock sale in Independence just last fall. And the other is one of the Fawcett boys. They lived near the Fords outside Liberty." He began to feel a little calmer as he saw that the course of the two fleeing riders would lead them into the woods a good twenty or thirty feet to the north of where he and Jesse were.

"Maybe that's who they were," Jesse said, rising unexpectedly, incredibly, to his feet, "but in a minute they won't be anybody at all!" And with that he burst from behind the cover, gun in hand, straight into the path of the two horsemen.

His appearance, coming as it did when the soldiers were on the very brink of safety, caught the men and their mounts completely by surprise. The horse Joe Ford was riding reared high on his hind legs, nearly throwing Ford off his back, but the other rider, the one Daniel had identified as Fawcett, was able to keep better control, and with a savage yank on the reins he turned to ride directly at Jesse James. Jesse snapped off a couple of quick shots with his revolver as he ran, but in the excitement of the moment his bullets struck neither man nor animal.

Fawcett's horse charged right at Jesse. At the last instant, Jesse was able to dodge slightly to the side, but the shoulder of the big animal still struck him solidly, tossing his slender body aside and dislodging the Colt from his hand. Then the Union soldier spun his horse around again, saber in hand, to finish the job that his first assault had begun. Jesse, stunned and disarmed, lay helplessly on the ground, unable to do anything to protect himself.

"No! Don't hurt him!" Daniel yelled out, leaping to his feet and rushing out into the field. His sudden appearance brought his friend a momentary reprieve, but an instant later Daniel found himself being confronted with the same sort of charge that had put Jesse out of action. He leaped aside as the big animal raced past, hearing the saber swish through the air only inches from his head. He hit the ground on his side, rolled once, and was instantly back on his feet to meet the next charge.

"Get the gun, Dan! It's right at your feet!"

Jesse called out urgently from somewhere behind him. Daniel risked a momentary glance downward and saw the Colt was indeed lying on the ground beside him. He stooped to pick it up, then made a desperate leap sideways to avoid yet another charge.

There was no time for reflection, no time to waste on the realization that he was about to do something that would change his life forever. Daniel Hartman simply raised the pistol and pulled the trigger. The shot caught Fawcett under his chin just as he was hauling this horse around for yet another charge. His head snapped back as if he had been punched, and his body toppled sideways out of the saddle.

Throughout much of the fight, Joe Ford, the second Union soldier, had been preoccupied with simply staying atop his excited, bucking mount. He finally gained full control just at the instant that Daniel leaped to his feet and pointed the pistol at him.

"Oh God! Please don't shoot me!" Ford exclaimed in terror. "I've got two little boys at home, both just babies!"

"Kill him, Dan!" Jesse yelled out, still lying flat on his back on the ground.

Daniel tried to will himself to squeeze the

trigger, knowing that this man was supposed to be his enemy, but he couldn't do it. He knew Joe Ford and liked him. Last fall at the stock sale, Ford had even led him into an empty stall at the sale barn and had given him his first taste of corn whiskey. They were friends.

The muzzle of the pistol wavered, then Dan slowly lowered it toward the ground.

Joe Ford took immediate advantage of the opportunity. Without another word, he swung his horse around, dug his spurs into the animal's flanks, and bolted into the woods. By the time Jesse had made it to his feet and wrenched the gun from Daniel's hands, it was too late to fire a shot.

Quantrill's men, under the leadership of Bill Gregg, were already beginning to search the bodies of their dead victims by the time the two young men reached the settlement. They had lost three of their own men in the fight and they were in a grim mood.

Daniel, leading his grandfather's mule as well as the horse of the soldier he had killed, was glad to find that his brother was not there. He didn't want to have to go through any long explanations about why he was there, not after what he had just been forced to do.

During the walk across the field, Daniel and Jesse had talked in fairly somber terms about the mess they were in. It hadn't occurred to Daniel at the time he was doing it that by sparing Joe Ford's life, he was sparing a man who could identify both him and Jesse as participants in the ambush of the mail detail. It had all started as a lark, a boyish excursion to get a glimpse of how the war was being fought, but now, suddenly, they were full participants instead of simple spectators.

They couldn't go home again, not even to bid their parents goodbye and tell them where they were. It would be too dangerous, not only for Daniel and Jesse, but also for their families.

The first man the two youths met when they entered the settlement was George Todd, who took them to meet the leader of the group.

"Bill, these boys are John Hartman's and Frank James's little brothers. Their names are Daniel Hartman and Jesse James," Todd explained to Gregg by way of an introduction. "They were the ones over yonder in the field that got those two Federals that slipped away from us."

"We only got one of them," Daniel admitted. "I brought his horse and rifle over with

214

me. But the other one . . . I'm sorry, but I knew him . . . I had a chance, but I just couldn't . . ."

Gregg seemed to understand without hearing a complete explanation. "So you were seen, then?" Gregg asked. "The one that got away can identify the two of you?"

"The fellow's name was Joe Ford," Jesse spoke up, "and he knows the both of us."

Todd and Gregg exchanged significant glances, and then Gregg told them, "You know, I guess, that you can't go home again. You'll have to come with us."

"We'll go if you'll have us," Daniel said. "But we've got to get word to our families. We have to find some way to let them know we're all right."

"We have ways," Gregg said. "That will be taken care of. But right now the most important thing is to get out of here before word of this ambush spreads and the Federals start looking for us. How are you two mounted? We'll probably be riding all night and most of tomorrow, so you'll need good horseflesh under you."

"Jesse's horse is fine, but all I've got is my grandfather's mule," Daniel explained.

"What about that other horse you brought in with you?" George Todd asked. "He looks like a pretty good animal to me."

"But it's not mine!" Daniel answered automatically.

His answer made both Todd and Gregg chuckle grimly. "Think about it, boy," Todd exclaimed. "You just killed yourself a Federal soldier. Do you think if they catch you that they're going to try you for horse-stealing? The horse is yours, and so is that rifle you're carrying, and anything else that you want to take along. That's how we get damn near everything, boy. We take what we need."

"You can put the mule out there in Clark's pasture and we'll get word to your grandfather to come and get it," Gregg added. "One thing we don't do is steal from our own. Times are hard enough for folks in these parts without men like us adding to their miseries."

About fifteen minutes later they rode out of Clark's Crossing, leading the Union horses they had captured and carrying an assortment of captured weapons, uniforms, and personal effects. The bodies of the three bushwhackers who had been killed were left with Art Clark, the owner of the store, for burial, and he was also given two hundred dollars, taken from the mail wagon, for his time and trouble.

They rode due south, heading, Bill Gregg

216

explained, toward Jackson County, where the main body of Quantrill's forces were gathered.

Daniel and Jesse rode side by side as darkness arrived and the group pressed on into the night. It took them a while to adjust to the idea of what had just taken place and to realize their lives would never again be the same, but neither of them could find it in himself to regret what had happened. After all, it was a time of war. With their families and most of the people they knew battling for their very survival against a relentless and brutal foe, why shouldn't they do their part? Why shouldn't they join Quantrill?

Chapter Nine

Mollie watched her brother pace from one side of the room to the other, pounding his fist in his hand as he cursed General Thomas Ewing with every ounce of malice his soul could muster.

"If I could just get my hands on him, just for one minute," Jason snarled. "I wouldn't care what they did to me afterward. It would be worth it just for the satisfaction of ending the career of that animal forever."

He still walked with a pronounced limp, the result of the injuries he had received two years before at Wilson's Creek, and Mollie found herself wondering if the furious grimaces which he sometimes made might not be caused as much by real pain as by the emotional anguish he was going through. His body had never healed properly, and she knew that from time to time he still fell victim to sudden flare-ups of fever and debilitating internal infections.

218

But any discomfort his old wounds might now be causing him could not compare with the mental pain he was suffering.

Two days before, General Ewing, the commander of the Western Missouri Military District, had issued one of the more heartless orders of his wartime career. Since the beginning of the war, a multitude of men had been arrested for guerrilla activities in the area, but this time it was women — the wives, sisters, and mothers of suspected bushwhackers — who had been taken into custody in a massive sweep through a four-county area.

Two of the women arrested were Jason's wife, Arethia, and his nineteen-year-old daughter, Ruth. They were being held now in an abandoned warehouse building right here in Kansas City along with about forty other female prisoners. The message Ewing had caused to be broadcast throughout the area was that they would stay in custody until the men in their families who were members of bands such as Quantrill's turned themselves in.

"Listen, Jason," Mollie told her brother, "John and Daniel are bound to try and get in touch with you or me when they hear about this. They'll want to know what you want them to do."

"I don't know what to tell them, Mollie. If I said the word, they'd surrender themselves in an instant, but how can I do that? It would be like passing a death sentence on both of them. Surely there must be something else we can try, somebody we can talk to."

"I've tried already," Mollie admitted. "As soon as I heard what had happened, I went to talk to some Union officers I know, but they told me Ewing was standing firm on this one. None of the women are to be released unless the bushwhackers they are related to turn themselves in. While I was there, I found out that they also have Cole Younger's sister and George Todd's aunt —"

"And Bill Anderson's mother and sister, and Bill Gregg's mother, and John McCorkle's sister . . ." Jason added.

"I'm going back this afternoon before I go to the theatre," Mollie told her brother, "and I'll at least try to get you permission to visit them. I've already talked to Genevieve, and she has said you can stay here with us until this thing is over. But you've got to promise me that you won't try something desperate and stupid."

"I wouldn't have any idea what to try, Mollie," Jason admitted dejectedly. Now that the wave of anger was past, his features were etched with lines of sadness and his voice seemed almost a whisper. He was only thirty-six, but at that moment he looked decades older.

"We'll get through this thing, Jason," Mollie told her brother. "I promise you I'll do everything I can, and we'll find some way to get Arethia and Ruth out of there. We'll work our way through it."

"We'll get through it," Jason agreed. "What other choice do we have?" But there was no self-assurance in his voice, no trace of confidence that either of them could transform their words into deeds.

That evening, after Mollie had left for the theatre, Cole Younger arrived, accompanied by John and Daniel Hartman. None of them seemed concerned with the risks they were taking. They hid in the stable until well past dark, as Cole had done during his previous visits, then sneaked into the house to join Jason. Genevieve de Mauduis welcomed them all into her home with warmth and compassion, then discreetly retired to the back portion of the house so they could be alone.

Jason had not seen either of his oldest sons in nearly a month now, and he was surprised at the changes that had taken place in them. Both were filthy from the trail, their clothes disheveled and in need of a good scrubbing, and each was heavily armed with a variety of handguns and knives. But Jason paid little attention to their appearance, knowing that these things were simply indications of the life they now led. Instead, what struck him the deepest was the cold, determined look in their eyes. He had seen that look before and he knew very well what it had taken to put it there. Even Daniel, who had been with the bushwhackers for only a short time, had already left all traces of his boyhood behind.

"It was hell getting here," Cole said as he leaned his rifle against a table and dropped tiredly into a chair. "Ewing must have pulled in reinforcements from somewhere, because the roads all around the city are packed with Federals. There are so many patrols out there that they're practically running into each other. We finally ended up riding around to the Kansas side and coming in that way because there were fewer Federals to deal with in that direction."

"Has there been any word from Mama and Ruth?" John asked hastily, impatient with Cole's small talk.

"Not yet," Jason said. "Mollie left early on

her way to the theatre so she could try to get in and see them, but I haven't heard anything from her."

"What can we do, Daddy?" Daniel asked his father. "What John and I are doing is not their fault and they shouldn't be punished for it. We've got to do something!" Both he and John had taken seats on a long, overstuffed couch, but despite the tiredness that showed on their faces, neither seemed willing to relax even slightly.

"I don't know what to tell you, son," Jason admitted. "I'm about to go crazy myself just sitting here waiting to find out something, but I can't figure out what else to do. The only thing I am sure of is that I don't want you two to even consider turning yourselves in. Not under any circumstances."

"We talked about that on the way in," Daniel revealed, "and if it would help at all, we would. But we know too much about how these bastards are to believe it would really change anything."

"If I have to go in at all, I'll go in shooting," John added bitterly. "Right now there's probably at least a hundred of Quantrill's men who have already made their way into the city just like we did. I just keep thinking that if all of us could get together someplace and come up with some kind of plan —"

"Damn it, John! Shut up with that kind of talk!" Cole said sharply. "You remember the last orders Bill Quantrill gave everybody before we split up. Nobody is to try any damn fool rescue attempts!"

"The hell with Quantrill!" John replied. "It's easy enough for him to give an order like that. They don't have any of his family locked up like they do Mama and Ruth!"

"That may be true, son," Jason said, "but I still think Quantrill is right. If I were Ewing, I'd be expecting the bushwhackers to make an attack, and I'd be well prepared for it. I'd *want* them to try it, because I'd have that building and all the ones around it filled with riflemen. It would be wholesale slaughter, and for all the men you lost, I bet you wouldn't get one single woman out alive."

Their talk was interrupted when Genevieve de Mauduis came in with a large tray filled with sandwiches. She put it on a table, left the room, and returned a minute later carrying four glasses and a full bottle of liquor.

"I don't keep any whiskey in the house," she told them almost apologetically, "but I did find this brandy in the cupboard. Under the circumstances, I thought you might prefer it to lemonade or tea."

"We're much obliged to you, ma'am," Jason told her. "And I want to apologize to you for whatever danger we might be putting you in by being here."

"I haven't given it a second thought," Genevieve told them with no apparent concern. "What are they going to do to an old woman like me? Lock me up like they've done with your womenfolk? If they did that, just for spite I might decide to up and die on them just so they'd look bad."

"Well, I promise you we'll be careful," Jason said, "and if there's any hint that the Federals know we're here, we'll leave immediately."

"There's no need," she assured them. "I'm going upstairs now to turn down beds for all of you, and you're welcome to stay as long as necessary."

After she had left the room, Cole and the boys attacked the plate of food. Jason watched without comment as his sons accepted their share of the brandy, knowing that that was a part of the change too. Such things were their right now, no longer subject to his permission or approval.

As they ate, Cole, John, and Daniel talked with Jason about some of the things that they and the others in Quantrill's band had been doing lately. The Clark's Crossing raid had been one of their most talked-about recent successes, but Quantrill's men had kept the pressure on the Federal authorities in a number of other areas as well.

"It's getting so you don't see any Federals out in the countryside in numbers of less than fifty anymore," Cole announced with obvious pride, "and even a group that size will ride half the night to get to safety rather than bivouac out in the open."

"We've stopped the mails completely in this part of the state, too," John added, "and every stagecoach is stopped and searched for disguised Federal soldiers and hidden dispatches. If you're a grown man riding from one town to another in western Missouri, you'd better be well acquainted with somebody in Quantrill's Raiders or you don't stand much chance of making it where you're going."

"I'm all for what you're doing," Jason told them, "but you know, don't you, that this sort of thing is bound to bring reprisals. This business of arresting our women is only the start. I can guarantee you that Ewing has plenty more tricks like this up his sleeve. And we can't forget Lane's and Jennison's Jayhawkers over in Kansas, either."

"But that's the way it's been ever since

the war started, Daddy," John reasoned. "All along they've been killing us and burning our homes and carrying us away to prison, and the only difference now is that we're giving them back some of what they've been giving us for the past three years."

"Don't think that what you're saying isn't on our minds, though, Jason," Cole told him. "Right now we bear the blame for everything the Federals and the Jayhawkers do to the people in the western counties of the state. But they'd be doing the same things even if we weren't here. The only difference is that now they can call what they're doing 'reprisals' because of us."

"I know," Jason agreed reluctantly. "I understand that very well, because it's the same sort of thing we went through back in the fifties. We raided into Kansas because of what John Brown and his kind were doing to us, and then they came right back on us because of what we had done to them. The only thing that's different is that most of the men who did the raiding back then are dead now, and the hate has been passed on to another generation. It makes me wonder sometimes if anybody will be left alive when the whole thing is over."

"But we don't have a choice, do we, Daddy?" John asked quietly. "You didn't, and we don't. We're caught up in it, like leaves in the wind."

"There never seems to be a choice, son," Jason conceded, his voice laden with immeasurable sadness.

They all looked up expectantly when they heard the front door open, and instinctively Cole reached to retrieve his rifle. There was a moment of absolute silence in the room as they listened to the sounds of footsteps crossing the entryway, and Jason seemed to sense, even before Mollie opened the door and came into the room, that something was terribly wrong.

The elegant gown she wore, apparently one of her onstage costumes, was streaked with soot and blood, and her thick blonde tresses hung in tangled disarray. Her arms and face were smoke-blackened, and her cheeks were streaked where her tears had sliced through the filth.

Even now she was so stunned and distraught that she was barely able to speak, but at last she choked out her grim announcement. "There's been an . . . an accident . . ." she said, her voice constricted and harsh. "The women's prison building . . . it collapsed . . ."

"No, damn it! *Nooooo!*" Jason shouted, his voice filled with rage and grief. He leaped to his feet and grabbed his sister by the shoulders, shaking her as if she might be trying to perpetrate some monstrous lie. He only released his furious hold on her when Cole appeared at his side and pulled his fingers loose. Mollie simply stared at him, dazed, seemingly unaware of what was going on.

"I saw Arethia," Mollie said. "They're taking care of her and I think she'll be all right, but Ruth . . ." Her voice caught in her throat and the tears began to stream from her eyes in a fresh flood.

"What about Ruth, Mollie?" Jason asked.

"She wasn't with her mother," Mollie said. "The guards had let her go visit a friend, up on the third floor on the side that fell. When I left they were still digging . . ."

"What about my sister?" Cole demanded. "Was there any word about Laura?"

"I saw her, Cole," Mollie told him. She was beginning to calm now that the worst of the announcements were past her, but her voice was still heavy with the impact of the tragedy. "She had a broken leg, but they were taking care of her. She was with Arethia, and there were lots of people helping out. The soldiers weren't trying to guard anybody anymore, and the people of the city were taking care of everybody they found in the rubble, taking them to their homes and to the hospital."

Slowly, over the next few minutes, the entire story of the tragic evening began to emerge in more coherent detail as Mollie gained control of her emotions and began to reveal the facts to her stunned listeners.

She had been in the midst of her evening performance when the theatre was shaken by the shock waves of the collapsing building several blocks away, she told them. Later she had heard someone in the crowd who flocked to the scene say that the building had been declared unsafe long before the decision was made to house the women prisoners in it. It was said that Ewing had been aware of the building's unstable condition but had decided that his charges didn't deserve any better, or more costly, accommodations.

"I bet the bastard planned this!" John shouted, his voice harsh with bitterness.

"It's possible," Mollie agreed. "At this point, I wouldn't put anything past that devil."

The theatre had quickly emptied when the building went down, and Mollie told them she was one of the first ones on the scene. A fire had started up in a part of the collapsed building, and she began to care for the victims that the soldiers pulled out of the flames.

"It was like visiting hell," Mollie said. "They were laying the bodies out in the middle of the street, the living and the dead side by side, and everywhere you turned women were screaming in pain and begging for somebody to help them. I stopped to try to do something for a young girl and saw that her right arm was gone. She was so stunned that she didn't even know it. She died in my arms a couple of minutes later . . ."

Once again she choked with emotion, and the others waited in strained silence until she was able to speak again.

"As soon as I could, I went looking for Arethia," she continued. "A woman was taking care of her and Laura, and she told me that her husband had gone to look for a doctor. But there was no sign of Ruth. After Arethia told me about her being up on the top floor, I searched all through the crowd, but I still couldn't find her . . . The fire was out when I left, and they were still digging, but —"

"Do you know where they took Arethia?" Jason interrupted. "I have to go to her."

"The woman gave me her address," Mollie said, producing a grimy piece of paper from somewhere in her clothing. "She said she would get some help and have Arethia and Laura carried there. I told her I would come there as soon as I came back here and got you."

"And we'll go and help with the digging," Cole announced. "There still may be some hope."

"Are you crazy?" Mollie demanded, horrified. "That place is crawling with Union soldiers!"

"They won't know who we are," Cole stated. "And how many of them are going to suspect that any of Quantrill's men would show up at such a place?"

"I agree with Cole," John announced decisively. "It's worth the risk if there's any chance of finding our sister. We can't just sit around here."

"But we'll have to leave our guns here," Cole said. "The Federals will get suspicious if they see the kind of hardware we're used to carrying around."

Their conversation was interrupted unexpectedly by the sound of a furtive knock on the front door. Cole, John, and Daniel immediately drew their pistols, and Jason picked up Cole's rifle from where it leaned against a table.

"Were you followed, Mollie?" Cole asked quietly.

"Someone could have been two steps behind me on the way back and I wouldn't have noticed it," Mollie admitted. "But who would do something like that at a time like this?"

"Well you have to answer it," Cole told her. "Come on, I'll go with you. And the rest of you, be ready to bail out those windows in a hurry if you hear any commotion."

They left the room, pulling the door nearly closed behind them, and crossed the vestibule to the front door. Cole stood out of sight behind the door, his pistol drawn, while Mollie eased the door open a few inches.

"Are you Mollie Hartman?" a gruff male voice asked from the shadows outside.

"Yes, I am," Mollie told him, sounding impatient. "Who are you and what do you want?"

"My name's Gregg, ma'am," the visitor told her, "and I've come here looking for a man named Younger . . ."

Before he had a chance to say more, Cole pulled the door open and greeted his friend. "Come on in, Bill," he said, stepping back to let Gregg enter and then closing the door behind him. "I guess you've heard about what happened tonight. We've got to leave to see if we can help, but you can stay here and wait for us to get back if you want."

"I can't stay, Cole," Gregg announced. "I just came to deliver a message from Quantrill, then I have to get going again."

"Quantrill?" Cole asked. "Is he here in the city too?"

"That's right, he's here," the bushwhacker said. "And after what the Federals did to those women tonight, he decided to put out the call. He wants everybody to get to the Lee's Summit camp as quick as they can."

By this time Jason and his two sons had realized that everything was all right and had come into the vestibule to listen. Gregg greeted them with a hurried nod, then continued with his message.

"Quantrill said he plans to make the Federals pay dearly for this stunt, and he wants to hit them quick and hard before they have time to brace themselves and get ready for us."

"We're not going anywhere, Bill," John said. "Our mother was hurt tonight, and our sister's still missing. We're not leaving 'til we find out about them."

"I won't try to make you go, John," Gregg said, "or your brother either, but I will tell

234

you this: Chances are you won't be able to do much for your mother or sister if you stick around here, but you can bet your last dollar that you will be able to sample the sweet taste of revenge if you come with us. I don't know where Quantrill plans to hit or when, but I'll wager it'll put to shame anything else we've ever done!"

"You go, John," Daniel told his brother. "You and Cole go, and I'll stay here. The two of you will be worth a lot more in a fight than I would be, and as soon as I get any definite word about Mama and Ruth, I'll come to the Lee's Summit camp or wherever you are by then."

"Daddy . . . ?" John Hartman said, turning to his father, a look of uncertainty on his face.

"Go, son," Jason told him. His features were drawn and his voice was laced with bitterness. "If I had a good pair of legs under me and a gut that would stand the ride, I'd be right there alongside you. But I don't, so it's your fight now, yours and Daniel's. Make the bastards pay like they never have before for this night's work!"

CHAPTER TEN

August 1863
Lawrence!

The mere mention of that town's name was enough to put a bitter taste in the mouths of countless loyal Missourians. Almost since the day of its founding a decade before, Lawrence had been nothing to them but a breeding ground for abolitionist fanaticism and unyielding anti-Missouri sentiments. Before the war, Lawrence had served as home base for various bands of Kansas Jayhawkers who frequently conducted anti-slavery raids across the border. Now many of those same groups served in loose alliance with the Union army to continue their destructive practices in Missouri under the leadership of James Lane and Charles Jennison.

Surprisingly enough, the town of Lawrence itself had prospered despite the turmoil that had swirled around it constantly since the day the first sod hut had been erected. It served not only as a commercial center for the surrounding farming community, but also as a stopping-off place for many of the countless thousands of westbound travelers who had passed through the area in the late 1850s. Even men like Jim Lane lived reasonably normal, prosperous lives when they returned to their own home soil in Kansas, though they wreaked such havoc when they crossed the state line into Missouri.

But all that changed early on the morning of August 21, 1863. That was the day William Clarke Quantrill and nearly 450 of his followers descended on Lawrence.

They came in from the south, riding hard and fast, shooting everything that moved. The few townsmen who had the courage and presence of mind to snatch up a weapon and try to fight back during those first few devastating minutes were immediately slaughtered, and it soon beame apparent that the raiders intended neither to take prisoners nor to leave alive any male in Lawrence who even approached fighting age.

They fanned out over the town in a brutal horde, slaughtering, pillaging, and burning everything in their path. Quantrill had ordered his men to split up into small groups to search every house, store, and barn for male inhabitants, and a number of men and boys who were able to hide successfully from the enraged Missourians were burned to death when the wood-frame structures where they were concealed were put to the torch.

Both Cole Younger and John Hartman were assigned to a special detail led by Bill Gregg. On the north side of the Kansas River across from Lawrence, a few hundred Union soldiers were bivouacked, and it was the job of Gregg's bunch to destroy the ferry before the enemy could cross and come to the aid of the town's residents.

During the initial assault, Gregg led his twenty-man force around the east edge of Lawrence, and they reached the ferry landing just as the first shots were beginning to sound within the town.

"Stop them before they can cut her free, boys!" Gregg shouted urgently, pointing with his saber toward the ferry ahead. After spotting the approaching raiders, the boat's operator was working desperately to launch his craft before they arrived. He had already cast the stern line free and was standing on one side of the boat, pushing against the bank with a long pole. A few feet away from him at the bow one of the crewmen was hacking away at the three-inch bow rope with a hatchet, and other members of the crew were tumbling out of the cabin onto the deck, utterly confused by the sudden commotion outside.

John Hartman, astride his fleet-footed bay, was the first to reach the levee. He swung his right leg over the saddle when he was still ten feet from the boat, cast the reins aside, and hit the ground running. The ferry had already drifted out a couple of feet into the channel, but John was easily able to leap onto the bow.

The startled crewman who had been chopping on the bow rope turned and came at John, his hatched raised menacingly, and John shot him in the middle of the chest. With a roar of agony, the man tumbled off the edge of the boat into the shallow water.

John turned immediately, his pistol ready, intending to shoot the man with the pole, but Cole Younger got his shot off first. The ferryman released the pole and staggered back clumsily. His right shoulder was a mangled, bloody mess and his face bore a stunned look of disbelief. Cole waded into the edge of the water and fired again, finishing his victim with a bullet in the head.

By that time the remaining crewmen had

been driven back into the cabin by a storm of gunfire, and more raiders were beginning to scramble onto the deck.

John and several others charged the cabin where the crew had fled, kicking in the bolted door and breaking out the windows to fire blindly inside. A couple of the crewmen made it out the other side and into the river, but they were able to swim only a few feet before being picked off.

Less than two minutes after it had begun, the fight was over.

Bill Gregg had stopped his horse on the edge of the levee and was watching the brief foray with calm satisfaction. When he saw that all the ferry's crew had been killed, he called out to his men on deck, "Good work, boys! Now burn the son of a bitch and let it go. That ought to keep those damn Federals over on the other side and out of our hair for a while."

John found a lamp hanging on a hook near the bow of the ferry and dashed it on the deck, then struck a match and tossed it into the spilled oil. Within an instant the fuel was transformed into a puddle of flames that flowed across the deck and down the side of the boat toward the water. At the stern another of the raiders had started a similar fire; dark smoke was already beginning to issue from one of the broken windows of the cabin.

The ferry had drifted several feet downstream by the time the attackers began to evacuate. John leaped over the side and landed waist-deep in the river, then began to wade laboriously toward the shore five feet away. Cole met him at the edge and reached out a hand to pull him up the rest of the way onto dry ground.

"You're getting to be a regular firebrand, aren't you, John?" Cole said. He held a pistol in his free hand, and his face was still animated with the excitement of the fight.

"Well, I just didn't figure I could afford to wait for the rest of you slowpokes to lend a hand," John said.

"Another minute or two and we would have had hell to pay getting on that deck," Cole admitted.

A couple of hundred yards away in the heart of Lawrence the gunfire was continuing at a steady level. Dozens of mounted men were in view, riding in all directions, still fanning out to the remaining portions of town to carry out their deadly mission.

As John and Cole watched, a man still dressed only in a nightshirt and trousers appeared from behind a distant house and went tearing out across an open stretch of ground toward a nearby field of corn. Close behind were two horsemen, both laughing and waving their pistols wildly as they pursued their hapless victim.

Rather than killing him straight out, the first of the two riders literally rode over the top of the fleeing man. Then he spun his horse around, and he and his companion pranced their horses around their fallen captive, taunting him even as he rose to his knees to plead for his life. When they began to fire at last, it was obvious that they did not want their first bullets to be fatal. Over and over they fired their revolvers, reducing their victim, at last, to a writhing, pathetic form. Finally one of them took more careful aim and finished the man off, then the two of them turned their mounts and rode back toward the town.

"It looks to me like some of our fellows might be enjoying this a little too much," Cole commented.

"Well, their blood's up and they've got a lot of getting even to do," John said. "I feel the same way. I've got me one of these Kansas bastards already, but I still don't feel like I've spilled enough blood. The Federals killed my sister Ruth when the women's prison collapsed. And ever since that day I've been praying to God I'd be able to get even."

Cole made no reply as they started toward their horses, but his thoughts began turning, quite unexpectedly, in a disturbing new direction. Killing the men on the boat was one thing . . . it had been necessary, and it had been carried out with skill and dispatch . . . but there was something about the scene he and John had witnessed moments later that left an odd, almost guilty feeling in the pit of his stomach.

How could a man tell, he wondered, when he had passed beyond simply killing when he must and had reached the point of actually *enjoying* the killing? The thought that he might someday pass that point, or that he could have passed it already without realizing it, struck a note of terror within him. There would be no going back when that happened. For a man who had passed beyond that threshold, the future could only hold more death and more destruction until he himself was, in effect, put out of his misery.

"Are you all right, Cole?" John Hartman asked. Cole looked over and was startled to see that John had already mounted and was sitting there waiting for him.

"Sure, I'm fine," Cole replied. He stuck his foot in the stirrup and swung up into the saddle.

"Then come on," John said. "I want to get on into town and see what's going on."

Gregg left a few men behind to sound the alarm in case the Union soldiers on the other side of the river found some way to attempt a crossing, then the rest of his band scattered and started for the main part of Lawrence.

Cole and John headed for the center of town via a side street lined with small frame houses. The roadway ahead of them was littered with bodies, and a number of the buildings they passed were already ablaze. Here and there a few women and young children were attempting to salvage what household goods they could from their burning homes, but there were no townsmen in sight.

Thus far none of the businesses in the center of Lawrence had been set afire, mainly because the raiders had not yet finished their looting and carousing. In various places, men were busy loading goods from the town's stores into wagons parked along the town's main thoroughfare, and numerous horses were tied to the rails outside every saloon they passed.

"Look down there, Cole," John said, pointing toward the opposite end of the street. "Isn't that Quantrill?"

"That's him," Cole confirmed, "but don't ask me what he's doing in that rig."

Their leader was riding toward them in a shiny black surrey drawn by a prancing black horse. Quantrill appeared to be in high spirits, laughing and joking with the men as he drove by. He wore a silk stovepipe hat which was so tall that it brushed the canvas top of the surrey whenever he moved his head.

As he approached Cole and John he stopped his horse and greeted them with a broad grin.

"Where in hell did you get that thing, Bill?" Cole asked Quantrill.

"It's the undertaker's!" Quantrill exclaimed with a laugh. "I didn't figure he'd mind me using it, not after all the business we've given him today."

"It does seem appropriate," Cole said wearily.

"How did everything go down at the river?" Quantrill asked.

"We burned the ferry and killed the crew," Cole reported matter-of-factly. "I guess it'll be a while before any of those Federals on the other side find a way to make it across."

"Good. Good," Quantrill replied. Then he shifted his gaze to John and asked, "Have you killed yourself any Jayhawkers yet, boy?"

"I shot a fellow on the boat," John answered, "but I don't know what he was. Probably just a deckhand with bad luck."

"He was the enemy, John. If he lived in this place, he couldn't be anything else. You know, years from now, when this raid is in the history books, you'll be proud to tell your grandchildren that you were here with me and that you helped stomp out the worst sort of border trash that ever walked the face of the earth!"

"We can worry about those years later," Cole suggested. "Right now we should just worry about getting back across that state line alive. Have you given any thought to how soon we'll be pulling out, Bill?"

"We can't leave yet because we haven't killed Jim Lane," Quantrill explained. "But he's here somewhere, and we'll get him. I've sent about a hundred men to the west side of town, and they're working their way in this direction, searching all the buildings and then setting them on fire when they're through. But damn the luck," he added, "I just found out a little while back that Charles Jennison left two days ago on a trip to Wichita, so I guess we'll have to take care of him next time."

"Sure," Cole mumbled. "Next time."

After their leader had passed on down the street, Cole and John dismounted and tied their horses in front of a general mercantile store. The plate-glass windows on the front of the building were broken out, but it had not yet been set afire and looked as if the looters hadn't finished stripping it of merchandise.

"I bet we could find us something to eat inside there," Cole suggested. "But let's be careful. Remember what happened in Olathe."

"I remember all right," John said, leading the way inside with his pistol drawn.

They found some tinned beef and peaches in the scattered debris on the floor, and then settled on a bench near the front door to eat.

"You know, I used to have an uncle named Charles who lived here in Lawrence," John said, fishing a thick slice of peach out of a can and putting it in his mouth. "And a whole flock of cousins, too. Daddy doesn't talk much about them, but I remember back before my Uncle William was killed by the Jayhawkers that he used to cuss Uncle Charles like a dog. Daddy said the two of them never did get along, not even when they were kids, but then when Uncle Charles came out here to support the abolitionists they became bitter enemies."

"I knew Charles and William both before they died," Cole admitted. "They were about the most bitter men I ever met. But you know what's funny about the whole thing? Even though they were on opposite sides of the fighting, the two of them were a lot alike."

"I can't imagine what it's like to hate your own brother," John said. "Dan and I haven't always got along, but I could never do anything to really hurt him, no matter what he did. I don't think I could ever truly *hate* him."

They continued their meal in silence for a few moments, watching the activities in the town with an almost casual air. Across the street, two men were wrestling with a huge oak dining table, trying to hoist it onto the back of a wagon. It was senseless to load up wagons with large objects, Cole thought, because they would never get them back to Missouri. Despite their present superior numbers, he knew that soon the enemy would be preparing to descend on them from all directions and that the trip home would probably turn out to be one bloody battle after another. If any of these men hoped to get home with the loot they were now gathering, Cole thought, they should be choosing things that would fit in their pockets or in a saddlebag.

"You know, Cole," John said, "I think I'm glad my brother didn't come along on this one. Dan's made a pretty good fighter of himself in a short time, but I feel like all this would bother him. It's a lot to take, being a part of this much killing."

"There's not much glory in it, is there?" Cole replied. "It's not like being back home and hearing somebody tell about it. And I'm not sure I agree with Bill Quantrill about how the history books are going to treat this thing, either. I guess all this had to be done, but it's still a pretty ugly mess when you look straight at it."

"It'll probably depend on who writes the history books," John said. "And that'll depend on who wins the war."

A commotion down the street caught their attention, and they watched as a group of half a dozen bushwhackers dragged a battered, struggling prisoner toward the center of town.

"I bet they've got Jim Lane!" John said excitedly, leaping to his feet and staring outside. Cole set his half-finished can of food aside and followed John out. A crowd was beginning to gather as the prisoner was dragged down the street.

"I've seen Lane before," Cole said after he got a look at the prisoner, "and that's not him. But he must be somebody important or they wouldn't have bothered to keep him alive this long. I guess they're bringing him to Quantrill."

The bushwhacker chief was approaching from the opposite end of town, still riding in the undertaker's buggy, and he stopped when he met the group coming toward him.

"Will you look here!" Quantrill drawled, stepping to the ground with a broad grin and moving close to the prisoner. "Damned if it isn't Rafe Barstow."

"I told them you would want to see me, Bill," Barstow replied quickly. "I knew you wouldn't want them to kill me."

"I do indeed want to see you, Rafe," Quantrill said. "I'm glad you were able to talk them out of killing you right off."

A look of utter relief flooded the man's bruised features, and he shrugged his arms free from his captors, as if trying to reclaim a measure of dignity. But whatever hopes might have been stirring in him were totally destroyed by Quantrill's next words.

"I hear you've fallen in with some bad company, Rafe. You've been seen two or three times riding with Jim Lane's bunch over into Missouri, and they tell me that you and him have got thick as thieves since the war started."

"Hell, Bill, you know how it is," Barstow said. "If you live here, you've got to do them things once in a while. They'll kill you if you don't."

"And we'll kill you if you do," Quantrill replied coldly. "Looks like your fat's in the fire either way."

"But we were friends, Bill!" Barstow pleaded. "I even gave you a job one time. Don't you remember? I helped you out!"

"Yeah, you helped me out, letting me do nigger work around your place for fifty cents a day," Quantrill said with sudden disdain. "But the tide's turned now, Rafe. Now I'm in charge, and as far as I'm concerned, your life isn't worth a tow sack full of that shit I used to shovel out of your horse barn."

"Don't kill me, Bill! Please. Please!" Barstow begged. His voice was beginning to take on a panicky, desperate tone that Cole had heard too often before in the voices of men so suddenly confronted with their own fragile mortality. But Quantrill didn't seem ready to completely destroy all the man's hopes yet.

"There might be a way for you to stay alive, Rafe," Quantrill said, as if he'd just thought of it. "I want Jim Lane one hell of a lot more than I do you, and I know he's somewhere here in town. You tell me where he is and I'll let you live. It's a simple trade. Your life for his."

"I don't know where he is!" Barstow announced desperately. "I was still in bed when your men rode into town. I didn't see anybody. All I did was run straight to my storm cellar and hide."

"Yeah, but you were in tight with him," Quantrill answered. "He's bound to have made some preparations or laid some plans in case of a raid like this. I think you know where he'd go."

"I swear to God, Bill —"

Quantrill drew his revolver and laid the muzzle on the bridge of Barstow's nose. Barstow's whole body began to tremble, and a look of complete terror ravaged his features.

"You're a lying son of a bitch, Rafe Barstow," Quantrill hissed. He pulled the hammer of the gun back with his thumb, but then, instead of shooting his victim in the head, he lowered the muzzle and squeezed the trigger.

Barstow howled in agony as the bullet shattered his right knee. He would have fallen but the men standing on either side of him quickly grabbed his arms and kept him on his feet. At the same time, the bystanders on all sides began to draw back cautiously to be out of the range of the gunfire.

"Tell me where he is!" Quantrill demanded. He shifted the aim of his pistol and put a bullet through Barstow's right shoulder.

"I don't know! I don't know!" Barstow screamed, his voice rising to a frantic, sobbing falsetto.

"Then I guess you're dead, Rafe," Quantrill said, shifting his pistol once again until it was pointed at the center of Barstow's chest. Everyone fell awesomely quiet as the eyes of the two men, executioner and victim, locked in a final contest. Then Quantrill's finger tightened on the trigger and the shot rang out. Rafe Barstow was dead even before the two men who were supporting him had the chance to release his arms and let him fall.

Before doing anything else, Quantrill removed the three spent cartridges from the cylinder of his revolver and replaced them with live rounds. Then, for a moment, he stood gazing down at the man he had just killed. The look on his face was nearly indescribable. It was an expression as cold and unfeeling as any Cole Younger had ever seen.

"Somebody get me my horse," Quantrill said at last, breaking the silence. "It's tied in front of the undertaker's a couple of blocks down. And unhitch that black from the buggy. I'm taking him back to Missouri with me."

Life immediately began to return to the crowd. A couple of men went to carry out his orders, and some of the others began to talk among themselves about the scene they had just witnessed. But all the discussion was short-lived because Quantrill was ready for action now, and he began to issue a stream of orders to the men around him.

A group of about twenty men were instructed to set fire to the buildings up and down the main street, and a number of others were dispatched throughout the town to spread the word to all the scattered bushwhackers that the band would be leaving soon. Bill Gregg was sent back down to the river to round up the men he had left there, and Cole Younger and George Todd were put in charge of organizing a thirty-man force to serve as a rear guard when they began their retreat back to Missouri.

Even as Quantrill was making his final plans for their withdrawal, a man came running up to him with a piece of paper in his hand.

"You need to see this, Bill," the man said, handing the paper over. "It just came in at the telegraph office."

Quantrill read the paper quickly, then announced to the men around him, "Listen up, boys. This will give you a pretty good idea of what we're in for on the way back. 'Your request for help received. Forces being dispatched immediately from Leavenworth and Kansas City. Send word if possible about numbers and route of enemy.' And it's signed 'General Thomas Ewing.' "

The telegram added a note of urgency to the preparations being made for departure, and within half an hour, most of the men had already gathered on the southern fringes of Lawrence. Across the prairie to the south, a long row of wagons was already starting out ahead, but gazing at them, Cole Younger guessed that few if any of the slow, heavily laden vehicles would ever make it across the state line.

Quantrill had already dispatched outriders to scout the route ahead, but the bushwhackers understood from the intercepted enemy message that if troops were being sent from Leavenworth and Kansas City, most opposition would come at them from

255

behind rather than in front as they made their way southeast back toward Missouri. That made Cole's and George Todd's rear-guard assignment doubly important to the safety of the entire band.

John Hartman and Frank James hung back with the rear guard after the main force had departed across the prairie. Both had volunteered for the duty. During those final few tense moments they sat on their horses watching the town of Lawrence burn to the ground while they waited for orders to leave. Cole had sent half a dozen riders back into town to look for stragglers, and he didn't want to go until those men had returned.

This was the first time the two young men had had the chance to talk since the night before, and although the luster of their adventure had already worn off for John, Frank was still aglow with the importance of what they had done.

"I got me one of the men on Bill Quantrill's execution list," Frank announced proudly. "I killed Hymie Boulting in the front parlor of his house and then burnt the damn place down right on top of his corpse. They say he's the one that beat those two Sharp brothers to death with a wagon spoke last fall over near Liberty. He was supposed to be one terrible customer, but he didn't act all that brave when I got to him. When I drew down on him, he started blubbering like a baby. He offered me a thousand dollars if I wouldn't kill him, said he had the money right there in the house. But afterward I couldn't ever find it. I guess if it was there, it burnt up when he did."

"I shot one of the men on the ferry," John replied. He felt like the revelation was expected of him, but somehow it seemed to come out sounding more like a confession than a boast.

"Yeah, you fellows did a good job over there," Frank conceded. "If you hadn't got to that ferry the way you did, we would have had hell to pay once those Federals got on this side of the river. But as it was, we killed maybe a hundred fifty or two hundred of them, and we didn't lose a single man. Think of it, John! We didn't lose one man, and we did all this!" He waved his hand expansively toward the inferno nearby, still beaming with pride.

"Yeah, Frank," John said. "We did all this." But in the excitement of the moment, the irony in his voice was wasted on his friend.

Concealed behind the thick trunk of a mulberry tree with his rifle resting in the fork of two branches, John Hartman welcomed the growing shadows of dusk which finally began to gather in the western sky.

The Federal pursuit had been fierce and relentless, turning the long afternoon of warfare into what seemed like days of steady fighting. A full third of the men that Cole and George had assembled for the rear guard were dead or missing by now, and the survivors were dazed and exhausted. John had lost track of Frank James a couple of hours before and no longer knew whether his friend was alive or dead.

The bushwhacker band had done all right for the first few hours of their retreat. None of the scouts had turned up any sign of trouble ahead, and the men in the rear guard had proceeded at an almost leisurely pace, the speed of their progress determined by the movement of the slow, heavy wagons loaded with booty. Quantrill's only mistake during the entire foray into Kansas, it seemed, was in deciding too late that the wagons and the goods they contained would have to be left behind. But that one error was gross enough by itself. Already it had cost the lives of more than a score of his men, and still there was no relief in sight from furious Union pursuit.

About a hundred yards away, across the

broad flat prairie to the west, John saw a Union soldier ease up out of the depression where he was hiding and start to crawl cautiously forward. John squeezed off a shot, and though the bullet did no apparent damage, it did strike close enough to the enemy soldier to drive him back into cover.

Although they had yet again succeeded in slowing the Federal soldiers to a dead stop, John knew full well what a dangerous situation they were now in. The soldiers they had pinned down were only the advance units of a much larger Federal force, and when the main body of troops came up on line, they could easily surround and overwhelm the scattered bushwhackers, who were now dug in amidst a copse of trees straddling the main road back to Missouri. But still they planned to remain for as long as they could, knowing that once they left this cover they might not come across any more as good for several miles down the road.

A movement to one side caught John's attention, and he turned his head to see Cole Younger scurrying through the underbrush toward him.

"How are you holding up, John?" Cole asked as he reached his friend's side.

"I guess I've got a few more hours of fight left in me," John answered tiredly, "but when we get back, I swear I'm going to find myself a big feather bed somewhere and sleep for a month."

"I've got a feeling there'll be a lot of that going on," Cole said. "But first we've got to get ourselves back in one piece."

"Has there been any word from Quantrill?" John asked.

"Yeah, finally a rider got through. That's what I came to tell you. They ran into a big fight about five miles east of here. Ewing must've sent a couple hundred troops southeast out of Kansas City to cut us off, and they hit Quantrill out of nowhere. The messenger said our men had no choice but to split up and hightail it for the border."

"Which means that we're fighting a rear guard for nothing," John said.

"That's about the size of it," Cole agreed. "But it's still not going to be so easy for us to cut and run. The rider Quantrill sent told me that he had to skirt around a company-sized Federal outfit east of here, and he had to outrun a couple of patrols to make it in from the south."

"Then we're surrounded?"

"Something like that."

John turned his eyes back to the western sky, as if trying to will the final layers of hazy daylight to fade away into darkness.

One good charge would be all it took to push them out of this small bit of cover, and once they were out in the open, there would be nowhere to run.

"We've just got one thing going for us," Cole said. "I don't believe those Federals out there know how many of us are in here. We've been keeping up a pretty steady fire, so maybe they don't know that there's only twenty or so of us left. But at any rate, the horses are ready, and at the first sign of a push from any side, we'll get the hell out. If they'll only hold off for another fifteen or twenty minutes . . ."

The next time the Union soldier tried to come up out of hiding was his last. The light was nearly gone, but there was still enough left for John to draw a bead and for him to see the distant man buck with the impact of the rifle bullet. He lay still for a moment, and then another figure rose up behind him and quickly drew him back out of sight.

Without warning an eruption of gunfire sounded on the eastern side of the clump of trees about fifteen yards from John. He turned immediately and sprinted toward the horses, knowing they would have to leave now or they would never leave at all.

Cole was already mounted. He was holding the reins of John's horse in his hand, waiting for him to arrive. All around him men were leaping onto the backs of their excited animals. The air was filled with the deadly hiss of Federal bullets, and only a few of the bushwhackers were even bothering to return the fire. Getting out was all any of them had on their minds right now.

John bounded astride his horse and dug his heels into the animal's side. In a moment they burst from the trees in a jumbled mass, scattering in all directions as they raced across the open prairie. A few enemy soldiers on both sides of them began to shoot, but the light was nearly gone now and the swift-riding bushwhackers made poor targets.

Cole Younger and his horse were transformed by the growing darkness into little more than a shadowy form ahead, but John followed him doggedly, knowing that if there was one man he could trust to lead him out of this mess, it was Cole. They raced for nearly a mile, pushing their horses to the very limits of their endurance.

John had no inkling that they might be running into trouble until he heard the angry bark of Cole's revolver and saw the yellow tongues of flame licking rapidly out into the night. There was no chance to turn aside. The momentum of the bay was such that John had little choice but to plunge right into the middle of the fight. Quickly looping his horse's reins around the saddle horn, he drew a revolver in each hand and began blasting away at the multitude of shadowy forms that seemed to engulf him.

For one horrendous moment the air was thick with the roar of gunfire and the acrid scent of black powder smoke. John felt something slam against his left thigh, but there was no time to pause and consider how badly he might be injured as he jammed his two now-empty revolvers into his clothing and drew out two more.

Then suddenly, remarkably, he was in the clear. The roar of gunfire still sounded behind him, but the explosions no longer seemed like they were going off only inches away.

Out of nowhere a dark, mounted form rushed at him from the side, and he almost squeezed off a shot before he heard the sound of his friend's voice. "Are you hit, John?" Cole asked quickly. Neither of them slowed his pace as they hurtled forward away from their enemies.

"Yeah," John answered huskily. "In the leg."

"How bad?"

"I don't know yet. I think I'll be all right

for a while. At least until we get away from these bastards."

"If you feel like you're going to pass out, give a yell so I can tie you in the saddle. One way or another, we've got to put some miles behind us in a hurry!"

"I'll let you know," John replied, gritting his teeth as waves of nauseating pain swept over him. It was going to be a long, hard night.

CHAPTER ELEVEN

Charlie Fulton's eyes glowed with desire as he grabbed Mollie by the wrist and pulled her roughly toward him. "Yes I *will* have you, Susan Pendleton!" he proclaimed, his voice rising to an insistent roar that echoed to all corners of the packed theatre. "You cannot resist me!" Laughing diabolically, he reached up to stroke his waxed, pencil-thin mustache. Mollie struggled against him, turning her head aside when he tried to kiss her and pounding vainly against his chest with her free hand.

"Never, you beast!" she screamed. "I'll die before I'll ever submit to you, Manfred Blunt!"

"As you wish, my dear," Fulton said, chuckling under his breath as he released his grip on her arm. Then a shrewd grin crossed his face as he added, "But don't forget that you'll be choosing death for your brother Jim as well. Only I can save him from the hangman's noose by testifying that he was not the man who robbed and killed the Widow Jarvis."

Mollie turned aside and, bringing the back of her right hand up to her forehead, she took a couple of steps forward on the stage so the audience could more clearly witness the depths of her suffering.

And then she saw him . . .

He was seated several rows back on the left side of the theatre; tall and proud in his Union officer's uniform, he looked even more handsome than she remembered him. When their eyes met, suddenly it seemed as if they were the only two people in the theatre, or perhaps in the whole world. His confident, intimate smile was so familiar to her that she might have last seen it only a day or two before instead of ten years ago and a thousand miles away.

". . . I said, what will your choice be, Miss Susan!" Charlie Fulton said irritably from behind her.

"Why are you so heartless, sir? How can a man be so cruel as you?" The words from the script droned from Mollie's lips, coming instinctively like a verse from an oft-repeated poem. She scarcely knew what she was saying. All she knew, the only thing that was real to her at that moment, was that

Kurt Rakestraw was here watching her perform. Her gaze was torn away from him only when Charlie Fulton grabbed her from behind and spun her roughly around.

"What's the matter with you?" he demanded angrily under his breath. "You're dropping cues right and left!"

"I'm sorry," she whispered. "I saw someone . . ." In the wings to her right she noticed Brian Kerr, the theatre owner, mopping his forehead frantically with a large red bandanna. Suddenly the scenery on stage began to swirl around her, and she might have fainted dead away had not Fulton begun to shake her angrily.

"There is time still to save your brother's life," he roared, "but if I do that, you must swear to me that we will wed tomorrow!"

"What choice do I have?" Mollie replied. She was struggling to regain the pace and flow of the play, but she could scarcely force herself to think about her lines. Even now, with her back turned to the audience, she could still see his face.

Somehow they finished. Through the remainder of the performance Mollie avoided looking back at Kurt Rakestraw, afraid of what would happen if she did. When the play was over she raced into the wings, brushing blindly past the red-faced

Brian Kerr and ignoring the audience's clamors for a second curtain call. Once inside her dressing room she quickly closed the door and leaned back heavily against it, as if to bar all intruders.

"Lord, Miss Mollie!" Eliza Franklin exclaimed. "You look like you've been dipped in chalk!"

"I saw someone out there, Eliza," Mollie announced breathlessly. "A man I knew a long time ago . . ."

"Was it that no-'count preacher you said tried to molest you once?" Eliza asked with concern. "If that's the trash you saw, I'll just go round up some of the stagehands and we'll —"

"No, it wasn't him," Mollie said. "It was a man I was in love with back when we still lived in Virginia." Here, safely cloistered in her dressing room, she was beginning to calm down at last. "I don't know why seeing him again has had such an effect on me, though. After all, it happened more than ten years ago. I was little more than a girl back then, and we knew each other for such a short time."

"It must have been something special to make you this way after ten years," Eliza said.

"Oh, that it was, Eliza," Mollie said, smiling suddenly at the memories. "That it was."

"Well what are you going to do when he comes back here?" the maid asked.

"Comes back here?" Mollie exclaimed. Somehow she had not considered that possibility.

"Well, he recognized you too, didn't he?"

"Yes, I'm sure he did."

"Then I'd say he'll be back," Eliza announced. "What fool would pass up the chance to try and be friends again with a woman who looks as good as you do when you go out there on that stage every night? Yes, I'd say he'll be back here just as soon as he can walk around back to the stage door and slip old Frank a dollar to let him in."

"My God . . ." Mollie whispered.

"So will you see him when he gets here?" Eliza asked. "Will you talk to him?"

"Yes, I'll see him," Mollie said after a moment's hesitation. "But first I have to change. If he does come, I don't want you to let him in until I'm ready." And with that, she and her companion began the process of getting her out of her stage costume and into her street clothes.

Mollie's pulse quickened when she heard a light tapping on her door, but she fought to maintain the control that she had regained over the past few minutes. After making sure her hair was in place, she laid aside the hairbrush she was holding and turned to face the door.

"You can leave after you let him in, Eliza," she said. "I'll be all right."

"I know you will." Eliza smiled back at her as she went to the door and opened it.

Standing in the open doorway, Kurt Rakestraw didn't seem quite as tall as Mollie remembered him, and the decade that had passed since they last saw one another had added a sprinkling of gray to his thick dark hair and beard. But she still thought he was the handsomest man she had ever seen.

He simply stood there for a moment, fingering the brim of his officer's hat, staring at her with eyes filled with appreciation and fond recollection. Unnoticed, her shawl in hand, Eliza slipped by him and disappeared before either Mollie or Rakestraw had spoken a word.

"Come in, Kurt," Mollie said at last. "Come in and close the door. It's . . . it's good to see you again after all these years." She stepped forward and, before he had the chance to attempt any other sort of greeting, took his hand and shook it warmly.

"I couldn't believe my eyes when I saw

your name on that marquee this afternoon," Rakestraw admitted. "I thought it surely couldn't be the same Mollie Hartman I knew so long ago back in Virginia, but I still had to come and make sure . . . And here you are, a successful actress, and even more beautiful than my memories of you."

"I was a little surprised when I saw you in the audience, too," Mollie admitted. "You probably noticed, along with everyone else in the theatre."

"I saw that I caught you off guard," he replied. "I suppose I should have sent word to you that I would be there."

"Well, you never were one to send word, were you, Kurt?" Mollie asked pointedly.

"No, I wasn't, Mollie," Rakestraw told her with no hint of apology in his voice. "But that doesn't mean that I haven't thought about you over and over again since those weeks we spent together, or that I haven't lain awake more nights than I can remember since then wishing that we —"

"There's no need to go into all that," Mollie stated, interrupting him brusquely.

"No, I suppose not. But l do want you to know that I did go back and try to find you, Mollie. It was two years after I left, but you and your family had already moved away, and my brother wasn't sure where you had gone."

"I believe you, Kurt," she said. "But that all happened a long time ago, and this is now. So tell me, what brings you to Kansas City?"

"Well, as you can see, I'm in the Union army now," Rakestraw said. "I joined up about two years ago in Colorado, and I've spent most of my time out there patrolling the gold fields and trying to keep the Indians in check. But now I've been transferred here on special assignment. I just got to Missouri a couple of days ago."

"On special assignment?" Mollie asked.

"Over the years I've gained quite a bit of experience dealing with the Indians out west," he explained. "I've learned a lot about the way they live off the land, the way they fight, and even the way they manage to stay out of the way and hide when they don't want to fight. And now it seems like the army believes I can put that experience to work in dealing with the kind of problems they're having in this area. I brought a specially trained company of troops from the Colorado District here to Missouri with me."

Mollie tried to act as if she were only vaguely interested in Rakestraw's assignment, although she knew that the "kind of problems" he had mentioned could only refer to the deadly activities of Quantrill's Raiders. She quickly changed the subject rather than give him any indication that his military duties concerned her in any way.

"I suppose you've been all over the country since we last saw one another, Kurt, just like you wanted to do."

"I've seen a good-sized piece of it," he admitted. "After I left you, I headed back out to California for a while, but I hated seeing what gold fever had done to that beautiful place in just a few short years. I lived with the Sioux for a while in 'fifty-seven, 'fifty-eight. Then, in the late fifties, I started drifting south, scouting for the army now and then to pick up some pocket money, other times just living off the land. I was in Mexico when the war broke out, but when I saw how bad it was going to get, I headed on back north to join up. I guess I never will have sense enough to keep my hand out of the fire."

"That sounds about like the life I would have predicted for you," Mollie said. "I guess the only thing that surprises me about the whole thing is that you're still alive to be here now. Your kind of men don't always live so long, do they Kurt?"

"I suppose not," Rakestraw said and smiled broadly. "But we sure do get our money's worth while we're here."

They talked on about what had happened in their lives since their last meeting, and Mollie was pleased to find that she could maintain a calm, composed front in his presence. But despite her cool appearance, she had little control over the rage of memories that raced through her mind.

She had been only seventeen when they first met, and Kurt Rakestraw had swept her off her feet as no man had ever done before or since. During the few short weeks they had spent together as lovers, she had immersed herself completely in their affair, believing with the blind innocence of youth that this was the man she was destined to be with and love for the rest of her life.

In all fairness to Kurt, she had to admit, he had never made any empty promises. He had told her that he loved her, but he had never vowed to stay in Virginia or to take her with him. In fact, he often talked glowingly of the places he had yet to see and the things that he felt he still must do. He loved the western frontier, and even in the midst of their love affair, it had still called to him.

Mollie remembered thinking she could hold him simply by the strength of her love, but in the end he had left her.

For a time she had been sure that he would come back, that someday, lying alone on a barren prairie, he would realize what he had given up and would come flying back into her arms. Then eventually, as the lonely months passed without any word from him, the healing process had finally started. Other men had entered her life to claim her thoughts and affections, and other hopes and dreams had been born to replace those that had died the day Kurt Rakestraw had started west again.

"I know it's probably unfair of me to suggest such a thing, Mollie," Rakestraw said, "but I would like to see you again. Would that be possible?"

Mollie's first instinct was to quickly reply that it would, but she didn't want to give him the satisfaction of seeing her so eager.

"I'll need some time to think about that, Kurt," she answered.

"I understand, but I hope that after you've thought it over, you'll decide in my favor. I know we can't turn the clock back to the way things were ten years ago, but that doesn't mean that we can't be friends. It doesn't mean that we still can't enjoy each other's company here and now."

"Of course it doesn't, but I'm not sure I

want that to happen, Kurt," she told him. "I have a full, complete life already, and I'm not sure there's a place for you in it any longer. Give me a few days and I'll have an answer for you."

"As you wish, Mollie," Rakestraw said, smiling as he turned to leave. "I'll come back and see you next week, and you can tell me then what you've decided."

After he was gone, Mollie dropped into the chair at her dressing table. She felt drained by the encounter. Dealing with all the complex emotions that had raced through her while they were together had left her tired and confused. Yet she still could not deny the spark of excitement caused by the arrival of the man she had longed for so many times over the years.

She knew that the days between now and when he returned would be long and anxious ones for her, and she was also starting to understand what her answer would undoubtedly be when he came again.

Now that the fall frosts had begun, the western Missouri countryside was splashed with the resplendent colors of autumn. There was a sharp chill in the air at this early hour of the morning, but Jason Hartman hardly noticed the cold as he drove his wagon southwest out of Lee's Summit toward the western part of Jackson County. He had too much on his mind to spend even a moment considering the vagaries of the weather.

He had just left a farmhouse outside Lee's Summit where his son John lay ill with a leg wound suffered during the trip back from Lawrence. The injury was not serious enough to be fatal, but the fact that he was immobilized was dangerous enough by itself to cause Jason grave concern for his son's safety. If any of the Federal troops in the area learned that a wounded bushwhacker was hiding at the farm, John would have no chance of escape and would probably be killed on the spot.

Daniel was there with his brother, however, and he had sent his father on his way this morning with a solemn pledge to take care of John until he was well enough to travel. Their plan was for Jason to pick his son up with the wagon on his way back through the area and take him to Clay County, where he could be with his family while he recuperated. Jason knew that would place them all in great danger, but he could not stand the thought of his son being at the mercy of strangers while lying injured and vulnerable.

Under any other circumstances, Jason would not even have considered leaving John at such a time, but the mission he was on was one of even greater urgency. He was on his way to help, and perhaps even save the lives of, the wife and two small children of a dead friend.

For the past three weeks since the death of his daughter Ruth in Kansas City, the string of brutal and deadly events in the area had continued at a horrible pace.

As if to show his total lack of remorse over the collapsed building in Kansas City, only four days later General Thomas Ewing had issued his General Order No. 10, which banished the families of all known bushwhackers and Southern sympathizers living within a specified zone along the Kansas-Missouri border. Because they were beyond the specified area, Jason's family had been exempt from the order, but scores of other people had been forced to leave behind practically everything they owned and either to move deeper into the interior of the state, or to flee southward in hopes of eventually reaching Confederate-controlled territory.

The Lawrence raid by Quantrill's forces had followed close on the heels of that order, and Jason and Arethia had lived through five agonizing days afterward before finally receiving any news about John's fate.

Then, on the very day they had learned that John was alive, though wounded, they had heard about yet another decree by the vengeful General Ewing. This one, officially titled General Order No. 11, mandated the almost total evacuation of a twenty-mile zone along the west central border of the state. Only those residents living in or near the Union-protected cities and towns in the area would be permitted to stay, and even they would be subjected to stringent loyalty oaths before the necessary permission would be granted.

The publicly stated purpose of General Order No. 11 was twofold — to deprive the bushwhackers of all sources of support in the area, and to move the law-abiding residents in that part of the state beyond the reach of retaliatory raids from enraged Kansans. Once enforcement began, however, it became clear that the results of the order would be far different from the stated goals.

Immediately after Ewing issued the order, stories began circulating about armed bands of Kansans roaming the area of evacuation, pillaging and burning homes indiscriminately and slaughtering all who had the misfortune to end up in their path. It was said that Ewing had done little to protect families and assist them with the evacuation and that he had ordered his troops to let the Kansans do as they wanted without opposition.

Had the circumstances been different, Jason would probably have done little during all the turmoil but stay close to home and protect his family as best he could. But soon after the issuance of General Order No. 11, he had received news that the widow and children of his friend Bill Witherow were in great peril. Eileen Witherow had been ill and unable to travel alone when the order was first issued, and during the initial rush to get out of danger, her neighbors had callously left her and her two small daughters behind. A raiding party had stolen all the livestock from her small farm, and now she and her two little ones were virtually stranded in what was fast becoming a barren wasteland.

Jason had no idea what he would find when he reached the home of Bill's widow. He knew there was a strong possibility that Eileen and her children were already dead, but still it was a chance that he had to take. Bill had been a close friend all during the difficult times when they had traveled with General Price's army at the start of the war, and the last promise Jason had made to Bill before he died was that if the time ever came when Bill's family needed help, he would be there for them.

A Union patrol stopped him as he entered the edge of the evacuation zone and warned him of the dangers of going any farther, but they reluctantly let him proceed after he explained his mission. They did not, however, offer to escort him to the Witherow farm, making him believe even more strongly in the popular contention that General Ewing actually *wanted* the marauding Jayhawkers to do their worst in retaliation for Quantrill's raid on Lawrence.

The countryside became more and more desolate as Jason traveled westward. The buildings of every farm he passed had been reduced to charred piles of blackened rubble, and most of the crops, which should have been ripe for harvest at this time of year, had been burned as well. Here and there along the road he passed the bloated, rotting bodies of civilians who had been murdered by the raiders even as they fled, and other than a few occasional birds and small animals, there was little sign of life anywhere about.

It was, Jason thought, as if the vengeful hand of a furious God had simply reached out and swept the land clear of all that man had built and done. But he knew only too well that God had nothing to do with anything he saw here. It was men who had done this, men whose hearts had been turned to stone by the blind hatred that filled them.

He reached the Witherow farm without meeting anyone else on the road, but whatever hopes he might have clung to up until then died when he saw the blackened ruins of the house and barn. A knot caught in his throat as he drove the wagon up to what had once been the yard of the neat frame house and stepped down to the ground.

Nothing was left of the hopes and dreams to which Bill and his wife had dedicated their lives before the war. A tall stone chimney rose starkly from one end of the twenty-by-thirty heap of cinders. Near the center of the ruins the twisted remnants of an iron bedstead protruded at an angle. Where the kitchen had once been, the handle of an indoor pump pointed crazily toward the sky. Farther away, across the back yard, the remains of a small vegetable plot lay in tram pled disarray, and beyond that was a pile of rubble where the chicken coop had once stood.

He was turning to leave, knowing it was

senseless to stay any longer, when a faint noise caught his attention. It wasn't exactly like the sound of a voice, but still it was a noise that somehow seemed too human to be ignored.

He skirted the ruins of the house and hurried in the direction from which the sound seemed to have come. He had gone only a few dozen feet when he heard it again.

It would have been easy enough to overlook the entrance to the small storm shelter if he had not been walking almost straight toward it. It was tucked back in a small clump of trees between the house and barn, and the hummock of dirt that covered its roof looked almost like a natural feature of the landscape.

As Jason neared the door, he detected the sound of a child whimpering, and then the soft reassuring voice of a woman. His spirits soared as he bounded to the door and flung it open. The splash of light that poured into the storm shelter fell upon a pathetic scene.

Three pitiful forms were huddled on the dirt floor of the shelter. Although Jason knew this must be Eileen Witherow, he scarcely recognized her. Covered with dirt, and a look of sheer terror on her face, she held her two small, frightened daughters tightly against her. She stared up at him in wordless dread as if he had already announced that he had come to serve as their executioner.

"It's all right, Eileen!" Jason told the woman quickly. "It's me, Jason Hartman. I've come to help you!"

"Jason?" Eileen whispered, as if his name were incomprehensible to her.

"That's right! Your husband's friend from the Home Guards. Remember? I came here two years ago to bring you Bill's things, and then I returned to visit again last year with my son Dan. He fixed your roof while we were here. You remember that, don't you, Eileen?"

"The roof's gone," Eileen said dully. "The house is gone too. They burnt it. They burnt everything. And then we hid out here."

"Well, it's all right now," Jason said, moving forward and gently urging the woman to rise to her feet. "I'm going to take you and your girls away from here where you'll be safe."

"But we can't go out there," Eileen replied, refusing to be led out of the storm shelter. "*They're* out there and they'll see us. They'll kill us! We can go out a little bit at night for water, but that's all."

"Don't worry, Eileen," Jason assured her, pulling her closer to the door. "I've looked

284

all around and there's no one here right now. We can leave now, but we must hurry. They might come back at any time."

Slowly, with great patience, Jason encouraged the three terror-filled fugitives to leave the cellar. For a moment they just stood looking around apprehensively, as if every tree concealed a danger, then Eileen turned to Jason and whispered, "They come back every day. Sometimes they just ride by, and sometimes they stop. But we always stay in there except at night. Then we can go out and get water. It's good at night because it's dark and safe and we can get water."

"I understand, but it's time to leave now, Eileen," Jason told her, steering them toward the wagon. "I know it's daylight and you're afraid, but we have to leave right away. We have to get out of this area right away, and then we'll all be safe."

Jason made a place for his three charges to sit on a piece of canvas in the back of the wagon, then gave them some bread and cold chicken to eat before he turned the horses and started back east. There was no telling how long it had been since any of them had had any proper food to eat, he thought. They all looked gaunt and pale, like dazed convicts released into the open after long confinement in some dank cell, and the stench that rose from their filthy bodies and clothes was almost overpowering.

It was midmorning now, and Jason figured they had about three hours of traveling ahead of them before they reached the relative safety of a populated area. He had been fortunate in not encountering any Jayhawkers on the way over, but he knew that he could not count on being so lucky on the way back. Despite the assurances he had given to Eileen Witherow, he still wasn't certain any of them would survive even another few hours. But surely, he thought, glancing back at his beleaguered charges, the sight of these three would be enough to light a spark of humanity in even the most brutal Jayhawker heart. What reason could there be, what cause could be served in doing them any further harm?

They had been traveling east for less than an hour when Jason spotted the band of mounted men approaching them down the road ahead. He didn't bother to try and turn aside, nor did he reach for the rifle that lay in the wagon bed behind the seat. He knew there was no point. Either they would be allowed to live or they wouldn't, depending on the mood and temperament of the men who were now galloping toward them.

His heart pounding, he stopped the wagon

when the men were still about fifty feet away and waited for them to come up. Behind him Eileen Witherow and her daughters huddled together once more, silent, their faces masks of fear.

Jason was relieved to find that he did not recognize any of the men in the eight-man Jayhawker band, knowing that certain of his enemies in Kansas, even now, would like nothing better than to catch him out alone and defenseless like this.

The raiders fanned out and surrounded the wagon and team, sizing him up with stern, dark gazes. They were all heavily armed, but for the time being, none of them brandished their weapons in any particularly threatening manner. It was obvious that Jason and the females with him posed no great threat to even such a small band of men.

"I guess you know you folks ain't s'pose to be in this part of the county," one of the Jayhawkers told Jason. He was a hawk-nosed fellow with dark eyes and an ugly scar across one temple. "Maybe you just better tell us who you are and what you're doing here."

"My name's Paul Roundtree," Jason lied, knowing that his real name might be familiar to some of these men. "I do know I'm not supposed to be here, but I came to get my sister-in-law and her girls and take them back to my place. I got word they were in trouble, so I'm taking them back to Booneville with me. You see, her husband, my brother Bill, was killed in 'sixty-one when that bastard Sterling Price marched his army of traitors through this part of the country."

"Your story sounds like a crock of shit to me," the Jayhawker announced with more boredom than malice in his voice. "If somebody made me lay my money down, I'd have to wager that you're a goddamn rebel bastard just like all the rest of the white trash we've dealt with in these parts over the past couple of weeks."

"Damn you!" Jason exclaimed, feigning a sudden flurry of indignation. "The only thing that's rebel about me is the Confederate bullet that I'm still carrying around in my leg from the Battle of Booneville!"

"Booneville, huh?" the Jayhawker said, unimpressed.

"Look, what's the point in all this?" Jason asked, deciding to let his elaborate story alone before he got too entangled in his own lies. "It won't hurt anything at all for you fellows to let us pass on by. No matter what you think I am, I don't have any part in the war anymore, not since I got crippled up, and you can see that the woman and her daughters in back are harmless enough. Hell, they're half out of their minds from spending so much time hiding and starving since the trouble started around here."

Jason could hardly believe what he was hearing when one of the other men spoke up in his defense. "I think he's right, Matthew," a second Jayhawker said, easing his horse up beside the first. "What could it hurt to leave them be? It's like we were talking about this morning in camp. A man's bound to get tired of the killing after a while. We don't know who these people are, but it's easy enough to see that they're just trying to stay alive and get the hell out of here. I say we let them go."

Glancing around, Jason saw that some of the other men in the group were of the same mind, but the apparent leader seemed unconvinced either by Jason's tale or by his companion's arguments.

"You know what Jennison's orders are," he said. "After all, we didn't ride all the way over here for a goddamn picnic!"

"Yeah, but where does it all stop, for Christ's sake?" the other man argued. "Hell, Matthew, that little girl back there, the blonde one, she looks a little bit like my daughter Rebecca. If we kill this fellow and take his team, that woman and those little girls might die out here. They got nothing to eat, no place to go, and nobody to help them."

The hawk-nosed leader turned and gave his companion a curious, irritated look. "I reckon you'll be staying back in Franklin the next time we ride out, Murphy," he said. "Seems to me you've done got softhearted all of a sudden."

"Maybe I have, Matthew," Murphy replied. "And maybe it's time somebody did. I say we let them go." This time a couple of the others actually expressed their approval of the idea out loud.

"Well then, mister," Hawk Nose said, turning his attention back to Jason, "I guess this must be your lucky day. You take your womenfolk and you get the hell on out of here. And when you get back with your bushwhacking friends on east of here, you tell them how you mush-mouthed your way past a gang of addleheaded Kansans who had you dead to rights but didn't have sense enough to put a bullet in you."

"We're much obliged to you," Jason said, clicking his team into motion before the Jayhawker leader had a chance to reconsider. "And you've done the right thing, I swear you have. All I ever wanted was to get these three away to safety."

The Jayhawkers lingered for a moment, watching Jason drive away, then turned their horses and proceeded down the road. After they had disappeared from sight, Jason turned to Eileen and said, "I sure am glad you kept quiet back there. That was too close for my liking."

Eileen Witherow looked up at him for a long moment, her eyes dull and confused, and then she asked, "Who is Paul Round-tree? I thought you said you were Jason."

CHAPTER TWELVE

Jason and his father had constructed a fifteen-foot plank table under the large mulberry tree in Will's back yard, and the women were busy filling it from end to end with platters and bowls of food. At this time of year, with the harvesting nearly finished, most of the fall slaughtering done, and the remainder of the garden produce hanging ripe on the vine, the tables of most country folk were cornucopias of good things to eat.

A cautious air of festivity permeated the reunion of the Hartman family. It was the first time they had all been together in nearly two years, and they had a lot of getting reacquainted to do. The war had changed each one of them, making them in an odd sort of way, strangers to each other, although they still remained the closest of families.

Jason had encountered no problems in returning home with his wounded son John,

Eileen Witherow, and her two daughters. Daniel and Cole had enlisted the aid of several of their fellow bushwhackers to serve as escort on the way back from Lee's Summit, but they had met no Union troops along the back-country route they had selected. The trip had been a rough one for John, but after carefully examining his son's wound when they reached Will Hartman's farm, Jason decided that the long healing process was well under way at last. No damage had been done to the bone in John's thigh, and the two holes in his leg had finally stopped oozing the bloody pus that marked the presence of infection and decay.

After receiving word that the rest of her family was gathering at her father's farm, Mollie had decided to join them. She was anxious to see everyone again, but in fact, she had a second reason for wanting to return home. She knew there was a good chance that Cole Younger would remain with the others to visit for a few days, and she urgently needed to talk to him.

When the meal was ready at last, Arethia called everyone out and they took their places at the table. Will Hartman sat at the head with Jason at the opposite end. Flanking Jason on either side were Daniel and John, and Cole took a seat at Will's right hand. Jason's other children, fifteen-year-old Benjamin and fourteen-year-old Cassie, found places to sit along the middle of the table, as did Eileen Witherow's two daughters, Tess and Laura. Mollie took a seat beside Cole, Eileen sat across from her daughters, and Jason's older sister, Sarah, filled the empty place on her father's left. Arethia, who spent much of her time going back and forth from the kitchen, set her place at John's side.

When everyone was seated, Will Hartman rose to his feet to bless the table. Wordy, eloquent prayers were one of his specialties, as his family could testify from spending countless Sunday afternoons trying to ignore the tantalizing smells of dinner while Will held lengthy discussions with his Maker on a variety of personal and political topics. But today he was mercifully, and surprisingly, brief. He asked God to make a special place in His kingdom for his dead granddaughter, Ruth, and beseeched Him to guide and protect his son Tyson who had disappeared into the western wilderness many years before. A true Southerner, he threw in a sound condemnation of all things Federal and Northern and begged the Lord to provide every young man fighting for the Confederate cause true aim and long life.

Then he said his "amens," sat back down in his chair, and reached for the chicken. The table immediately became a hive of activity as everyone began to fill his plate with food, passing bowls and platters in every direction.

"So, Cole," Will Hartman asked with typical abruptness, "have you decided yet whether you'll be going along when Quantrill leads his bunch south to Texas?"

"No, sir, I haven't quite made up my mind yet," Cole replied, casting a quick, anxious glance in Mollie's direction. He had intended to discuss that topic with her, but there hadn't been any chance for the two of them to be alone yet. "I can't say that I relish the thought of spending the whole winter that far away from home, but with most of the outfit gone, there won't be much that a handful of stragglers can do in these parts."

"Folks are pretty worried about what's going to happen when they leave," Will admitted. "Now that Price's army has been ordered way the hell across the Mississippi, it doesn't look like there'll be any Southern forces anywhere in the state to offer us the hope of liberation. We'll be at the complete mercy of both Ewing's Federals *and* the damn Jayhawkers."

"Well, it might not be as bad as everyone thinks, Dad," Jason said. "For the past two years, nobody's seemed all that anxious to do much fighting during the winter, and it's not like they'll be gone for good. Come spring, I'm sure Quantrill will head back in this direction."

"Yeah, unless that fool Jeff Davis takes a notion to order him east like he has all the rest of our best fighting men," Will grumbled. As a dedicated devotee of General Sterling Price, Will Hartman had become extremely critical of Jefferson Davis after he learned of Price's less-than-amiable relationship with the Confederate president. But there were solid reasons for his complaint as well. Now that the Confederates were steadily losing ground on all fronts east of the Mississippi River, Davis had increasingly drawn on the manpower and resources of the states west of the river to bolster his crumbling cause.

"I don't think there would be much use in Davis trying something like that," Cole said. "Not many of the men I know would go, even if Quantrill himself ordered them to."

"That's right, Grandpa," Daniel spoke up. "The way we see it, those other states over there like Tennessee and Virginia should do their best to hold on to their own soil, just like we're doing. We're Missourians, and our fight's here."

"Good boy!" Will announced. "You're thinking straight on that, Daniel, and I'm proud of you."

Arethia Hartman had just returned from the kitchen with a full pitcher of tea, but instead of serving it immediately, she paused behind her husband, her hand resting on his shoulder, to listen to the conversation. For several days now, she and her husband had been aware of Quantrill's plans to lead his men south out of the state, and the two of them had held a number of long discussions about that topic.

Finally they had decided to advise their sons not to go, but to stay here and hide out either on or near the family farm instead. It would be risky, not only for John and Daniel, but for the rest of the family as well, but the reasons in favor of their staying seemed to outweigh the disadvantages. Foremost on their minds was the fact that John was still in no condition to survive a long, difficult trip, and he probably wouldn't be for at least another month or two. But on a deeper, emotional level, neither of them could bear to face the idea of seeing their sons travel so far away during a time of war, perhaps never to return.

Just the night before, Jason and Arethia had broached the topic, and both John and Daniel had agreed to at least try staying close to home for a while. The long summer of fighting had been physically and emotionally exhausting for both of them, and John in particular, after the brutality he had witnessed and the danger he had faced, was eager to live some sort of life other than that of a bushwhacker. None of them knew how long this period of relative peace and recovery might last, but they were willing to take their chances and to face each new day as it came.

When the meal was finished, the men drifted back inside Will Hartman's house to smoke and talk while the women began clearing the table and carrying everything inside.

A few minutes later when Mollie saw Cole come back out of the house and head for the barn, she begged off helping with the rest of the cleanup and hurried to catch up with him.

"You aren't leaving, are you, Cole?" Mollie asked.

Cole waited on the path for her to reach him, then the two of them proceeded toward the barn.

"No, I'm just going to check my horse,"

Cole explained. "I pushed him so hard during the ride back from Lawrence that he strained a muscle, and it's been slow in healing. I thought I might rub a little liniment on it."

"This business about going to Texas came as a complete surprise to me," Mollie admitted. "It's been nearly six weeks since I've seen any of you, and I guess I'm out of touch."

"I meant to talk to you about it the first chance I got," Cole told her. "I would have come to see you before now, but since Lawrence and this Order 11 business, it's been a little tough for any of us to slip into Kansas City and back out again."

"So will you be going, Cole?" Mollie asked.

"Well, it's like I told your dad. I'm not sure yet. I might be able to do more down there than I could here, but things are getting pretty strange in Quantrill's bunch these days. There's more infighting and arguing than before, and I think a lot of the men are beginning to lose some of their confidence in Quantrill. After the job we did at Lawrence, some of them started wondering if he hadn't gone too far, if he wasn't just beginning to kill for the sake of killing rather than for some good reason.

And yet there's others, like Bill Anderson and some of his cronies, who would turn right around and do the same thing in Topeka or Ottawa or Pittsburg, or anywhere else across the line if they could put enough men together to pull it off."

"You'll have to decide soon, won't you?" Mollie asked. "I guess since they're going, they'll be wanting to leave before the cold weather hits."

They stopped at the door to the barn and Cole gave Mollie a long, serious look. "It sounds almost like you *want* me to go," he said curiously.

"No, it's not that at all, Cole," she replied hurriedly. "I want you to do what you think is best. It's just that . . ." She wanted to tell him about Kurt Rakestraw, and in fact urgently needed to talk about the matter with him, but now that the time had come to do it, she just couldn't find the words.

"Come on, Mollie," Cole said. "Out with it. What's on your mind?"

"Something happened, Cole," Mollie began at last. "Something that I didn't expect, and really didn't want, but now it's changed everything." She raised her hand and rested it lightly on his arm, then withdrew it again. There was something about touching him that just didn't feel right, not now, not with what she had to say.

If Cole noted the abortive gesture he did not react to it in any way. Nor did he speak. He simply stood, waiting for her to go on.

"Do you remember me telling you about a man named Kurt Rakestraw that I knew several years ago back in Virginia?" she asked him.

"I do. And if I recall correctly, you said you had a pretty hot romance going with him before he ran out on you."

"I loved him very much, Cole. As much as I've ever loved anybody in my life. I thought I had got over all that, that I had put it behind me long ago. But then he showed up in Kansas City a couple of weeks ago, and we talked, and he said he wanted to see me again . . ."

Even as she watched, the muscles of Cole's jaw began to tighten and his gaze narrowed to a dark, intense stare. She had seen this mood sweep over him only a few times before in all the years she had known him, but she knew what it meant. More than any other man she knew, Cole Younger had the ability to harden himself suddenly and totally in order to face any difficulty without feeling or remorse. He had been this way the day the two of them carried out their plan to kill Major Rudolph Benjamin.

"So you think you might still be in love with him, then," Cole concluded, his voice chilling in its detachment.

"I don't know, Cole," Mollie said, her voice rising as her frustration grew. She was beginning to understand that, although she was turning this man away as her lover, she still very desperately needed him to be her friend. But suddenly she realized that was not the way it was to be. That's not the way these things worked. "All I know is that I have to find out. As I said, he's been here two weeks already, but I swore I wouldn't be alone with him again until I found some way to see you and explain how it is. But now that he's here, I don't think I have the strength in me to stay away from him forever. I have to find out."

"So do it, damn you!" Cole snapped. "What do you want from me? My blessing?"

"No, I didn't expect that," Mollie said. "But I guess I did expect . . ." She fell silent, feeling the impact of his cold, dark stare. Suddenly she realized that there was no graceful, compassionate way to end a scene like this one. The only merciful thing to do was simply to end it as quickly as possible. "Never mind what I expected, Cole," she told him finally. "I'm sorry if I've hurt you, but I've told you as honestly as I can how things are. From here on, you can think and do what you want." On the way here, when she considered what she must confess to Cole, she had also decided that she would reveal that Rakestraw was a Union officer. But now, considering the seething rage Cole was in, she was afraid to say any more. There was no telling what he might do if she poured that additional measure of salt into the fresh and painful wound she had just inflicted.

"Well, life is not without its little consolations, my dear," Cole told her with a snarl. He reached for the barn door and yanked it open, nearly striking Mollie in the shoulder before she dodged out of the way. He plunged into the dimly lit barn, continuing to talk even though Mollie did not follow him inside. "There's a young woman named Belle down in Texas who's been writing me for months now, asking me to come and see her. I've heard talk that her family and mine are related somewhere back down the line, but if that's the case she's more of a kissing cousin than a regular one . . ."

Even as Cole continued to talk, Mollie turned and started back toward the house. She was back in the kitchen helping with the dishes when she heard the sound of a horse's hoofbeats thunder past the house.

Across the room Arethia, standing with her hands in a pan of soapy dishwater, turned her gaze toward Mollie, silently offering to listen to whatever she might want to say. Mollie simply shook her head. She would probably tell her brother and sister-in-law about everything eventually, but not now. It was still too soon, and still too utterly confusing to discuss.

It was a cool, crisp November afternoon, the kind of day when a man would work up a sweat performing whatever labor he had to do and then would find himself needing to pull on a jacket as soon as he laid down his tools to take a break.

Jason and his sons had been at work all day on the new house, which he was putting up on the same site where Jim Lane and his men had burned down his old one two years before. Because of the uncertainties of the war, Jason had waited much longer to rebuild than he otherwise might have, thinking that there was no good reason to go to the effort and expense of rebuilding if the Jayhawkers were just going to come along and burn him out again as soon as he was finished.

But he was beginning to think that maybe the Union forces finally had the Jayhawker problem under control. There had been no reports of raids for more than two months now, ever since the atrocities that had resulted from Ewing's General Order No. 11, and it seemed as if the Union commander in the region might have finally decided it was time to put a stop to the destructive excesses of Kansans like Lane and Jennison. And, besides that, Jason knew that deep within, his wife Arethia yearned to have a home of her own again. After two years of accepting the hospitality of her father-in-law and sister-in-law, she needed to have a house that she could call her own.

They had made good progress that afternoon despite the fact that Daniel was the only one of the three of them who was still nimble enough to do much of the required climbing. Nearly half the rafters were up now, and finally the structure was beginning to look more like a house than a box-shaped wooden skeleton.

"What would you say to quitting for the day, boys?" Jason said, pulling the tie on his nail apron and removing it from around his waist. "We've done more than I expected, and I think we owe ourselves a break."

Neither of his sons offered any objections

to stopping work a little early. Daniel started climbing down a fifteen-foot ladder; John finished hammering in a last nail before beginning to gather up his tools.

"It's looking good, Daddy," John said, pausing to survey their work. "Mama's going to be pleased as punch when she sees how far we've come."

"Yes she is. I thought I'd drive her over Sunday after church to see it," Jason said. "If it were just a little warmer, we could bring a picnic lunch and make a day of it, but I guess it might be a shade cool for that."

"I bet Mama wouldn't think so," John said. "If you left it up to her, I bet she'd start moving stuff in tomorrow, and by the time we got the walls and roof closed in, she'd already have housekeeping set up." After laying his tools in the back of the wagon, he picked up his rifle and checked the load as if by reflex.

Both he and Daniel remained heavily armed even while they worked, a carry-over from their days with the bushwhackers. But despite the fact that they were no longer with Quantrill's band, there was still good reason for their precautions. Two of Quantrill's men who, like John and Daniel, had remained behind in Missouri had been caught and shot by Union troops just the week before in Jackson County, and the word was out that General Ewing still held with his no-quarter policy toward all bushwhackers in his district. If they were discovered, they would be killed on the spot, no questions asked.

While his sons were loading everything onto the back of the wagon, Jason hitched up the mules. Then he climbed onto the seat, picked up the traces, and John and Daniel climbed in back. Jason was both pleased and surprised at how quickly John was recovering from his wound. Although the muscles of his thigh were still sore, all traces of a limp were nearly gone from John's stride, and by Christmas he would probably be as good as new.

"When we get back, maybe we could uncork a bottle of that peach wine you have working in the wellhouse," John suggested as Jason clicked the team into motion and turned them toward the road.

"We might be able to arrange that," Jason said, "although I know your mother will have something to say about us drinking, especially before supper."

"Well, maybe we could sneak it out to the barn or something," John said. "I haven't had anything stronger than black coffee to drink since I got home, and I'm about ready for a nip or two. That was one thing about being with Quantrill's bunch. There was always a jug or a bottle around somewhere for a man to pull on now and then if he was so inclined. It helped pass the long days in camp, and sometimes you could use it to forget about something you'd just done or were about to do."

"I'll round Dad up when we get back," Jason promised, "and we'll sample that first batch I made in September. It should be strong enough now to warm a man's innards."

Jason drove north for about half a mile on the narrow dirt road leading to his house, then turned the team east onto the main road which led toward his father's farm. They had gone about another mile when Daniel spoke up to point something out to his father and brother.

"I've been looking at the tracks in the dust behind us," he said, "and I think maybe there's something strange going on here."

Jason stopped the wagon and turned to see what his son was talking about.

"See those tracks on top?" Daniel asked, pointing toward the road. "Those are the ones our team made just now. But look how many others there are. And they've all been made since that shower we had a couple of hours ago. There shouldn't be that much traffic on this road on a weekday afternoon."

"And all headed east," John added. "You're right. It does look strange."

"Just to be safe, you boys better get off here and circle around to the woods north of Dad's place," Jason instructed. "When I get home, if there's no problem there, I'll send Benjamin out on a horse to follow the tracks on east and make sure they don't turn off the road anywhere. Then, if every-thing's clear, I'll signal for you to come on in."

John and Daniel picked up their weapons and climbed to the ground at the side of the road. "The usual signal?" John asked.

"That's right. Two lanterns in the kitchen window, one above the other. If you don't see anything by the time the moon comes up, head on over to the dugout at the Slate Springs Hollow. I'll send Benjamin over to let you know what's going on as soon as I can. Now you two boys take care."

"And you too, Daddy," Daniel said.

Jason watched until his sons had dis-appeared into the woods at the edge of the road, then started toward home again. His rifle was on the wagon seat beside him, but as always, he knew that there was little chance that he could use it in case of trouble. If there were soldiers or Jayhawkers at his father's farm, any resistence they encountered would no doubt cause them to wreak fierce retribution on the family.

But still it galled a man to be so frequently victimized and never to be able to fight back, Jason thought bitterly. Whenever he met these men, it seemed that he was always heavily outnumbered and that there were always loved ones nearby whose lives he had to consider in addition to his own. Someday he would not be able to reason or lie his way out of one of these encounters, and he might die without ever raising a finger to resist his killers.

Jason's worst fears were realized when he neared his father's farm and saw that the tracks of the large mounted band turned off the main road there. As he approached, he spotted eight or ten men milling around the front of the house and at least that many more up near the barn. It looked as if they had just finished searching the place, no doubt looking for John and Daniel.

None of the men wore a military uniform, which led Jason to believe at first that they must be Kansans, but then, as he drew closer to the house, he began to recognize a few faces in the group. They were men from right here in Clay County, mostly business-men and merchants from Liberty with unquestionable Union loyalties. Their apparent leader was Isaac Paul, the man whose harassment a year before had, in part, driven John to join Quantrill's bushwhack-ers.

Jason spotted his father standing in the middle of the front yard, loosely guarded by a couple of the townsmen. The rest of the family were gathered on the front porch silently eyeing the intruders. Shrugging past his would-be captors disdainfully, Will Hartman started toward the wagon as Jason drove to the edge of the yard and stopped. Relief at seeing his son arrive alone showed clearly on the old man's features.

"They came looking for John and Daniel," Will explained as Jason stepped to the ground. "I told them it's been three, maybe four months since we saw either of your boys, but they don't believe me. That goddamn Isaac Paul called me a liar right to my face!"

"Well just let them search, Dad," Jason said. "We've got nothing to hide, because we both know neither of my sons are even in the state anymore."

"It won't wash, Hartman," Isaac Paul exclaimed, approaching the wagon from the direction of the house. "Them two bush-whacking whelps of yours were seen right here on this farm just three days ago! We know they didn't go to Texas with the others, and we know you've been hiding them out for at least a month now, maybe longer."

"You think I'd be stupid enough to take that kind of chance, Isaac?" Jason asked. "I told John and Daniel when they joined up with Quantrill that they were on their own from that day forward. I still love both my boys, but I don't want them coming back here to put their mama and everyone else in the family in danger."

"I'll give you this, Hartman," Paul said with a crooked sneer, "you're about as smooth a liar as I ever seen, but it won't work this time. They're here, or at least they were as recently as three days ago."

"Damn you, Isaac Paul!" old Will exclaimed angrily. "I've known you for years now, and I never did think you were worth the cost of the rope it would take to hang you with. You ain't nothing but a no-good, thieving Federal bootlick, and if you think you can get away with coming on a man's place like this —"

His diatribe was cut short by the punch that Isaac Paul landed in his midsection. As his father staggered back against the wagon,

Jason sprang forward to throw his body between the two men before Paul could strike again, but he made no attempt to fight back, knowing it would only make things worse.

"There'll be no peace for you until we get them two sons of yours, Hartman," Isaac Paul vowed angrily. "We've had enough of their kind rampaging across the county, terrorizing good loyal citizens and resisting the rightful military authorities in our country. We're going to get them, and we're going to shoot them down like rebel dogs, just like they deserve."

"I don't want to see them die, Isaac," Jason said, "but all that has to be between you and them. I've got women and children here to think about, and I'm staying out of the middle of this mess because of that."

"You may think you're a pretty smart fellow, Hartman," Paul sneered, "but you ain't getting out of this scrape that easy. No sir! This time you lose the barn because they got away from us. The next time it'll probably be the house, and then after that . . ."

Jason sensed his father's movement behind him, but realized too late what the old man's anger and frustration had driven him to try. He turned his head in time to see Will grab the rifle from the wagon seat and swing the muzzle around.

A shot rang out from across the yard before Will Hartman could manage to take aim at Isaac Paul, and with a startled cry of pain, the old man tumbled forward into his son's arms.

Slowly, gently, Jason lowered his father to the ground. The lower part of his abdomen was bathed in blood, and a fierce grimace of agony contorted his features. Arethia came running toward them, and the rest of the men with Paul began to crowd in closer to witness the results of the gunfire.

"Who shot him?" Jason demanded, gazing up desperately at the faces of the men standing in a circle around him. Then his eyes fell on a tall, stern-looking stranger who stood a few feet away, still holding a smoking revolver in his hand. The man gazed down with a cold, malicious lack of concern at Jason and his injured, nearly unconscious father.

"Oh, I forgot to tell you about this fellow," Isaac Paul crowed. "He's the fellow that seen your sons here Monday afternoon, and later he came to Liberty to talk the sheriff into sending this posse out. Says he has a special interest in seeing you and all the rest of your people get what's coming to you."

Jason stared into the stranger's chilling dark eyes. "Who are you?" he asked.

"My name should be pretty easy for you to remember," the stranger replied. His voice was deep and harsh like the distant growling of thunder. "My name is Morgan Hartman. My father was Charles Hartman, your brother."

From beside her husband, Arethia looked up in surprise, her face a mask of grief and desperation. "Do you realize who you shot? Who you might have already killed? This man is your grandfather!"

"He means nothing to me," Morgan Hartman replied impassively as he holstered his gun and turned away. "None of you do."

Jason was scarcely aware of anything going on around him as he lifted his father in his arms and started toward the house, his family trailing along in stunned, tearful silence. He carried Will to his bedroom, and he and Arethia gently stripped the old man's shirt off and began trying to stem the rushing flow of blood from the wounds in his stomach and back.

Some time later their son Benjamin came into the room to tell them that Isaac Paul and his men were finally gone but that in their wake they had left the barn in flames as Paul had threatened to do. Jason told him to let it burn, that there was nothing they could do and that it didn't matter.

He kept his vigil at his father's side as the sun went down and darkness claimed the land. After a couple of hours Arethia went out to talk to the children and put together a simple supper for them, but Jason never budged.

Finally, long after the clock in the front room had chimed out the midnight hour, Jason appeared in the doorway. Arethia, Benjamin, and Sarah were waiting there, but everyone else had gone to bed.

"Son, I want you to go to Slate Springs Hollow and find your brothers in that old dugout there," Jason instructed Benjamin in a monotone voice filled with exhaustion and grief. "Tell them what happened here, and tell them that they can't come home anymore. It will probably be a long, long time before it will be safe for them to return here again. And Ben, you also need to tell them . . ." His voice suddenly choked with emotion, and tears began flowing from his eyes, but he faintly managed to get the words out at last. "Tell them that their grandfather is dead, shot down by a heartless devil named Morgan Hartman . . . their cousin from Kansas!"

CHAPTER THIRTEEN

The first thing Mollie saw when she opened her eyes in the morning was Kurt's uniform tunic hanging neatly on the back of the hotel room chair. A Federal uniform. A Federal man. A Federal lover.

This is crazy! she thought. *This could turn out to be one of the biggest mistakes I've ever made in my life.* But still, any feeling of regret or guilt could hardly diminish the happiness and fulfillment she felt at that moment.

He lay beside her, his right arm barely touching her hand. She could tell by the sound of his even breathing that he was still asleep despite the sunlight that now poured into the room. The night before had been a long one for them, long and wonderful.

Moving gently, she rolled over so she could study his features in the bright morning light. It was a good face, handsome but not rakishly so, hinting even in repose at the strength and character of its owner. His dark hair was tangled and matted, but still the mere sight of him so close, so real, beside her sent a chill of delight through her body.

Thinking about the night before, which had been their first encounter since Mollie's return from the reunion at her father's farm, she realized that there was never much doubt in her mind that they would end up like this. And most of it had been her doing, she knew.

Kurt had responded immediately to the message she'd sent him the day after she returned. They'd met for dinner, then took a long quiet walk through the empty streets of the Quality Hill area. Kurt had been a perfect gentleman, and it was apparent from the start that he had no intention of pressuring her to renew their long-abandoned love affair. They had talked of many things, including Kurt's adventures in the West and Mollie's life in Missouri. On a number of occasions their conversation touched upon the subject of the war, but never once did Kurt give any indication of the special duties that had brought him here. And Mollie had never once felt inclined to talk about how deeply her family was involved in the conflict for the opposing side. There would be time to deal with that later, she promised herself.

It was all over for her after the first kiss. Standing on a bluff overlooking the moonlit Missouri River, Kurt took her in his arms at last and touched his lips to hers. It was a gentle kiss, and yet it struck her with devastating force. Her breath had quickened, and she could feel the desire surge through her veins. It had always been that way with him, she remembered, but until that instant she had not permitted herself to think that it could still be the same, not after so long a time. And yet it was. Suddenly she was seventeen again, kissing the tall dark adventurer, yearning to give him everything that it was in her power to give.

She had little recollection of what happened from that moment until they were naked together in this bed in this room, making love with mindless abandon. Kurt, she knew, had fallen victim to the same overwhelming storm of physical need. This morning Mollie felt stiff and sated from the experience, but she soon began to realize as she continued to gaze at his face that the fire was still not out. Not quite.

She ran her hand up under the covers, sliding her fingers gently across Kurt's muscular chest. He began to smile even before he opened his eyes to look at her, but she raised a finger and touched his lips before he could speak a word. Understanding immediately, Kurt snaked an arm around her shoulder and drew her to him for their first kiss of the day.

Their lovemaking had a different mood and texture this morning. For a time Kurt was content simply to lie back and let Mollie minister to his body, to let her lead him slowly from sleep to sexual arousal. And even when he did, at last, raise and ease her over onto her back, his movements and caresses had all the careful gentleness of a man handling some delicate treasure which he was afraid to damage with even a single careless touch.

Mollie closed her eyes and let reality dissolve as Kurt's strong body covered hers.

The café was run by a woman named Helga Wagner, a stocky middle-aged hausfrau who doted over her customers like an anxious mother. Although the tiny restaurant was situated on a side street and seldom received the attention of the more elite diners in the city, it was one of Mollie's favorite places to eat, especially in the morning because of the rich European pastries Helga baked with her own hands.

It was that time of morning when the breakfast crowd had already come and gone and the noon diners had not yet started to arrive, so Mollie and Kurt had the place all to themselves. They were seated at a small table in the corner, lingering over their coffee and pastries, unwilling to let their time together end.

"So what are your plans for the day?" Kurt asked, picking up a piece of sweet roll and putting it in his mouth.

"Well it's Saturday, so I have a matinee at three, and I have to go back by the house before that and let Genevieve know that I'm still alive and well," Mollie answered. "I told her about you, so she probably has a pretty good idea of where I've been, but she still might worry if I don't stop in."

"This is quite an unusual woman you live with," Kurt noted. "Practically any other landlady her age would give you hell about staying out all night, or perhaps even evict you from her house."

"No, Genevieve's not like that at all. In fact, she'll probably be tickled by the idea, and maybe a little envious as well. You see, she hasn't always been just a rich old widow who lived in a big house in the society district. In her younger years, she traveled all over this country, and she's done a lot of living along the way. Back in the thirties, she followed her husband-to-be, Jean de Mauduis, all the way down from Quebec to St. Louis, and she even made one trip into the western wilderness on a fur-buying expedition. She's probably one of the few white women in the country who actually witnessed a fur-trading rendezvous in the northern Rockies, and she told me once that she and Jean lived together for nearly eight years before he finally made an honest woman of her. They only settled in this area about ten years ago, after Jean had made his fortune and they had grown too old to enjoy roaming any longer."

"I've seen a few women like that out in the wilderness," Kurt said, "but they're a rare breed, and few live long enough to enjoy their old age in a place like this."

"Genevieve is rare," Mollie agreed.

In a minute Helga appeared from the back room to refill their coffee cups, but she sensed that they wanted to be alone so she did not linger to chat or urge more food on them. After she was gone, the couple sat silently for a moment, each lost in thought.

Now that she was away from the hotel room, distanced from the intimacy she and Kurt had been sharing little more than an hour before, Mollie's innermost doubts and guilts began to plague her once more. After last night she knew that she would have to see Kurt again, that her feelings for him were too strong simply to ignore or put aside, but she wondered how, in the days and weeks to come, would she be able to reconcile herself to the fact that the man whom she still loved so completely was a Union officer. It was terrible to consider the deceits she would have to engage in, the lies she would have to tell, and the terrible secrets that she would have to bear alone.

Mollie looked deeply into Kurt's eyes for a long moment and then realized it was all hopeless. She couldn't possibly conceal the facts about her family, not from this man, not if she ever expected to hold on to his love. "Kurt," she began and then stopped as if unable to find the words. "My . . . my brother Jason fought at Wilson's Creek . . . for Price . . . for the South." The words were almost impossible to say, but once she'd said them she was glad she had.

"I know," Kurt said, smiling gently as he reached out to touch her hand. "And I know about your nephews John and Daniel as well. I've read reports on them."

"And still you wanted to be with me?" Mollie asked. "Aren't you afraid that I'm . . . that I might —"

"Be a spy?" Kurt interrupted. "Yes, of course I am. With your family supporting the other side and you living right here in the heart of the Union camp, so to speak, only a fool wouldn't consider the possibility. But my doubts weren't strong enough to keep me away from you."

"The whole thing is so confusing to me, Kurt," Mollie confessed. "If it were any man but you, there would be no problem because I'd simply walk away. But I can't with you. I simply can't make myself do it."

"Does your family know about me yet?" he asked. "Do they know I'm here?"

"I don't think so. I didn't tell any of them about you when I was home. But that doesn't help much with the guilt I feel. I know in my heart that I'm not doing anything wrong, but I feel like such a traitor to them. I just don't know what to do."

Kurt reached out a finger and brushed away a solitary tear which had started down her cheek. She turned her face to him and smiled, but it was a desperate sort of smile, filled with pain and uncertainty.

"The South has lost the war, Mollie," he told her earnestly. "They're only fighting on out of habit now. They're just too stubborn to admit the truth, even to themselves."

"You're probably right," Mollie admitted,

"but that doesn't change this situation much. It doesn't change who my father and brother and nephews are, does it?"

"No, it doesn't change them, but what about you? I don't want to know what you might have done in the past, but whatever it's been, couldn't you just give it up, make your own separate peace? If you did things for the South because you believed in the cause or because you were trying to help your family, that's fine, and perhaps even admirable, but if you agree that the war is truly lost now, why do anything to prolong all this madness? Why not just quit?"

"Jason tried that," Mollie said. "He tried to quit after Wilson's Creek, but they wouldn't let him. They destroyed his home and killed his daughter Ruth. They ran his sons off and forced them to become bushwhackers, and probably a night never passes when he doesn't wonder if this will be the night the Jayhawkers come again. I've never known of anyone who was allowed to quit, not even the ones who applied for amnesty and gave it a sincere try."

Mollie paused for a moment, staring down at her coffee cup. Then suddenly and unexpectedly, her expression brightened. "But what if we left, Kurt?" she exclaimed. "Just you and me. Surely there must be places in this country where the war is just something people read about in the newspapers. I bet you know of someplace we could go and be together without all these troubles. California maybe, or Oregon. I'd go anywhere with you, Kurt. I'd leave today, right now . . ."

"I can't go," Kurt replied, his face filled with deep concern and apology.

"Why not?" Mollie asked desperately. "You asked me to quit because the war is lost for the South, so why can't you quit if you're so sure that your side will win? Is it because you think they might not be able to pull it off without you?"

"No, of course not," Kurt told her. "The reason I can't quit is because I believe in this cause. I believe this fight to hold our nation together is a good one and I want to see it through. And I also believe that I am uniquely qualified to carry on the small part of it that has been assigned to me."

"Your *mission*!" Mollie said with growing disgust.

"That's right. My mission."

"Tell me, Captain Rakestraw," Mollie said, almost sneering now, "what is this grand and glorious *mission* that only you of all the men in the Union army are qualified to carry out?"

Rakestraw simply stared at her for a moment, obviously trying to control himself, struggling against the urge to let his temper flare as hers had done. When he spoke at last, his voice was quiet, yet seemingly filled with a multitude of emotions and regrets. "I've come to kill Quantrill," he said. "My assignment is to track these bushwhackers down and to kill as many of them as I can lay my hands on. My men and I have been dealing with the Indians out west for nearly two years now, and we know how to fight the kind of war this man Quantrill has chosen to fight."

"Kurt! My God!" Mollie muttered, her worst fears realized. "Then part of your job would be to kill John and Daniel!"

"If we have to," he said. "If we find them with Quantrill after he gets back from Texas . . ."

"But they didn't go with him to Texas! They stayed here!" Mollie exclaimed, filled with the sudden unreasonable impulse to plead for their lives. She immediately regretted her words, however, realizing that any thoughtless thing she said at this point could truly endanger her family.

"I know," Kurt assured her. "We have our ways of finding out who went and who didn't. My only hope is that they don't join him again when he returns. Believe me, I do not relish the idea of hunting down and killing any member of your family."

"Of course it could be the other way around," Mollie pointed out, regaining control of herself. "These men are very good at what they do. If they weren't good, they wouldn't have remained alive this long."

"It's all a roll of the dice, my dear," Kurt agreed. "My life has always been like that, and I'm used to it by now. But what concerns me more is that you and I find some way to stay together, some middle ground someplace. I told you that first night when I saw you in the theatre that I have thought of you many times over the past few years, but that's not exactly true. The truth is that a hundred times I've ached to have you in my arms, and as many times I've cursed myself for a blind stubborn fool for letting you go.

"I'm like you, Mollie. I wasn't sure if it would work for us to try to get back together after all these years, but now that we're here, and now that we've found out how good things can still be together, I don't want to give that up. I need you with me."

The words warmed Mollie's heart like the blaze of a fire on a cold winter morning. No matter how deeply her feelings ran, she would never have asked for such a profession of commitment from him, nor would she have imagined him capable of making one, not Kurt Rakestraw the wanderer, Kurt Rakestraw who could never tolerate not knowing what lay beyond the next river or the next horizon. But now that the words were spoken, now that he had left no doubt about the depth of his feelings for her, she felt instinctively that it was her lot to do whatever it took to keep the two of them together.

She knew that, as a matter of course, love came and went from the lives of most people like the changing of the seasons, but she also knew that the type of love she now felt for Kurt was, for most people, a once-in-a-lifetime experience. For some it never came at all. Even if tremendous sacrifices were required of her, she knew she had to do everything in her power to make this last.

"We'll figure it out, Kurt," Mollie promised him softly. "Even in the midst of all this trouble and confusion, there must be a way for us to stay together. I'll do everything I can, and I'll never give up hope until the day you tell me that you don't want me anymore."

"You'll have a long wait before you hear those words coming from me," Kurt swore.

Genevieve was back in the kitchen with the maid when Mollie and Kurt reached the house. Kurt felt a little uncomfortable about coming in and being introduced, but Mollie reassured him that nothing but a gracious welcome awaited him inside.

At first Mollie thought she was going to have to eat her words when she saw Genevieve coming toward them down the hall from the kitchen. Her friend had no smiles to spare for the new arrivals, and when she drew closer, Mollie saw that she looked drawn with exhaustion and worry. Mollie still attempted to make her introductions, but Genevieve had no more than a nod and a quick hello to spare for Kurt Rakestraw.

"Mollie, you had a visitor last evening," Genevieve began in a quiet voice heavy with concern. She seemed uncomfortable talking in front of Kurt, but apparently the importance of her news was such that it could not wait even another moment. "He arrived about an hour after you left. I had never seen him before, but he said he was a neighbor of your brother's from Clay County. At first he insisted on speaking only to you, but when I explained you might be quite, uh, late, he finally decided to leave a message with me."

"Yes?" Mollie asked urgently. "What did he say?"

Genevieve's expression became even more somber, and tears welled in her eyes as she attempted to pull together the words and phrases to communicate the message. "It's your father, dear," she said. "Some men came to his farm looking for your nephews, and apparently he attacked one of them . . ."

"Oh no . . ." Mollie mumbled dully. A feeling of dread swept over her as she suddenly knew what she was about to hear. Her head swirled, and her knees threatened to give way. ". . . Daddy . . ."

"There was some gunfire, and your father was shot," Genevieve continued, gathering her strength to complete the dread announcement. "The man said he lived for a short time afterward, but he never regained consciousness. He never suffered."

Mollie turned her face from Genevieve to Kurt, her features a mask of shock and disbelief. Her lips moved, but no more words came forth, and she gazed at her lover as if waiting for him to tell her that some horribly cruel mistake had been made, that it was not her father who was dead but some other man instead.

Without speaking, Kurt took Mollie in his arms and pulled her to him, holding her tightly against his chest as the first sobs of grief began to rack her body.

"I'm so sorry, dear," Genevieve murmured, placing a consoling hand on Mollie's shoulder. "I'm so very sorry this has happened."

For the first few moments Mollie was able to do nothing but cling to Kurt, crying uncontrollably. Myriad wretched and vengeful thoughts swirled through her mind as she wrestled to accept the grim announcement. Despite all the people she knew and loved whose lives had been in jeopardy during these troubled times, and despite all the deaths that had already taken place, somehow it had never occurred to her that this terrible war could ever possibly claim the life of her father. He was the one who had always been there, the anchor to which all the Hartmans attached themselves when life's tribulations became too overwhelming to bear alone. But he was dead now. Gone forever. Somehow she couldn't quite grasp the reality of that fact.

When Mollie's tears began to subside at last, she turned to Genevieve and asked, "Did he say . . . did he tell you when the . . . the funeral . . ."

"He said the services were to be held today, dear," Genevieve answered. "Your brother didn't know how long it might take for word to reach you, nor when you might be able to get there, and they couldn't wait. But they still want you to come home. Your brother sent word that he wants you to come home."

"Who did it?" Kurt Rakestraw asked. Those were the first words he had spoken since entering the house, and they reflected the anger and resolve of his present mood.

A worried look crossed Genevieve de Mauduis' features, and she hesitated a moment before speaking. Her reluctance made Mollie stare at her intently, adding her own unspoken insistence to that of Rakestraw.

"I was waiting," Genevieve began uncertainly. "I thought you had enough on you already."

"Who killed my father?" Mollie demanded.

"His name was Morgan Hartman," Genevieve admitted at last. "I didn't want to tell you right away because the man said he was —"

"My nephew!" Mollie finished in a shocked, disbelieving tone. "The oldest son of my dead brother Charles. And he killed Daddy? My nephew shot Daddy?"

"Apparently he came with a posse of local men looking for John and Daniel," the old woman explained. "I can't imagine it. No matter how heartless and cruel a man might be . . ."

Mollie said nothing, but she could imagine it with no difficulty at all. Years before, during the undeclared Kansas-Missouri border war which had preceded the Civil War, she had witnessed firsthand the deadly, unyielding fanaticism that seemed to plague that particular branch of the family. Yes, she could imagine it all too easily.

"This nephew of yours," Kurt asked Mollie, "this Morgan Hartman, is he a local man? Does he live somewhere in this part of the state?"

"As far as I know he still lives somewhere in Kansas," Mollie answered dully. "After his father was killed several years ago we lost all contact with that side of the family, but once in a while I still hear a rumor or a name mentioned in passing. Charles had a big family, and as far as I know, most of them are still in Kansas."

"This stinks of murder to me," Rakestraw announced, "and I promise you I won't let the matter drop until I find out everything about what happened."

"Exactly what are you going to find out,

Kurt?" Mollie asked angrily. "That Kansans have been coming across the border and murdering our people at will ever since before the war began? That the Jayhawkers are allowed to ride over here any time they want to burn our homes and gun our loved ones down in their yards like rabid dogs? Those things aren't exactly a secret, you know!"

"No, of course they aren't a secret," Kurt replied. "But it's time they stopped. The problems here are military problems, and perhaps it's time that we found some way to impress that fact on the men of Kansas once and for all. Perhaps it's time that someone like this Morgan Hartman was arrested and made to face up to his evil deed."

Mollie pulled free of his grasp, almost enjoying the wave of fury that had surged in to replace the anguish in her heart. "Sure, you do that, Kurt," she said. "You go over there and arrest Morgan for shooting his own grandfather. And the minute you get him back here, your own commander, General Ewing, will set him free again and pat him on the back for putting another rebel bastard out of commission."

"I'm trying, Mollie," Kurt said. "I swear to you, I really want to do something that will make a difference to *everybody* in this part of the county. I want to put a stop to what Quantrill is doing, but I want to stop men like Morgan Hartman just as much. Wrong is wrong, no matter which side a man is on when he does it."

Mollie somehow managed to muster a hint of a smile to let him know that it wasn't him she was angry at. "I know you mean well, Kurt. I know you want to do the right thing, and I love you for that. But you haven't been here over these past few years and so you couldn't understand how the hatred has built up, layer by layer, until whatever might once have been beneath it has long since been smothered forever.

"Sometimes I just despair for all of us," she went on in a voice laden with grim resignation. "Sometimes I believe that even if this war ever finally ends, it will still be too late for all of us. It will be too late for anybody who this hateful business has touched to ever live a normal, happy life again."

"You're right, Mollie. I don't understand all this the way you do because I haven't been here and seen it all. But I do know this. If it is within my power, Morgan Hartman will be made to face some kind of justice, either God's or man's, for what he did. That I promise you."

After Kurt was gone, Mollie and Genevieve went upstairs to Mollie's room and began packing the things she would need for the sad journey home to Clay County.

CHAPTER FOURTEEN

September, 1864

Pell Durham's living room looked more like an indoor trail camp than the central room of a home. Most of the furniture was pushed back against the walls to make more space, and the place was littered with packs, weapons, and a variety of riding gear. The seven bushwhackers had spread their blankets in various places on the plank floor and were sitting on them now, passing around a jug of Pell's outstanding home-brewed whiskey. The whiskey and Margaret Durham's good cooking were, in fact, the two main reasons why the small band had decided to stop here for the night rather than ride a few miles farther east toward the rendezvous which was to be held near Lee's Summit. After making sure that their guests were taken care of for the night, Durham and his family had retired to their upstairs bedrooms and were now fast asleep.

"Now don't get me wrong, fellows," Cal Penny said. "I ain't trying to tell you that I don't want to ride on and join up with Bill Anderson like we planned. All's I'm saying is that Anderson just ain't the leader that Bill Quantrill was. Ever since he split off from Quantrill and George Todd, he's led his boys into one nasty scrape after another, and most of it without any rhyme or reason that I could make out."

"We've lost a lot of good men this past spring and summer since we got back from Texas," Paul Grimsley agreed. "But it ain't all Anderson's fault. Hell, we got two, maybe three times more Federals to deal with than we used to, and these new sonsabitches they've put out against us don't fight like any Federals ever did before. They fight like we used to in our prime, and they've got spies everywhere, seems like. It's got so you can't trust anybody anymore," Grimsley continued. "Not even people you grew up with and have known all your life." He was sitting off to the side of the room, reclining on one elbow, a tin cup of whiskey sitting in front of him. He was half drunk already and seemed bent on completing the process as quickly as possible.

"That's the whole thing about it," Penny said. "Three times in the last two months men from Anderson's outfit have been ambushed and nearly wiped out. Now what I'm saying is that it ain't because the men ain't good or careful, it's because of where they were sent and what they were sent out to do. I like Bill Anderson personally. He's about as brave and determined a man as I ever knew, but I'm starting to think that he's just too damn reckless with his own life and everybody else's to be a good leader. He's just in charge now because he's so goddamned dangerous. Nobody wanted to stand up to him and tell him he couldn't be the boss because they knew he'd shoot them dead."

From over near the kitchen door came a mumble of disgust which caused Penny to turn his head sharply in that direction. "You got a dollar you wanta throw in this pot, Jesse?" he growled.

"Sounds to me like you're just losing your taste for this line of work, Cal," Jesse James replied dryly. "Maybe you need some time off to go someplace and find your nerve again."

Cal Penny's anger was readily apparent in his eyes, but he made no immediate response to the insult. As was their frequent habit, both Frank and Jesse James were sitting with their revolvers drawn and lying in their laps, and Penny had sense enough to know that any argument that got started at this point might end in gunplay.

"Damned if we couldn't all use some time off from this business," Homer Jackson interrupted. At twenty-seven, he was the old man of the group, and even the young hotheads like Frank and Jesse James often found themselves listening to his advice and counsel at times when they might not listen to anybody else. "I can tell you for a fact, I would sure rather be home raising a crop this year than wandering around the countryside looking for somebody to kill and waiting to be killed. But it's gotta be done, boys. It's gotta be done."

John and Daniel Hartman, who were seated by the front door, had been taking little part in the conversation up to this point. But finally John decided to speak up. "I just wish we'd all stayed together like we were last year," he said. "Quantrill might have had his faults, but at least when he was in charge it seemed like we were getting a few things done. We were together in spirit back then, and we all had more or less the same idea of why we were doing what we were doing. But now Quantrill's disappeared to God knows where, everybody's split up — some under Todd, and some under Anderson, and some headed off to join the Regulars — and it seems like we spend more time bickering and mixing it up amongst ourselves than we do fighting the enemy."

"It's different because we're different," Homer Jackson said, a distinct note of sadness in his voice. "After all the things we've done, all the fighting and killing and dying, we were bound to change. Just look at the way things were in Texas. There wasn't any enemy to fight so we turned on ourselves like a pack of wolves just because we had to fight. We needed it. Most of us have forgotten by now that there ever was another way to live."

A silence fell over the room as the men considered Jackson's words. Nobody could really deny the truth in what he said. Texas had been a mess.

At first they had been welcomed as heroes by the Confederate military authorities in Texas. Quantrill had offered the services of his men for whatever tasks they might be suited to perform, and he had finally been awarded the formal military commission for which he had yearned so long. But his men soon tired of the tedium of camp life, and they had long since grown unaccustomed to conforming to the restrictions of any civil authority. The local civilians in the towns near their camp soon came to dread the raucous visits of the bushwhackers, and all efforts by the Confederate military leaders to control their activities met with strong, and often violent, opposition.

With too much time on their hands, Quantrill's lieutenants and their various supporters began to feud among themselves. At one point George Todd had been forced to flee the camp under threat of death by Bill Anderson and several of his followers. Bill Gregg had left in disgust to join the regular army in Arkansas, and Cole Younger had left to join a Confederate recruiting expedition to New Mexico.

By spring, Quantrill had lost all control of the band, and when he returned to Missouri, it was in the company of an offshoot group under the leadership of George Todd. The remainder of the men either came back with Bill Anderson or straggled back on their own, confused, disillusioned, and no longer sure whether the cause they had supported for so long was still worth fighting for.

Frank and Jesse James had opted to follow Bill Anderson simply because he was the sort of recklessly dangerous man that they looked up to. Both now fostered a hatred for the Federal forces as deep and bitter as could be found, and young Jesse in particular had developed a murderously ruthless temperament during his year with the bushwhackers.

The decision had not been quite as clear-cut for the two Hartman brothers. Cole's departure had a heavy impact on both of them, leaving them feeling cast adrift in an insane world. Finally they had decided to stay with Anderson's band simply because they didn't know what else to do. They knew they could not go home for fear of causing further danger to their family, and they had lost considerable respect for George Todd the day he fled the Texas encampment rather than stand up to the threats of Bill Anderson and his cronies. If they wanted to return to their home at all, it seemed they had no choice but to do it in the company of Anderson.

All summer Anderson had either been leading or sending small parties of his men out on reckless, sometimes almost suicidal missions which seemed to have little impact on their vastly strengthened foe. Dozens of good men had fallen in pointless charges on fortified enemy positions and the like, and the increasingly blind brutality of the men under Anderson's command had even be-

344

gun to erode their base of support among the local populace.

"I tell you, boys, it's gonna take some kind of almighty miracle to turn this here war around," Paul Grimsley announced dejectedly. "I swore when I joined up with Quantrill two years ago that I wouldn't quit fighting till the last minute of the last day, but I'm starting to think now that that time won't be long in coming."

"You could be right, Paul," Homer Jackson said. "The war might be pretty well lost already, but sometimes I wonder if it will ever really be finished for any of us. After the things we've been through, it seems like most of us will spend the rest of our lives fighting the war again and again in our heads and our hearts. That's what will be left to us, and probably nothing else."

Before settling down to sleep, the men agreed among themselves on a schedule for guard duty, and a few minutes later Cal Penny and Homer Jackson headed out to take the first shift. The rest of them turned the lamps down, placed their weapons within easy reach, and settled down to rest.

A few minutes later Daniel Hartman was nearly asleep when a sudden feeling of uneasiness swept over him, startling him fully awake again. For a moment, he simply lay there trying to decide whether it was something he had heard that had alarmed him or whether it might simply be one of those spells of unfounded nervousness that overtook all of them from time to time. He reached out to retrieve the pistol that lay on the floor beside him, and then he spent a moment taking stock of where the rest of his weapons were in case he needed to get at them quickly.

Outside, the night was as silent as a crypt. Even the cicadas in the big elm out front seemed to be taking a break from their droning chorus, and the cricket Daniel had noticed earlier just outside on the front porch —

That was it! he realized suddenly. It wasn't a sound that had awakened him. Instead, it was the cessation of all the natural night sounds he *should* have been hearing.

Slowly and carefully he rose to his feet and eased to the window along the front side of the house. He moved with almost total silence, but even the faint noise his feet made on the plank floor was enough to arouse such edgy, cautious men.

"What is it?" John asked, sitting up on his pallet, gun in hand. All around the room the other men were stirring and arming themselves.

"I don't know," Daniel said. "Probably nothing." But even as he spoke, his eyes caught a momentary glimpse of a shadowy movement near the corner of the house, almost out of his field of vision. It could be Cal or Homer, he thought, but they weren't likely to be out in the open like that so close to the house. They should be hiding farther out, one in front and one in back, as was customary with guards in situations like this.

And then for an instant he saw the twinkle of moonlight reflected off two circular polished objects, and immediately he recognized them as eyeglasses, which neither Cal nor Homer wore. Instinctively he swung his pistol to the right and fired straight into the wall at the corner of the house. Outside a man yelped in pain and reeled clumsily into view, holding the right side of his chest with both hands. Daniel shattered one pane of window glass with the butt of his revolver, then fired a second shot, which toppled the intruder to the ground.

Wasting little time on unnecessary conversation, the four other men in the room immediately sprang to the nearby windows and doors and took up fighting positions. They all had a pretty good idea of what bad luck had befallen them. For another minute all was still outside. The man Daniel had shot lay on the ground without moving, and the line of brush and trees beyond the front yard of the house revealed no trace of additional intruders.

Then suddenly a figure burst into the open at the far edge of the yard, waving his arms wildly above him as he raced toward the house.

"It's the Federals, boys! Dozens of 'em!" Homer Jackson shouted as he ran. "Get out while you can! Run for the —"

His voice was drowned out by the roar of a dozen gunshots fired at close range from behind him. An instant later his legs buckled and Homer tumbled forward in the thick grass of the yard.

"Homer's down," Daniel announced to the others. "It looks like we'd better try to make a break for it while we can."

"But which way?" Paul Grimsley asked excitedly. "If there's as many of them as he said, they've probably got the whole place surrounded!"

"Well I don't know about the rest of you, but I wouldn't mind having a horse under me," Frank James said. "I say we try for the barn."

By this time the men out front were beginning to fire at the house, and soon it was filled with the tinkle of shattering glass and the sickening sound of lead balls ripping through the plank walls.

"It's as good a plan as any, I guess," John said. "It's a sure bet we'll just get ourselves and Pell Durham's family killed if we stay here."

Bothering only to gather up all their available weapons, they raced through the kitchen and burst out the back door of the house. In a moment a few guns opened up at them behind a fence to the right and a garden patch to the left, but the utter brashness of their charge seemed to have taken their opponents by surprise.

Daniel, who found himself in the lead, cut a zigzag path across the back yard, firing wildly, a gun in each hand as he ran. At one point he heard somebody behind him scream and fall, but he knew he couldn't slow down to help or even to find out who it was that had been hit. From this point on, it had to be every man for himself until they had run the deadly gauntlet of enemy gunfire.

As he neared a side entrance to the barn, Daniel saw the door ease open a few inches, and a rifle barrel appeared in the opening. He emptied the revolver in his left hand at the door, then jammed the gun down in his belt and drew another. He slammed into the door running full speed. The momentum of his charge ripped it off its hinges and toppled it inward on top of the body of the man he had shot. Within seconds the others had piled inside after him.

"Who got it back there?" Daniel asked hurriedly as they spread out in the darkened interior to locate their mounts.

"Paul," somebody answered.

"Did anybody see any sign of Cal?"

"Nope. They must have grabbed him like they did Homer."

"Everybody got a horse?"

"Yeah, we're ready. Let's go!"

Somebody, Daniel couldn't tell who in the darkness, flung the front door of the barn open, and they all thundered out at a dead run, cutting immediately to the right and heading for the deep woods nearby. Men were racing toward them from the house, shouting and firing as they ran, but the five horsemen leaned low across their horses' necks and dug their heels in, demanding every ounce of speed their animals could deliver. All rode bareback because there hadn't been time to saddle up, but that fact was scarcely noticed by any of them.

When they reached the woods, Jesse James cut loose with a loud whoop of sheer exhilaration. "We did it!" he shouted. "We escaped the bastards!"

"Yeah, but don't forget, we lost three men in the doing," John yelled back. "Is anybody else hit?"

No one answered. Remarkably, despite the shower of bullets that had been fired in their direction, none of them had received a scratch.

A few hundred yards into the woods, Jesse turned his head to the side and called to the others, "Look up ahead. There's somebody up there. He's seen us and he's waving."

"Don't shoot!" the lone figure called out. "It's me! Cal Penny!"

A moment later the four of them reached him. Penny was out of breath from running, and his clothes were in shreds from his wild flight through the woods. Somewhere along the way he had lost whatever weapons he had been carrying when he left the house.

"You made it!" Penny exclaimed.

"Yeah we made it, but Paul and Homer didn't," Frank James said. "What the hell are you doing way out here, Cal?"

"Somebody give me a hand up and I'll explain on the way," Penny said. "In another couple of minutes, they're going to be on us like flies on shit."

"I think maybe you better explain first,"

Jesse told him. "There's time if you talk in a hurry."

"All right then, dammit," Penny barked. "They jumped us. They came out of nowhere, three fellows with rifles, and they had the drop on us before we knew what happened. But I managed to dive into a patch of brush and get away, and I guess they didn't want to shoot at me for fear of warning the rest of you. I worked my way out back of the house, but they were watching the barn, so I just cut out through the woods. I been running ever since."

"Homer Jackson died giving us a warning, Cal," Daniel Hartman told Penny. "He shouted out to us knowing that they would shoot him down the minute he opened his mouth. What about you, Cal? You were on your own. Why didn't you try to warn us?"

"There was so damn many of them and they were everywhere, all around!" Penny stammered nervously. "I'd have been shot too if I opened my mouth, and I figured you boys didn't stand a chance anyway. If I'd just known —"

His clumsy explanations were interrupted by the roar of Jesse's revolver. Penny was staggered by the impact of the bullet striking his shoulder, but he didn't fall. "Goddammit, Jesse!" he bellowed. "You shot me!"

"Wrong, Cal," Jesse said, leveling his revolver at Penny's panic-stricken features. "I killed you, you son of a bitch!"

Cal Penny's head snapped back as the second bullet smashed into his skull, and his body crumpled to the ground like a sack of meal.

"Come on," Jesse said, holstering his pistol and yanking his horse's head savagely to the side with the reins. "Let's ride!"

They reached Anderson's camp late the following afternoon, just as the rest of the hundred or so men in the band were completing their final preparations for leaving. The four new arrivals had now gone without sleep for more than thirty-six hours, most of those spent in the saddle, but after seeing what was going on in camp they realized that they would probably have to pass at least another dozen or so hours before they were finally able to rest. While Frank and Jesse went off in search of food and fresh mounts, John and Daniel Hartman sought out Bill Anderson to make their report.

"I just wish you'd brought that bastard Cal Penny back here to me," Anderson said after hearing of their narrow escape and of Penny's cowardice. "I'd have killed him slow in front of the whole group. As an example."

Below his heavy brows, his small dark eyes shone at the prospect. These days, the only thing that could still bring any sort of animation to Bloody Bill Anderson's tanned, bearded features was the prospect of violence.

"Well, we didn't exactly have the time to worry about things like that," John said. "I'd guess there was at least fifty Federals on our tails at the time, and after they rounded up their horses, they dogged us for another twenty miles before we finally lost them. I bet some of their trackers could follow a beetle's trail across a hard rock."

"It had to have been that Colorado outfit," Anderson said, "the one that's been causing us such grief for the past three months. But what I'm wondering is how in the hell they knew you would be there at Pell Durham's farm on that particular night. Did Penny or Grimsley slip away from the rest of you anywhere along the way?"

"Not for any longer than it takes a man to visit the bushes," John said. "And Pell didn't know we were coming till we got there, so it couldn't have been him. I just don't know how they found out, Bill. They've got their ways, I guess, just like we do."

"They sure as hell do," Anderson said and frowned. "But at least they won't be following us where we're going now, because I haven't told a living soul what our target is. Nobody knows but George Todd."

"George Todd!" John exclaimed. "You mean you've seen him?"

"We met two days ago and patched things up between us," Anderson explained. "I had a raid in mind that might be too big for my outfit alone, so we decided to join forces to do it. I still don't trust the bastard any farther than I could throw him, but he's got nearly a hundred and twenty men riding with him now, and I need them for what I have in mind."

"Did he say anything about Quantrill?" Daniel asked. He knew the question would not please Anderson, but he was curious about what had happened to their former leader.

"George said he's holed up somewhere with that whore of his, Kate King," Anderson answered offhandedly. "But where he is or what he's doing isn't our concern anymore. I'm in charge now, and he's of no use to me. He's lost his nerve, and he's lost control. He's through." Daniel nodded solemnly, knowing that those few words pretty well summed it up. After another moment of conversation with their leader, the brothers turned away to find their friends and to prepare for the trip ahead.

For the next three days they traveled mostly by night, not so much out of fear of attack as because they did not want the enemy to gain a clear idea of the speed and direction of their advance. On the night of September 26, 1864, they finally joined up with George Todd's forces north of the Missouri River at a farm in Boone County near the center of the state.

Instead of traveling on, they remained on the farm that night, leading most of the men to believe that their objective must be close by. Around many an evening fire speculation ran high as to what that objective might be. The town of Columbia was about fifteen miles southwest of them, Moberly was about the same distance to the northwest, and the town of Centralia lay a mere four miles due north of the camp.

Before dawn the following morning both Anderson and Todd called together their chosen lieutenants for a council of war. Frank James was one of those summoned, and when he returned to his companions about thirty minutes later, he was bursting with news.

"It's Centralia!" he announced to the others. "Bill says he plans to take the town and hold it for a full day just to show those

Federal bastards that they're still a long ways from taking Missouri away from its rightful citizens. Pack it up, boys, because we ride in twenty minutes."

The plan turned out to be a good one and showed the influence of George Todd's more cautious, sensible approach to ventures of this sort. Because there was no Federal garrison in Centralia and little resistance was expected, the force that actually entered the town under Bill Anderson's command would be relatively small. Todd, on the other hand, would be in charge of dispersing the bulk of their forces along the main approaches to Centralia to intercept any relief forces that might try to get in. To the special delight of his brother Jesse, Frank James announced that the two of them, along with the Hartman brothers, would be going along with Bill Anderson on the actual raid. Also chosen to ride with Anderson were Arch Clement, Frank Shepherd, and twenty-five additional men selected for their courage and outstanding shooting abilities.

Bloody Bill's small contingent caught the sleepy little town completely by surprise. Before most of the residents were even fully aware of what was going on, Anderson's men had full control of the place. As always, the raiders headed immediately toward the town's business district to confiscate whatever food, liquor, ammunition, and guns they could find, then dispersed to enjoy their plunder and to spread terror in all quarters. There was no true resistance, and the only men who were killed were townsmen shot down in cold blood by Anderson's ruthless followers.

For three hours, the lives of everyone in Centralia, Missouri, hung by a thread, subject to the whim of the unpredictable Anderson and his savage band. The telegraph lines were immediately cut so that no appeals for help could go out, and a pile of spare railroad ties were heaped across the tracks. Later someone set fire to the railroad depot, and for a time the men enjoyed the diversion of watching it burn to the ground.

About eleven o'clock the stage from Columbia arrived, and Bill Anderson himself took charge of robbing the passengers. But soon the half-drunk bushwhackers began to grow restless. All during the long ride they had expected some action on the scale of the Lawrence raid, and Centralia was proving to be too easy, too docile for their tastes. Some among them began to suggest that they simply burn the place to the ground and ride out, but Anderson vetoed all such ideas. He wanted not simply to destroy the town, but to hold it for an appreciable period of time in open defiance of the Federal forces who thought they dominated nearly every settled region of the state.

About noon the shrill, distant wail of a steam whistle heralded the approach of a train from the east, promising yet another diversion for the restive bushwhackers. The cumbersome black steam engine began to slow when it came within a quarter mile of the burning station, but a dozen of Anderson's men quickly mounted and rode out to force the engineer to come on in under the threat of death. As soon as the train stopped, the bushwhackers descended on it like a pack of wolves, herding the unfortunate passengers out into the open as they fired their weapons wildly into the air.

With vicious glee, Anderson's men soon realized that the arrival of the train was going to provide them with an unexpected bonus — twenty-five unarmed Union soldiers on their way home on furlough. Within minutes the soldiers were separated from the other passengers, lined up near the tracks, and stripped of their uniforms.

By this time, John and Daniel Hartman had gathered with all the rest of the men in Anderson's band to watch their leader parade up and down in front of the row of silent, fearful enemy troops.

"I tell you, men," Anderson exclaimed, "this has to be the sorriest pack of Federal whelps I ever have laid eyes on." The whiskey he had drunk that morning had added a trace of unsteadiness to his gait, and he carried a loaded revolver in each hand, waving them wildly at his victims as he spoke. "Why, look at this one here!" he said, swinging the pistol in his right hand around to point to one of the younger men before him. "He's done pissed all over himself already!"

In fact, the young man Anderson pointed to had lost control of himself, and his standard-issue long johns were stained and wet nearly to his knees. Tears were streaming down his cheeks, and the look of terror on his face was so stark that it stirred a momentary note of sympathy in Daniel Hartman.

"What do you do for Mr. Lincoln, boy?" Anderson demanded, jamming the muzzle of his gun so hard against the young man's chest that the youth staggered back slightly.

"Supply, sir," the young man responded, his voice choked with emotion. "I'm a supply clerk in Pittsburgh."

"Well, it looks to me like Mr. Lincoln must be getting pretty hard up for supply clerks, boy," Anderson sneered, "if he's having to take in babies like you that can't even hold their water. Wouldn't you say that's about right, boy?"

"Yu-yu-yes, sir," the youth replied, sobbing openly now.

Anderson continued his inspection of the prisoners, awarding almost every one of them an insult or a sneer before he finally reached the end of the line. Then at last he turned around to face the members of his own band.

"So what do you think, men?" he asked. "Looks like all we got here is a bunch of supply clerks and errand boys. So shouldn't we let them go? Don't you think we ought to just put them back on the train and send them on their way?" Some of the men looked at Anderson in surprise, but those who knew him best knew that his words were only a cruel ruse meant to fill the hearts of the prisoners with false, desperate hopes. "You, Arch Clement!" Anderson called out. "You've always had a soft spot in your heart for our brave enemies. What do you think?"

Clement was a short, ugly, wiry fellow, the kind who had spent much of his life in private warfare against those who sought to run over him or ridicule him because of his size and looks. He was soundly disliked by the majority of the bushwhackers because of his customary ill temper and his affinity for unnecessary cruelty, but those very qualities had gained him considerable favor in the eyes of Bloody Bill Anderson. Casting only a quick sideways glance in Anderson's direction, Clement raised the muzzle of his revolver slightly and called out, "Here's what I think of your idea, Bill!" He fired three shots in quick succession, swinging his weapon slightly to the left after each shot. Three of the Federal soldiers collapsed immediately to the ground, each with a bullet hole placed neatly in the center of his chest.

The remainder of Anderson's men needed no other signal. A storm of gunfire followed Clement's callous act, and within a matter of seconds the line of enemy soldiers had been reduced to a tangled, bloody row of dead and dying bodies.

When it was all over, Daniel Hartman stared down in amazement at the smoking revolver in his hand. Although he had fired the gun over and over with the others, almost as a matter of reflex, he could now scarcely believe what they had just done. He watched dully as Clement, Jesse, and a couple of others stepped forward to finish off the wounded, and his body jolted involuntarily as each additional shot ended the agony of yet another Union soldier.

"They were the enemy, Dan," John Hartman said, placing a calming hand on his brother's shoulder. "It was ugly, but it had to be done."

"I know," Daniel answered. "I'm all right."

The two of them turned away, and with the last shots still exploding behind them, started back toward the middle of town. For the first time in months, Daniel remembered the sobering warning that his father had given him during one of their last talks together before he and John left for Texas. *For any man with a heart in his chest, it never gets any easier. No matter how many times you have to do it, the last killing is just as hard as the first.*

The men in Anderson's group were in general high spirits that night when they returned to the camp outside Centralia and began telling their fellows about the slaughter of the Union soldiers. Jesse James in particular, primed by the bonded whiskey he had brought back with him, related his version of the incident over and over to anyone who would listen. Daniel Hartman had recovered from the shock he'd felt immediately after the massacre, but he was still quiet all evening and took little part in the general merriment that pervaded the camp.

There had to be a way out of all this, he kept thinking. There had to be an end to all of this, sometime, somewhere. The strain of this dangerous lifestyle they led was beginning to affect him more strongly than even his brother John realized, and he was not sure how much longer he could go on without the hope of seeing an end to it all somewhere down the road. He had turned nineteen earlier that summer, and though it was impossible to keep count with any certainty, there was a good possibility that he had taken a man's life for every year he had been alive. There had to be an end to it all.

Nobody seemed all that surprised when they began to hear the sound of gunfire in the woods about a quarter mile north of camp. They had all expected pursuit when the Union army found out about the Centralia raid, and no one had even bothered to spread their blankets or unsaddle their horses for the night. The return to the camp had been primarily for the purpose of cooking supper, and the word was that they would split up into smaller bands and start back west toward Jackson County as soon as the moon rose high enough to light the way for riding.

Jamming a last few bites of fried ham and biscuits into their mouths, the men quickly gathered up their cooking gear and mounted their horses. By the time they were all ready to go, a rider raced by to spread the orders Anderson had issued.

"We're gonna charge 'em, boys!" the man shouted excitedly. "There's more of us then there is of them, and Bloody Bill says we're gonna take 'em!"

No objections were raised. The majority of the men had spent the entire day riding the roads around Centralia with no victories whatsoever to show for their efforts, and now they were eager to face the enemy, especially if they had them outnumbered as the messenger had said. Whooping and hollering at the top of their lungs, they put the spurs to their horses and started north in a savage, noisy mob.

The commander of the Union troops, a man later identified as a Major A. V. E. Johnson, had made a serious blunder in strategy, one that was to cost the life of practically every man under his command. When he left Centralia earlier in the night, he had believed he was simply pursuing Anderson and his thirty or so men, and he was sure that the hundred men he led would be more than sufficient to challenge such a group. But then, even after learning the actual size of the force he was taking on, he ordered his men to dismount and move forward on foot in a defensive line rather than retiring from the field until he could send for reinforcements.

Even on horseback, Johnson's green troops with their awkward single-shot rifles would scarcely have been a match for the overwhelming firepower of the battle-seasoned bushwhackers, and the fact that they were on foot simply multiplied the fatal odds stacked against them. Todd's and Anderson's men swept over them like an overwhelming wave, riding so swiftly that it was impossible for their opponents to aim and fire at them with any kind of accuracy.

Few of the Union soldiers were alive after the first few minutes of battle, and those scattered survivors who had somehow remained on their feet in the face of the onslaught simply threw down their weapons and fled in terror. But it was futile. Their mounts had been left fifty yards to the rear of the line of battle, and the bushwhackers had them cut off from that line of retreat. They scattered in all directions, but there was no cover, no safe refuge on any side, and each in his turn was caught, ridden to the ground, and killed.

After the brief battle, George Todd immediately dispatched scouts in all directions to make sure that this Federal unit was not simply the advance ranks of a much larger body of troops. Then the remainder of the bushwhackers quickly dismounted and began searching the bodies of the fallen foe.

Daniel Hartman stopped his horse beside a man he had shot and studied the body for a minute, looking for any signs of life. Then, when he felt reasonably sure that the man was dead, he stepped to the ground and knelt beside his victim, poking him a couple of times with the barrel of his revolver before finally holstering the weapon. In the confusion, Daniel had momentarily lost track of his brother John, but he had little fear for his brother's safety. Only two or three of the bushwhackers had been injured in the fray, and he felt confident about his brother's ability to take care of himself.

With practiced ease he rifled the man's pockets, producing a couple of letters, a few dollars, a pack of playing cards, and a folding knife with one of its two blades broken. The letters and knife he pitched aside, and the money and cards went into his shirt.

The man's shirt was too torn and blood-stained to bother with, but Daniel did strip off his boots, trousers, belt, and cartridge box. More and more the bushwhackers had taken to using enemy uniforms on some of their raids, and good, serviceable Union tunics and trousers were always in short supply.

He had just finished with the body and was stashing his loot on the back of his saddle when Jesse James came striding toward him through the darkness.

"Hey, Dan! Look at this!" Jesse said, holding out something Daniel could not identify in the dim moonlight.

"What is it?" Daniel asked.

"It's a major's insignia!" Jesse announced proudly. "I killed their leader. I nailed the bastard with one clean shot in the head. He's right over there, dead as a rock!"

"Well good for you, Jesse. I'd say he deserves to die for leading his outfit into a mess like this."

"I see you got one too," Jesse said, nodding toward the dead soldier nearby.

"Yeah."

"Did he have much on him?"

"Not much. I got a little cash, seven, maybe eight dollars."

"I got twenty-eight off that major," Jesse

announced, "and a ring that looks like it might have a real ruby in it." Then, turning to survey the general carnage around him, his face still flushed with the thrill of conflict, he said, "Can you believe it, Dan? Twice in one day. First we hammered that bunch in Centralia, and then this. Hell, if we could keep things going at this pace, we'd have the damn war won in another six months or so."

"Well, before you get too carried away, Jesse," Daniel told his friend, "don't forget Pell Durham's. It's not always this way, and our turn to catch the short end of things will come around again one of these days . . . probably before we know it."

"You're just too much of a damn pessimist, Dan," Jesse complained. "Don't you see that this business here could turn everything around for us, that it could mean a new start for this outfit and the cause it stands for? Hellfire! It's like Lawrence all over again, or maybe better. Once word gets out about this, people will start believing in us again. It'll be like it used to be back at the start."

"No, my friend," Dan said sadly. "I'm afraid it can never be like that again, not for any of us. Our turn is coming around again, and from now on out, every time we catch hell from the Federals it'll be worse than the time before."

Jesse turned and walked away, shaking his head in disgust as he pocketed his prize, the insignia of rank from the dead major's uniform. "Say what you want, dammit," he called back over his shoulder, "but this thing will never be over, not unless we let it. And there are some of us who will never let it end."

CHAPTER FIFTEEN

Dressed in men's clothing and riding the best horse she could buy, Mollie Hartman slipped out of Kansas City in the dead of night and started east toward Independence. It had been years since she had used such furtive tactics to travel cross-country undetected, but once she got under way all the tricks she had once used during the Kansas-Missouri border wars quickly came back to her.

She knew the countryside well and limited her travel to the most obscure back roads and forest trails. Countless times along the way she eased her mount into the woods along the route until she had identified a suspicious sound. Twice she slipped around Federal roadblocks, and another time she waited patiently in the woods for more than twenty minutes while a large contingent of artillery and supply wagons crossed her path.

The trip was risky, but the true scope of the gamble she was taking went far beyond simply traveling across countryside that would soon become the site of one of the largest battles fought thus far in the state. She was risking her life, but what was perhaps more important than that to Mollie was the fact that she was also risking the love and respect of a number of people who were more dear to her than anyone else in the world.

As startling as it was, the slaughter of the Union soldiers in and around Centralia had soon been overshadowed by events of even greater import for the war-weary and be-seiged residents of western Missouri.

A few weeks earlier, General Sterling Price had finally started his long-awaited advance into Missouri. It had been nearly three years since his forces had been driven south into Arkansas and had joined the Confederate army to bolster their crumbling front in west Tennessee and northern Mississippi. Since that time, Price had campaigned long and hard to be allowed to come back and "liberate" his home state from Union oc-cupation in order to open a new western front in the war. His vehement protests had eventually plunged him into disfavor with the Confederate hierarchy in Richmond, and the year before, when he finally did return to Arkansas, it was without any of the Missouri troops that had followed him so faithfully throughout the first half of the war.

But now he was back in Missouri at last, leading a patchwork assemblage of cavalry and infantry borrowed from a number of Confederate divisions west of the Mississippi. He had come into the state at the southeast corner, marching north toward St. Louis for a time before finally turning west near the center of the state and heading toward Kansas City.

The general's victories thus far during the campaign had been shallow and costly, and in a number of places along the way he had been forced to make wide detours in his route to avoid direct confrontation with superior enemy units. Now, in mid-October, with Price's army reported to be somewhere near the eastern edge of Jackson County, the entire venture was beginning to seem more like running a deadly gauntlet than making a victorious advance into the heart of enemy territory.

Mollie had been following the saga of Price's campaign with great interest, gleaning what information she could from the spotty newspaper stories and the scattered rumors that had circulated among the Union officers she knew through Kurt. She realized, as even Price probably did not at this point, what strong opposition he would soon face when he reached the western part of the state. Thus far, despite the ponderous wagon trains of supplies and plunder which he was said to be dragging along, Price had moved quickly and unpredictably enough to avoid the largest bodies of enemy troops in his path. But if he kept pushing due west toward Kansas City, as was his apparent plan, Mollie knew he could not avoid colliding with the superior enemy forces there with all the devastating impact of a freight train crashing into the side of a mountain.

Mollie did not believe she could have any effect on Price's inevitable defeat, although the prospect saddened her, but she did have an idea that she could do something worthwhile on a much smaller scale. No one questioned the fact that when the Confederate army reached western Missouri, the bands of bushwhackers in the area would almost certainly join up with it. Their fighting abilities and their knowledge of the countryside would be invaluable to Price, and the bushwhackers themselves would certainly consider his coming a turning point in the war.

But knowing what awaited Price in Jackson County, Mollie could only believe that all the bushwhackers who stepped forward to serve the Confederate general, including her nephews John and Daniel, would pay the same toll in blood that would soon be required of Price's own troops.

It hadn't been easy to set up the meeting with her nephews and her brother Jason on such short notice. Finding out where John and Daniel were and then figuring out a way to get a message to them had been the hardest part, but somehow she had managed it. She had set up the meeting place at the home of a friend near Lee's Summit, an elderly widow named Maude Case whose husband Barney had been killed six years before in a skirmish against a band of abolitionist raiders from Kansas. That part of the county was still safer than any other for her nephews to enter, and it was a journey of similar length for both Mollie and her brother.

A few miles east of Independence her path turned southeast into the wild hilly country that was a favorite haunt of the bushwhackers. Maude Case still lived in the remote log cabin where Barney had spent the last twenty-five years of his life making moonshine whiskey. Although she was in her eighties now, Maude still kept the tradition alive, and some said the product she sold was as good as any her husband ever thought about making. She was a crusty old woman who feared neither man nor beast, and the ancient Hawken rifle she carried had become as much a part of her persona as her homemade grain-sack dresses and her outdated high-brimmed cotton bonnets.

Near the turnoff to Maude's cabin, Mollie cut off the side of the road into the woods, rode about a hundred yards into the underbrush, dismounted and tied her horse to a tree. Then she retraced her route on foot and spent the next half-hour crouched in the bushes at the side of the road. The skill of the trackers in Kurt Rakestraw's company had become the stuff of legends in the few short months they had been here, and she wanted to make absolutely certain that none of them had followed her before she went on to the meeting with her brother and nephews.

Waiting there in the darkness, so still that soon even the creatures of the night began passing close by without knowing she was there, Mollie found herself wondering once again how Jason and the boys would receive the revelations she would soon be making.

As near as she could tell, none of her

friends or family from Clay County knew anything about her recent affair with a Union officer. Both she and Kurt were very discreet about their meetings, and she had noticed no difference in the tone of the occasional letters she received from her brother and Arethia. Cole's being gone helped because he had been her most frequent visitor from back home. The fact that the army took pains to conceal the identities and activities of Rakestraw and his men also contributed to her success at keeping the love affair a secret.

But tonight she was going to tell them everything. She felt she had no choice if she expected John and Daniel to trust her and accept her advice. But . . .

Finally, assured that she had not been followed, Mollie rose to her feet, stretched the stiffness out of her legs, and started back to her horse. It was another mile back into the woods to Maude Case's house, and Mollie followed a stream bed for most of the way rather than venture onto the overgrown wagon path that led to the cabin. It was nearly five in the morning now, but she knew she would still have time to reach her destination before dawn.

She made no effort to conceal the sounds of her movements as she passed through the last few yards of brush and emerged into the littered patch of open ground that passed for a yard in front of Maude Case's home. It would be better for her brother and nephews to know she was approaching, and if there did happen to be any enemy troops near enough to hear her, it was over for all of them anyway.

A single lamp burned in a front window of the structure, and a lazy curl of smoke was drifting skyward from the blackened fieldstone chimney. She caught a glimpse of somebody moving around inside, and then, as she drew closer, a form rose from a chair in the shadowy recesses of the small front porch. Catching a whiff of the pipe smoke that filled the air near the porch, she realized that the dark figure was her brother Jason.

"Hi, Mollie," he said casually. "Did you have any trouble getting here?"

"I had to slip around a couple of Federal patrols," she said, "but it wasn't much of a problem. In fact, the most difficult part of the whole trip was locating a horse to make it on. The army has bought or commandeered just about every decent animal in the city, and the few that are still available don't come cheap."

As she dismounted, Jason stepped forward

to greet her. She noticed that he continued to walk with an awkward limp, and yet his arms still felt strong and reassuring as he hugged her. It seemed like forever since they had last been together, and seeing him now somehow made her life in Kansas City seem distant and lacking in reality.

"The boys are inside," Jason told her. "They're really anxious to see you again."

"I feel the same way," Mollie said. "It's been more than a year now. I haven't seen either of them since back before . . ."

"I know," Jason answered. "Since before Daddy was killed."

John and Daniel met her at the door, each taking his turn at hugging her and kissing her cheek. Then they all stepped back to take a second look at one another.

"My God! Both of you have changed so much!" Mollie exclaimed. "If I had seen either of you on the street, I'm not sure I would have even recognized you."

The metamorphosis of John and Daniel Hartman seemed complete now. Gone were the two wide-eyed youths she remembered so well. In their places were two dark, handsome men, hard of frame and visage, armed to the teeth, and even now during this hasty reunion, slightly detached from all things too familiar or sentimental. John was dressed in loose, comfortable clothing, a worn flop hat, and a scuffed pair of Union-issue riding boots. Daniel had on a pair of dark trousers, the blue uniform tunic of a Union army corporal, and a pair of confiscated cavalry boots similar to his brother's. The butts of no less than four revolvers peeked from various hiding places in John's clothing, and Daniel was similarly armed. Hugging them, Mollie thought wryly, was like wrapping her arms around a sack full of stones.

"So where is Maude?" Mollie asked at last, realizing that their hostess was absent.

"She's been down in the hollow all night keeping a watch on her still," Daniel said and chuckled. "Seems she's had some pilfering going on at night lately, and she said she's determined to dust the britches of anybody who tries to make off with a jug of her brew without paying for it."

"But isn't she worried that she might be biting off more than she can chew? Doesn't she realize that it's some of the bushwhackers who are likely to be doing the stealing?" Mollie asked in alarm. "These days, hardly anyone else would dare venture into these hills."

"Shoot, Aunt Mollie." John grinned. "That old gal is no more afraid of the likes of us than she is of the Federals. I bet she wouldn't hesitate to draw a bead on General Lee himself if she caught him slipping around through the woods too close to her still."

While Daniel poured coffee for all of them, Mollie, Jason, and John settled down around Maude Case's table to talk.

"Well, I'm sure you're all curious about the urgent messages I sent you," Mollie began, "so I won't waste time with small talk. We can catch up on that later, after you've heard what I came here to say."

"We have been wondering," John admitted. "It wasn't easy for Daniel and me to cut loose and come, but from the sounds of things, we decided we'd better try."

"It did sound like a life-and-death matter," Jason agreed.

"It is, Jason," Mollie told them earnestly. "At least, I feel like it could easily be that."

Daniel brought clay mugs of coffee to the table, then sat down beside his father, waiting quietly with the others for her to continue.

Mollie drew a breath and steeled herself for what was to come, knowing that the next few minutes could easily determine whether or not she was ostracized by her family for the rest of her life.

"Jason, do you remember back about ten years ago in Virginia," Mollie began, "when a man named Kurt Rakestraw came to visit his brother near our farm?"

"Sure I do," Jason said. "A tall, handsome fellow. Always wore that same buckskin shirt. And if I remember right, you were pretty sweet on him until he just up and left one day."

"That's the one," Mollie said. "And I was more than just sweet on him. I was so crazy in love with him that after he left I thought for a while that I might just as well die."

"Well, we never talked about that, Mollie, but now that you mention it, I guess I do recall you acting a little strange for several months after that. But I still don't quite see the connection. What does this fellow Rakestraw have to do with you bringing us here?"

"A while ago, Kurt Rakestraw showed up in Kansas City," Mollie announced nervously. "Things . . . well, things worked out between us, and we've been seeing each other ever since."

"That part I didn't know about," Jason replied quietly.

"I told Cole about it. I owed him that much, but I felt like I couldn't tell anybody else, not even you or Arethia. You see,

Kurt . . . well . . . you see, he's a major in the Union army." Mollie saw the expressions on the faces of her brother and nephews immediately begin to darken, but she plunged right on, knowing that the worst was yet to come. "He came here last fall from Colorado, and he brought a company of soldiers with him, a company with a very special assignment. For a while I didn't know what that assignment was, but later I found out —"

She was interrupted by the sharp, explosive crack of John's clay mug crashing against the stone of the fireplace across the room. Utterly enraged, he rose so quickly that the chair behind him flew halfway across the room. "God damn it, Mollie!" he roared, turning swiftly toward the door. "God damn it!" In another instant he would have crashed through the door and out into the night, but his brother leapt up to halt his furious charge.

"John, wait!" Daniel insisted.

John spun to face them, his face livid with rage. "I'm damned if I'll listen to any more of this, Dan!" he stormed. "You know as well as I do who this Rakestraw, this *Coloradan*, is, and she's . . . she's . . ."

"I don't understand any of this," Jason admitted, looking quickly from one to the other of his sons in confusion.

"Daddy, these Coloradans are the ones we told you about," Daniel said. "The ones that dog us everywhere we go, the ones that killed Paul Grimsley and Kyle Pettijohn and Homer Jackson and at least two or three other good men."

"They're the worst thing that's happened around here since order Number 11," John said. "And now our dear Aunt Mollie here is telling us that she's —"

"That she's in love with him," Mollie interrupted sharply. All three of the men looked at her in amazement, hardly able to believe her admission, but she met their gazes directly and went on without hesitation. "Days ago I vowed to myself that if I could get you here I would tell you everything, and part of it is that Kurt and I have been lovers for a year now . . ."

"That's it!" John exclaimed, turning toward the door again. But this time it was his father who kept him from leaving.

"Wait a minute, son," Jason said sternly. "I don't like what I'm hearing either. In fact I hate it, but we should hear it all before we make up our minds."

John hesitated, his hand on the door latch, and for a moment it looked as if he still planned to leave. Then, slowly, he turned and stalked back across the room in stony silence. He retrieved his chair from where he had knocked it, then sat down at the table again. The anger had by now left his features, but the cold, impersonal gaze that replaced it seemed even more terrible to Mollie.

"I want the three of you to know that I'm not proud of what's happened," she continued, her voice now controlled only by the sheer force of her will, "but I'm not ashamed of it either. What happened happened because the two of us are in love, and I can't bring myself to look on that as shameful or wrong. But I can also promise you on all that's sacred to me that I never gave him any information that could be useful to him or to the Union army." She ignored John's ugly growl of disbelief.

"Two and three years ago, when it seemed like there was still some sense and purpose in this war," Mollie continued, "I did what I could to help my family and friends and the Southern cause. Surely you haven't forgotten, Jason, that I found a way to get you out of that terrible detention camp when probably no one else could have."

"How could I ever forget something like that?" Jason answered quietly.

"And I did other things, too. More than

once I put myself in danger by passing information on to Cole about what the Federals were up to, and, almost without exception, each time I did something like that, it was in hopes of saving the lives of people I knew and cared about." When she stopped speaking, the room fell silent. No one could dispute her claims.

"And that's the same reason I'm here today," Mollie told them at last. "I came hoping to save the lives of at least two people that I love as much as I love anybody in the world. For the past year I've tried to ignore the war. I pretended that there was nothing more I could do, and I convinced myself that it wasn't my place to try and help either side. But knowing what's about to happen, and who it might happen to, I can't fool myself like that any longer. I can't sit back and watch two of my nephews continue on a course that will almost surely mean their deaths."

"What are you talking about, Aunt Mollie?" Daniel asked with concern.

"I'm talking about what's going to happen when General Sterling Price marches his army into Jackson County," Mollie told him earnestly. "It doesn't take a military genius to figure out that when he gets here, every bushwhacker for a hundred miles in any direction will rally to his flag and that those are the very men who will probably be in the front lines of every battle that Price decides to fight here."

"You're damned right we plan to join him," John announced defiantly, "and you can tell your Yankee boyfriend that when that day comes he'd better pack his kit and head on back to Colorado, because it's going to get pretty hot for the likes of him in these parts."

"For your sake, John, yours and Daniel's, I wish that could be true. After the long, hard fight you've had, I wish there was still some chance of your winning, but I know now that there is not. I wonder if General Price realizes that there's an army twice the size of his gaining ground on him from behind and that at least that many more Union soldiers are braced and waiting here, eager for him to arrive. And that's not counting any of the Union forces in Kansas, or the hundreds of Kansan volunteers who are preparing to ride over and lend a hand when the time comes. Price is rushing straight into the heart of the storm, and he's going to be destroyed for all his blind, foolish haste — he and every man who's with him when the fighting starts."

Mollie could tell by the solemn expressions on the faces of the three men that her dire prophecies had had their effect. Hoping beyond hope, most Southerners in the region clung to the desperate belief that Price could still manage to serve as their liberator, that his mere presence would be the catalyst for a popular uprising in the region so that the tide of the war could be turned around. But surely, Mollie thought, her brother and nephews could not ignore evidence as strong as that which she was presenting.

"I can't do anything to stop Sterling Price," Mollie continued. "Right now Jefferson Davis himself probably couldn't convince him to abandon his grand dreams and hightail it back into safe territory. But what I pray that I can do is persuade the two of you that there is no point in taking part in his campaign. What good can it do for two more lives to be sacrificed in this futile effort?"

Neither John nor Daniel attempted to answer her question, but she could tell by their expressions that she hadn't succeeded in convincing them yet.

"Even if you just decide to give it up," Mollie went on, "nobody who knows you could ever doubt your courage and dedication. It would simply be a matter of choosing to live rather than to die!"

Daniel stared blankly at his coffee for a moment, considering her words, and then he said, "I guess we all do know deep down that it's over just like you said, Aunt Mollie. The Federals own just about everything now, and even things like what we did over in Centralia are just a fluke, a matter of stumbling into one place where we weren't outnumbered four or five to one.

"But can't you understand that by now we've pretty much used up all our options? We can't go home again because they'd just find us and kill us there. And what would be the point of heading south and joining the regulars when they're fighting the same sort of last-ditch battles that we are here? If we left at all, it would be with the knowledge that we were abandoning our closest friends to the same fate that we were running away from. I wouldn't want to try to live with that for the rest of my life."

"And besides that," John added venomously, "why should we take the word of a damn Federal officer's . . ." He paused, choking back the word he wanted to use. ". . . a Federal officer's *woman*?" he spat.

"Because it's the truth, John," Mollie replied calmly. "No matter how deeply I might care for Kurt Rakestraw or any other man, I would never trick you and I would never lie to you."

"That's right. She wouldn't do that, son," Jason said, entering the conversation at last. "I can't say that I approve of what she's done with this fellow Rakestraw, and I won't ever attempt to try to tell you boys what to do. But I can swear to you that Mollie would no more lie to you about something like this than I would or your mother would. She hasn't got the stuff in her to do that."

"But truth or lie," Daniel told his father, "it still doesn't change what we have to do, Daddy." Then turning to Mollie, he added, "I believe that you came here to help us, and I suppose that, barring some sort of miracle, your predictions will come true. But when it happens, and whatever happens, John and I will be there. We chose a long time ago to see this thing through to the end."

For the first time since his outburst several minutes before, the hard expression disappeared from John's face and his voice softened when he addressed his aunt. "You've got to understand something about the way we are now, Aunt Mollie," he said quietly. "If you're going to try to change somebody's mind about something by warning him that he might die if he does it, you have to make sure that he still gives a damn whether he lives or dies."

Looking from one to the other of them, Mollie wanted to cry, to literally drown her feelings of helplessness and sorrow in a flood of tears, but she knew she would have to wait until she was alone to enjoy that sort of relief. And her brother wasn't even trying to help her. He understood their reasoning intimately, having felt the same unyielding commitment himself many times in years past. She bit her lip to halt its telltale quivering and took a drink of her lukewarm coffee to push the hateful lump back down her throat.

"Does he know you're here, Mollie?"

"Yes," she answered in a low, broken voice. "He urged me to come. He remembers you, Jason, and he remembers the boys. He's a good man."

"I'm sure he is," Jason told her softly. "And maybe in years to come, I'll be able to shake his hand and feel happy that you have someone like him in your life. But not now. Now he's the enemy."

"The enemy . . ." Mollie mumbled dully. And she wondered how such a fact could at once be so true and yet so senseless.

CHAPTER SIXTEEN

They charged like wild men, their eyes blood-red from the bite of gunsmoke, their throats raw from yelling shrill battle cries, their ears pounding from the constant roar of gunfire and the relentless explosions of artillery rounds.

The determined blue line fell back before them. Although vastly outnumbered, the Confederate cavalry led by General Jo Shelby swept the west bank of the Big Blue River clear of all opposition in a matter of minutes, then pushed on, insane with the thrill of battle, into the rim of trees and scrub brush beyond.

Once into the trees some of the Union soldiers simply threw down their weapons and fled, filled with blind primal terror, but far more chose to stand and fight now that they had at least some scant cover to shield them from the pack of screaming rebel banshees that had descended on them.

Lashing out from the shelter of trees and ditches, they emptied saddle after saddle until at last the cutting edge of the Confederate cavalry charge was blunted and turned aside.

There was no second charge. Taking stock of his decimated ranks after the first attack, Shelby quickly realized that he could easily end up a commander without a command if he ordered a second charge. Besides, there was no need for a second assault on the advancing enemy ranks because the first had accomplished precisely what he had hoped.

Only minutes before, a Union brigade in pursuit of Sterling Price's army had caught up to the infantry units in Price's rear guard just as they were crossing the Big Blue. As the Union cannons had pounded away at the soggy jumble of men and wagons scrambling up out of the water on the opposite bank, the enemy infantry had moved right down to the edge of the water to harass the last of the Confederate stragglers.

As desperate and hasty as it was, Shelby's charge bought the fleeing Confederate infantry a few precious minutes, time enough to complete the river crossing and form a respectable line of defense on the western bank. Then, on their leader's command, the rebel cavalry scattered like quail, racing their horses back across the river and to relative safety just as quickly as they had vaulted across it the first time.

Bullets continued to sing past Daniel Hartman as he urged his horse up a steep, muddy bank on the west side of the river and into the cover of the trees and brush beyond. He hadn't had time to pause and examine the bullet wound on his left thigh, but since he still had full use of the leg he guessed it must not be too bad. It hadn't started to hurt yet either, but he knew well enough that when it did he would be in for constant pain over the next few hours or days. There would be no hope of finding any medical help this close to the front, and heaven only knew when he could be spared from the battle so that he could have the wound tended to.

Once out of the direct line of fire, Daniel turned his horse to the southwest and headed toward the clearing Shelby had designated as a rendezvous point after the charge. The woods around him were filled with stragglers from Shelby's unit, some wounded and some not, but all who could still ride were headed in the same general direction. Behind him the cracking exchange of small-arms fire reassured Daniel that the Confederate infantry had dug their heels in and intended to prevent the enemy from crossing the river for as long as possible.

John was one of the first men Daniel spotted when he entered the clearing. As Daniel stepped to the ground, the two brothers exchanged grim smiles, both relieved to see the other still among the living. Then John quickly fell to work tending his brother's injured leg.

"It's not so bad," John said after he had cut away the leg of Daniel's trousers. Then, producing a small dented flask from his shirt pocket, he said, "Here, take a slug of this for the pain, and then I'll use the rest on this gash."

Grimly surveying the furrow the bullet had made in his thigh, Daniel tilted the flask back and gulped down a mouthful of Maude Case's white lightning, then passed the metal container back to John. The colorless liquid felt like pure acid as it splashed onto his open wound, but he knew that if anything could stop a deadly infection from eating into his flesh, certainly this stuff could.

"Have you got anything to use for a bandage?" John asked.

"In my saddlebags," Daniel managed to say, still gritting his teeth against the pain.

John retrieved the bundle of white muslin that Maude Case had given Daniel as a parting gift before he left her cabin. The bandage he fashioned was neat and tight, and Daniel began to feel better as soon as it was in place. As the pain began to subside slightly, Daniel rose tentatively onto the leg, tested it by walking around a little, and pronounced it usable.

While Daniel rested, John wandered away in search of food and ammunition, returning a few minutes later with a meager stock of both. Over the next ten or fifteen minutes, the regulars in Shelby's cavalry unit and the bushwhackers who had joined them continued to straggle into the clearing. Looking around, Daniel guessed that perhaps two-thirds of the men who had been involved in the charge had by now returned. Many were injured, but most of those, like Daniel, would still be able to ride and fight. The worst of the casualties had been left behind at the river, perhaps never to be seen again.

"Have you seen anything of Frank and Jesse?" Daniel asked as he gnawed on the hunk of dried bread John handed him.

"Frank's here, and he talked to a man who said he saw Jesse ride back across the river," John answered. "He must have got lost in the woods somewhere."

"What about the rest of our bunch?" Daniel inquired.

"I talked to George Todd, and he said he thought we'd lost about thirty. He and Bill Anderson are with Shelby now, taking stock of our situation and figuring out what we should do next."

"Well, then, I guess we'd better load up and get ready to ride again," Daniel said and sighed deeply, "because we sure as hell won't be staying here for long." He stuffed the bread into one of his pockets, then took his share of the ammunition John had brought and began reloading his collection of revolvers.

The band of bushwhackers John and Daniel Hartman were with had placed themselves at General Shelby's disposal two days before, and they had been in the saddle almost constantly ever since. At first the bushwhackers had been scorned by the regulars in Shelby's command, who considered them to be little more than savage outlaws who would be useless in any direct confrontation with the enemy. But after the first combined engagement with the Federals, the Confederates granted their new allies a great degree of respect, having witnessed their fearlessness and fighting ability firsthand.

Over the past forty-eight hours, Shelby's men had covered more than a hundred miles on horseback. Again and again the general had thrown his men against overwhelming numbers of the enemy, trying desperately to stem the determined Union onslaught long enough for the main body of Price's army to move away to safety. But everywhere they turned, it seemed, the numbers of their Union opponents multiplied while their own forces dwindled pathetically.

General Sterling Price had finally given up on his grand dream of capturing Kansas City and then plunging on westward into Kansas. The sketchy rumors that now reached Shelby's men placed Price's main army somewhere south of Kansas City, near Westport, and as incredible as it seemed, it was said that he still refused to abandon the wagon trains of plunder and military stores that had slowed his progress so much. To complicate things still further, hundreds of civilians with Southern sympathies had attached themselves to Price's entourage, hoping to travel under his protection as he retreated south toward Arkansas.

And all about the flanks and rear of the fleeing Confederate herd the relentless Union wolves snapped and howled, sensing not just victory at this point, but perhaps the total annihilation of their stumbling, beleaguered, and ill-led foe.

Daniel paused from jamming fresh cartridges into one of his pistols long enough to look up and survey the field of ragged, desperate men around him. Some lay sprawled on the ground like corpses, greedily claiming a few tantalizing moments of rest. Others gnawed on their starvation rations or treated ugly wounds. A few simply sat staring dully at nothing, their minds and bodies numbed beyond thought or action by the awful demands of warfare. Nearby the sounds of the battle were drawing undeniably nearer, which could only mean that the Federals had somehow made it across the Big Blue and were shoving forward again, confident and irresistible.

"She was right, wasn't she, John?" Daniel said. "Aunt Mollie was right about everything she told us, wasn't she?"

"We knew then that she was," John replied quietly. "As I recall, neither one of us tried to argue that this wouldn't be a big bloody mess."

"No, I mean that she was right that it was all for nothing, and that our being here wouldn't make any difference one way or another. We came back because we thought our presence might mean the difference between life and death for some of our friends. But if we fight to the last man . . . if every one of us dies for a lost cause . . . then whose life have we saved, John? What have we accomplished?"

John stuck the pistol he had been reloading in his waistband and studied his brother's features closely. Beneath the dirt and the grayish soot that acrid gunsmoke had deposited there, he could clearly see the fear, exhaustion, and bitterness that filled his brother's words with such stark intensity.

"Dammit, Dan," John answered finally, his voice containing more frustration than true anger. "I don't have any answers for you! Ask somebody else your questions if you must. All I know is that this is the game we picked, and this is the hand we were dealt. What choice do we have now but to play it out?"

"You're right, John," Daniel said. "I guess it doesn't matter much at this point, does it? When it's all over, all that will matter is who won and who lost."

On the far side of the clearing a few men began to rise lethargically to their feet and prepare to mount their horses. The realization spread that they were leaving again, and all across the open area men began to raise their leaden bodies and climb into their saddles.

John and Daniel followed as the stream of mounted men started down a road to the west. No one asked where they were going. At this point it didn't seem to matter, because each rode with a single unsettling certainty to keep him company. Wherever it was that they were heading, only more killing and dying awaited them at the end of the trip.

"Good God! What a mess!" George Todd exclaimed. He and half a dozen other bushwhackers, including John and Daniel Hartman, were sitting on a hilltop gazing westward into the long valley where, even as they watched, General Price's wagon train was being overrun by Union forces. Shelby had sent them on ahead to try to find out where Price's main force was located and to determine the best course for the cavalry to take to rejoin their leader.

The wagon train, or at least what was left of it, was scattered out along a quarter mile of road about fifteen miles south of Westport. The attackers were pouring in from the west and the north in large numbers, some mounted and others on foot, slaughtering both the hapless wagon drivers and the crowds of unarmed civilians who had the great misfortune to be overtaken by this deadly onslaught. A number of the wagons were already on fire, but it looked as if the Union forces wanted to seize as many of them as possible intact.

From all indications, Price had decided to try to salvage what troops he could from his ravaged divisions rather than commit them to the defense of the wagons. It was a wise choice, considering the overwhelming numbers of the enemy his soldiers would have had to face, but the men on the hilltop who witnessed the carnage agreed among themselves that it had been made much too late. Days before, if he had opted to take along only the most necessary food and ordnance, he could have traveled much faster than he had and this tragic scene would never have taken place. Now he had lost everything, and the men assigned to drive the overloaded wagons of plunder were paying for his mistake with their lives.

Judging by the civilian clothing as well as the blue uniforms the attackers wore, it appeared that the Kansas Jayhawkers were finally getting a chance to take part in the fighting. And it was precisely the kind of fighting the Jayhawkers were best at, shooting and killing helpless people, few of whom could shoot back.

"Well, it's plain enough there's not much

we can do for this bunch," George Todd announced at last. "But after the Federals finish here, they'll be hot on Price's trail again. Maybe we can slow that business down a little bit. John, you and Daniel and I will ride on south for a ways while the rest of these men head back to let Shelby know what's going on."

"All right, George," John Hartman agreed. "I'd guess that Price has at least got as far as Martin's Crossing by now, and maybe we can scout out a good location for an ambush there if Shelby can get there in time."

"Good idea," Todd said. Then, turning to the men who were headed back to rejoin Shelby, he said, "Tell the general to keep moving south for another three or four miles, then to cut due west until he reaches Martin's Crossing. Unless he runs into some Federal outfit that we don't know about, that should keep him from tangling with any of the bastards before he's ready to."

A moment later the two groups rode off in their separate directions. It took Todd and the Hartman brothers less than an hour to outdistance the vanguard of the Federal forces and to overtake the Confederate units that were bringing up the rear of General

Price's retreating army. Then they pushed on south a few miles farther until they reached the site of the ambush.

After talking it over, the three bushwhackers realized there was no guarantee that the last of the Confederate units would be past Martin's Crossing by the time the ambush was to take place, but it would just be their bad luck if they were caught in it and forced to fight for their lives alongside the cavalry. This was the last good place for such a trap before the road entered into another long stretch of flat, open territory, and if there was any hope of delaying the Federals long enough for Price to escape, the attack had to take place here.

Another hour passed before Shelby and his men finally caught up. Todd, John, and Daniel passed the time scouting out the best fighting positions in the area, and they were able to advise the general on the disbursement of his men when he arrived. By then the only stragglers still passing by were civilians, strays from the beleaguered rear-guard units, and the walking wounded. Many of those who still had weapons and the strength to wield them took up positions alongside Shelby's men and the bushwhackers to help with the impending fight.

They didn't have long to wait. Within

twenty mintues the head of the Union column came into view. Encouraged by their easy capture of the wagon train, and with the scent of blood still fresh in their nostrils, they pushed forward down the road in an eager, overconfident, and careless manner which played right into the hands of Shelby and his men.

The Confederate general had scattered his men out along a quarter-mile strip of the road, cautioning them to stay out of sight until the fighting started and to wait until the head of the Federal column had reached the southern tip of their fire zone before opening up. Had the Union commander sent riders out to flank the main column the ambush might have been discovered and ruined, but he was apparently so anxious to catch Price and gain an unconditional victory that he had abandoned normal military precautions. That was his undoing.

Seconds after the signal shot was fired, the Union forces were raked by a heavy crossfire. The situation was so confused for the first couple of minutes that the panicky Federal troops were scattering in all directions, scarcely aware of where their enemies were shooting from or what direction they should flee for safety.

After the first couple of volleys, most of

the cavalrymen and bushwhackers leaped onto their horses and charged in to deal with the foe at closer quarters. For the next five minutes they rode among the enemy, killing at will. Their revolvers far outweighed the firepower of the awkward, single-shot rifles most of the Union troops carried, and few of the three or four hundred blue-clad soldiers who had marched unwittingly into the ambush lived long enough to figure out how they had fallen into such a devastating trap.

As Shelby had expected, the fighting at the front of the advancing column caused the other Union units in the area to halt and dig in until they had figured out how many enemy soldiers they were up against and if the attack would be pressed against them as well. Some of the cavalrymen and bushwhackers wanted to do just that, but the Confederate general was smart enough to know that, with the element of surprise gone and the enemy now braced and ready, any further attacks could turn the moment of victory into one of utter defeat.

But they had done enough. It was early evening now, and the momentum of the Union advance was gone. General Price and his forces would certainly push on through the night, but it was less likely that the

Federal forces would do likewise, not after the surprising defeat they had suffered just at the moment when total victory seemed assured.

After the attack, John and Daniel Hartman turned south with the others until they were well past Martin's Crossing and the area where the recent fighting had taken place.

From this point on, they realized, General Price would be moving due south as fast as his exhausted, starving entourage could travel. Some of the other bushwhackers had already made inquiries about enlisting in Shelby's cavalry and were readily accepted into the brigade, but the two Hartman brothers were reluctant to travel southward as members of a regular military unit to witness the final death throes of the Southern war effort.

After discussing the matter quietly, about an hour after dark John and Daniel simply turned their horses aside out of the cavalry column and started east. Dozens of the other bushwhackers had already done the same thing, and neither Shelby nor any of his subordinate officers had made any attempt to stop them. It was understood that this was not an act of cowardice or desertion. The men who left had simply chosen to stay and continue the fight here.

Riding across the open, moonlit country-side, John and Daniel tried to decide where they should go and what they should do now that they were on their own again.

"Well, I don't know about you, big brother," Daniel said, "but number one on my list is sleep and some decent food. And I wouldn't mind stopping by Walt Tyler's place so his wife can take a look at this leg. She's bound to have some concoction that will make it heal."

"That all sounds fine to me," John replied. "And then maybe we can head to Wyatt's Cave and hole up for a few days. It's the nearest safe place I can think of, and some of the others will probably show up there. Maybe they'll have some news about who's still alive and where they are."

"I wonder if Anderson and Todd will try to put their outfits back together again after all of this," Daniel said.

"I expect they will," John answered. "We've both been around Bloody Bill Anderson long enough to know that nothing short of a bullet in the heart will end this war for him. And I expect George Todd is of the same mind."

"But how can they expect to do any good now, John?" Daniel asked. "Price was our last hope, and now that he's been driven out, what sense is there in going on?"

"Look, Dan, we took to the brush a long time ago because we weren't given any choice in the matter. It was that or be killed. And that part hasn't changed. There probably won't be any more Lawrences or Centralias for us. And there won't be any more hopes that somebody like Sterling Price will march through and drive the Federals out for good. But that doesn't mean we can quit fighting. If we quit, we'll die. It's that simple."

Daniel couldn't argue with the grim truth in his brother's words. It *was* that simple, he had to admit. It was that simple, and that crazy. The war was lost, but the warfare must continue.

CHAPTER SEVENTEEN

Kurt Rakestraw was waiting in Mollie's dressing room after the performance. She gave him a hug and a kiss as soon as she came in, then drew back slightly to study his face more closely. He was pensive tonight, his expression serious and slightly distracted, as if his thoughts were on some other matter besides being here with her. Mollie started to ask him what was troubling him, then decided against it. It was undoubtedly a military matter, and therefore something that she preferred to know nothing about.

"Did you get the room?" she asked, stepping around the partition she used to dress behind when she had company in the room. Eliza had taken the night off, but the costume Mollie wore in the last act of the play she was now in was simple and easy to remove so she didn't really need the assistance of her dresser.

"I got it this afternoon," Kurt replied, "but it looks like we won't have much time to use it. One of my informants came in late this afternoon with some news that has to be followed up. My unit will be riding out before dawn tomorrow morning."

Mollie tried to hide her disappointment. She had seen very little of Kurt for the past month, ever since General Price had entered the western part of Missouri and then turned south to begin his ignoble retreat back to Confederate territory. Kurt's company, in fact, had been one of the last units to give up the pursuit of the defeated Southerners, turning back only when they found themselves single-handedly pursuing and harassing an enemy force many times their own size.

The week that had passed since her secret meeting with Jason and his sons had been a particularly trying time for Mollie. The strain of knowing that Kurt was deeply involved in the Union defense of Jackson County and that her nephews were, without a doubt, equally active on the Confederate side was almost more than she could bear. While the fighting was going on she had hounded the Federal authorities daily, begging to see the casualty lists, and now that Kurt had returned safely she was just as eager to find out if her nephews had survived the tumult. None of the messages she had sent to Jason had yet been answered, and all her other efforts to gain some information about John and Daniel had been unsuccessful.

Tonight, for the first time in what seemed like ages, she had hoped to relax with her lover, putting aside, at least for a few hours, all her worries and frustrations. But apparently it was not to be.

After Mollie had changed, they went out the stage door and got into the buggy Kurt had brought. Neither of them had much to say during the ride to the small, out-of-the-way hotel where Kurt had rented them a room. Mollie felt almost angry at Kurt for deserting her tonight, although she knew he had no choice in the matter, and as the silence continued minute after minute, it began to seem like a wall between them.

When they reached the hotel, Mollie took the room key from Kurt and went in a side entrance while Kurt drove to the stable behind the building to leave the horse and buggy. She was standing at the window in the room, gazing out into the night, when he joined her there a few minutes later.

"How much time do you have?" Mollie asked, not even bothering to turn as Kurt sat down on the edge of the bed and began pulling off his boots.

"A couple of hours, I guess," he answered. "I should be back at the barracks before three so I can take care of some last-minute details before we wake the men."

"Well perhaps your time would be better spent sleeping than in being here with me," Mollie suggested, turning to look at him at last. She hated herself for the cold, impersonal tone that had crept into her voice, but she couldn't help it. She knew she was still unjustly blaming Kurt for the hurt and disappointment she felt, but blame him she did.

Kurt paused with one boot off and one on to look at her. "Perhaps," he answered quietly, "but I'd still rather be here with you. I've missed you and I want to make love to you tonight, even if it means being exhausted tomorrow."

"I'm sorry, darling," Mollie said, coming over to sit beside him on the bed at last. "I guess I'm just acting ugly because I was so looking forward to tonight and I hate the idea of your leaving again so soon." But despite her conciliatory words, Mollie could not rid herself of the feeling that the mood was all wrong tonight. For once the idea of undressing and getting into bed with this man did not stir any feelings of passion whatsoever in her.

"Well I'm not exactly looking forward myself to the idea of leaving so soon," Kurt told her, "and that's especially true considering the job we have ahead of us tomorrow. God damn it, I hate caves! I have ever since I was a little boy."

Ordinarily Mollie would have let a comment of that sort go by as if she had not heard it, but this particular exclamation was so unexpected that she found herself breaking the unwritten code between them.

"Do you have to go into some caves tomorrow, Kurt?" she asked.

"I guess we will," he answered. "The information we have is that a handful of bushwhackers are holed up in a cavern a few miles east of Independence, and that's where we're going in the morning. I hate the idea of blindly leading my men into such a place, but I don't guess we'll be able to just wait outside for them to come out and fight. There's too much of a chance that they'll just sneak out some back way and give us the slip entirely."

Mollie didn't envy him the job. She had visited enough of the natural caverns in the area to know how dank and dangerous they could be, and the idea of fighting in such surroundings seemed incredibly perilous.

"If there's only a few of them, why don't you just let them go, Kurt?" she suggested. "After all the losses they've suffered lately, they're bound to be pretty well whipped. Why not just let them alone to lick their wounds in peace?"

"I wish we could," he answered sincerely, "but I'm afraid it's far too late for that, Mollie. They're the ones who have made this a fight to the finish, and even though the war is so close to being over, I guess we're still going to have to track them down to the last man and kill every one of them. I don't understand what keeps them going anymore or why they even want to keep on fighting after all hope of winning is gone, but that's the way things seem to be."

Mollie thought of the meeting with her nephews, as she had so many times before. Where were they now? she wondered. Was it possible that they might be hiding out in the same caves Kurt Rakestraw planned to assault tomorrow, or had they already perished, their bodies buried anonymously in some mass grave with the countless others who had died in the recent fighting?

She realized that Kurt had turned to look at her and was studying her with rapt attention. His eyes were filled with a sadness and yearning that Mollie found hard to comprehend.

"I'm sorry," he told her, almost in a whisper. "I know you're thinking about your nephews and I am truly sorry about the way things turned out. I wish you could have changed their minds, but you couldn't, so now we have to deal with them. If they're still alive, we have no choice but to track them down."

Mollie had not told him anything about the meeting at Maude Case's cabin, but she realized that her very silence had been tantamount to an admission of failure.

"We've broken all our rules tonight, Kurt," Mollie told him at last. "We're talking about things that we shouldn't, that we can't discuss, because we both know that if we look too closely at all of this, it could mean the end of us. The final unchangeable truth in all of this is that John and Daniel are doing what they feel they must, and so are you."

"You're right, we shouldn't be talking about it, especially not when we have as little time as we do tonight," he said. "Do you feel like making love?"

"Yes," Mollie lied, trying to utter the pronouncement softly, willingly. Not an ounce of desire was stirring anywhere within her. Slowly she reached up and began working on the buttons of her blouse as Kurt started removing his own clothing.

His warmth and scent remained on the bedding even after he was gone. She had feigned sleep when Kurt rose softly from the bed and began dressing a few minutes before. She opened her eyes only to sneak a final glimpse of him as he slipped quietly out the door.

Mollie remained in the bed a short time longer, trying to will herself to sleep, but it was no use. Although the hour was late and she was tired, her mind was still racing, filled with a host of unsettling thoughts and emotions. Despite all her best efforts, the strain between her and Kurt tonight had carried over into their lovemaking, which had been brief and unsatisfying for both of them. Kurt accepted the blame, apologizing for his distracted mood and his early departure, but Mollie knew the problem went much deeper than that.

For many months now, ever since Kurt Rakestraw's sudden re-entry into her life, Mollie hadn't questioned her belief that if the war were not there she and Kurt would have nothing standing between them and a long happy life together. He sometimes

spoke eagerly about the two of them settling down somewhere permanently, and
Mollie thought that the only thing that
stopped him from proposing was the danger
and uncertainty of his military duties.

But suddenly, in one of those overpowering premonitions that come only a few times
in a person's life, Mollie realized that those
dreams of togetherness and happiness were
never to be. She fought the notion, thinking
that after all they had endured, and with
the war now so close to an end, surely they
would be able to enjoy the results of their
perseverance. And yet the feeling would not
leave, nor would sleep come to relieve her
of its burden.

Finally she rose and began dressing. The
hotel room seemed empty and oppressive
without Kurt, and the idea of tossing and
turning throughout the long hours that
remained of the night seemed unbearable.
She would go home so that if she had to
pass the rest of the night in restless insom-
nia, at least she could do it in familiar,
comfortable surroundings.

The streets outside were dark and deserted. It was past midnight now, and Mollie knew that this was not the best area of
town for a woman to be alone in late at
night, but she turned her steps toward the

Quality Hill area without a thought to the danger. Kurt had taken the buggy with him, thinking she would not be leaving until morning, when she would be able to hire a carriage. Though there were no such conveyances available at this hour, Mollie was glad to have the opportunity to walk and think anyway.

In an attempt to counteract her disturbing premonitions, she tried to imagine taking Kurt to meet her family after the war was ended. It would be awkward at first, she knew. Jason would probably try to be hospitable for her sake, although the strain of having a Union officer in his home would fill the air. And things would be even more volatile when Kurt first met John and Daniel. But surely, she thought, they would eventually be able to get beyond that.

Of course she would have to wait awhile before she could take him there, months perhaps, or maybe more, long enough for the flames of hatred to die down and for the wartime habits of fighting and killing instinctively to disappear. But it could happen, she insisted to herself, arguing against some hateful inner voice that kept telling her that such fantasies were laughably foolish. They were all good men, strong and reasonable, their lives shaped by worthwhile values . . .

Finding herself at the front door of her home, she let herself in, then eased the door closed behind her and locked it again. All the lamps were out, but she knew the way so well she didn't bother lighting even a candle. She was halfway across the foyer heading toward the stairs when a quiet voice spoke her name.

It was Jason, she realized in sudden excitement. They met at the door of the front parlor, where he had been dozing on a couch, waiting for her return. Mollie threw her arms around her brother's neck as if she had not seen him in months. The first words that tumbled from her lips were about her nephews.

"Have you heard from John and Daniel?" she asked urgently. "Are they both still alive? Are they all right?"

"I just came from seeing them about six hours ago," Jason announced. His smile was broad, filled with relief. "Somehow they managed to stay alive, although they looked like hell and their moods are none too good."

"I guess that's understandable," Mollie said. "Things must have been awful for them since that night at Maude's cabin."

"They said it was pretty rough, but they're

in a fairly safe hideout now, so they'll have a chance to rest and recover."

Mollie lit a lamp and the two of them settled on a couch to talk more comfortably now that the most urgent announcement had been made.

"Thank you for coming here to let me know," Mollie said, taking her brother's hands in both of hers. "I've worried about them every minute since I last saw them. I know that right now they might not be thinking many kindly thoughts about me, but I only did what I did because I love them so much, and I just wanted them to be safe."

"I know that, Mollie," Jason told her, "and so do the boys. And you'll be surprised to know that what you told them at Maude's that night has apparently had some effect."

"What do you mean?" Mollie asked.

"The boys want me to ask you about investigating the possibility of paroles for them," he announced. "Daniel, especially, is sick of this whole mess, and if there's any chance that he'll be allowed to walk away from it now and come on home, he'll be willing to take the chance. John's not as sure, but he is willing to hear what offers, if any, the Federals are making to the bush-whackers."

"It's been quite a long time since I've heard any talk of paroles," Mollie said apprehensively, "but I can find out easily enough what the policy is now. Kurt can find out for me, and he might even be able to help them in some way if John and Daniel are willing to accept his aid."

"I think they might," Jason said. "After all the years of hoping, the mess Sterling Price made of his invasion has been quite a revelation to everybody, including the bushwhackers. Given the chance, I think they might be a little more reasonable about things. Talking about fighting to the last man is one thing, but actually doing it is quite another matter."

"Just give me two or three days to find out what I can," Mollie told Jason. "Kurt has to be away for a while, but he should be back by then, and I'll talk to him as soon as he returns. I'm sure he'll do everything he can to help them out. He's like that, Jason. He's really a good man," she said earnestly.

"Well perhaps someday soon I'll have the opportunity to find that out for myself. He must have at least a couple of good points for you to love him as much as you do."

"Well, why don't you stay here and meet him?" Mollie suggested brightly. "You're not wanted for anything, and you are my brother. There's no reason why you shouldn't!"

"I promised the boys I'd head on back as soon as I talked to you," Jason explained. "They're short of food and medical supplies, and I told them I would try to smuggle a few things in to them. A couple of men in the cave where they're hiding are pretty bad off, and hardly a one of them doesn't have some sort of wound that needs tending to."

Just at the moment her most fervent prayers seemed about to be answered, all of Mollie's hopes were suddenly destroyed by her brother's words. "Cave?" she asked in alarm. "Did you say they're in a *cave*?"

"They're in one of those big caves in the hills between Independence and Lee's Summit," Jason said. "It's a good hiding place and they've used it dozens of times before."

"My God, Jason," Mollie moaned, stunned by the awful implications of the situation. "You've got to get to them in a hurry and tell them that they can't stay there, that they must leave immediately and go as far away as possible!"

"Why?" Jason asked. "What have you heard?"

For a few seconds she could not bring herself to speak, knowing that the moment she did she would be betraying the man she

loved. Kurt trusted her, fully and unques-
tioningly . . .

"Tell me, Mollie!" Jason demanded urgently. "No matter what it is, if the safety of
my boys is involved, you must tell me
everything. *You must, Mollie!*"

"They're riding out before dawn," she
began dully, "the Colorado company, Kurt's
company. He told me a little while ago that
one of his spies brought him some information about some bushwhackers hiding out
in a cave east of here. That's really all I
know, Jason. I swear to you —"

"Before dawn, you say?" Jason interrupted. "That means that if I leave now
there might still be time. Is there any food
in the house?"

"In the pantry," Mollie said. "Take all you
can carry, and I'll explain everything to
Ginny in the morning. But do hurry, Jason.
Tell them I'll get word to them when I find
something out about the possibility of
paroles, but for now they just have to get as
far away from here as they can. There are
too few of them left, and too many spies. It
will never be safe for them again."

"Damn you, Paul, you little weasel!" Kurt
Rakestraw growled.

"But they *were* here, Cap'n Rakestraw!"

Isaac Paul insisted. "I checked the ashes of that campfire over there, and the bedrock is still warm underneath. They were here, and just a little while ago, too. Somebody must have warned them."

They were standing in the main room of a large, dank cavern, the entrance of which was conveniently hidden behind a dense pine thicket. The stone floor of the twenty-by-forty chamber was littered with the considerable evidence that several men and horses had indeed found shelter here a short time before. Two passages led away from this main room, one due south, straight into the side of the hill, and another angling off to the southeast, but after a thorough search Rakestraw's men had pronounced them both quite empty.

"You promised you were going to watch them!" Rakestraw reminded Paul angrily. "And you said if they did leave, you would follow them."

"I was watching them, but I almost got found out!" Paul explained. "Two of them passed right by where I was, and I swear to God one of them looked just like Bloody Bill Anderson himself. After that I figured, hell, they're all shot up and worn out. It was nearly dark by then and it seemed to me they sure wouldn't be going noplace before morning. I was getting pretty hungry by then anyway, so I thought —"

"You were getting hungry!" Rakestraw scoffed. "I brought a hundred men, a whole company of United States cavalry, all the way out here for nothing because you were hungry!" He turned abruptly and strode away, knowing that if their conversation continued much longer he might not be able to resist the urge to knock Paul down.

Finally, convinced that there was no reason to stay inside any longer, Rakestraw headed back outside, and the men who had gone in with him began to follow him out. He followed the hidden, winding path through the pine thicket and emerged at last into the open, grassy area beyond. Most of his company was gathered there by this time, the men grumbling quietly among themselves about the situation.

A moment later the first sergeant, a burly, red-faced man named Mike Andrews, spotted Kurt and came over to make his report. "One of the scouts has found the bushwhackers' tracks leading east of here. He said there was about a dozen of them, and that the tracks are still fresh. No more than two or three hours old."

"Two or three hours is a long lead when you're dealing with these people," Rakestraw said grimly. "You and I both know that sometimes two or three *minutes* is enough for them to disappear completely."

"Yes, sir, but that was when they knew we were after them," the sergeant suggested. "They might not know that we're back here. They might have just decided to move on for some other reason."

The thought was an intriguing one, Rakestraw decided, and perhaps it was worth following up on. It was still fairly early in the morning, and his men and horses were fresh. Besides all that, Isaac Paul had mentioned that the bushwhackers in this group were in pretty bad shape. They had wounded men in their party, which would slow them down during a long flight, and the mere fact that they were tired and discouraged might make them ignore some of the routine precautions they might otherwise take.

"It's worth a shot, I guess," Rakestraw said at last. "Get the men mounted and we'll follow their trail for a while. I want six of our best scouts to stay at least a quarter mile ahead of the main column, and I want outriders spaced every hundred yards to the right and left of the trail. We don't want any surprises on this operation, Sergeant."

"Yes, sir. I'll take care of it," Andrews

promised as he turned to carry out his orders.

As they were preparing to leave, Isaac Paul sought Kurt out once again, sidling up to him hesitantly.

"I guess if you don't need me anymore, Cap'n . . ." Paul began.

Kurt turned his head, his brows furrowing in disapproval at the mere sight of the cowardly spy. "Are you getting hungry again, Paul?" he sneered.

"No, it's not that, Cap'n," Paul said, "but I just figured I wouldn't be much use to you when you go after them. I thought maybe I'd just start on back home now . . ."

"Well at least you're right about one thing," Kurt said. "You are useless."

"If you say so, Cap'n," Paul answered docilely. "But about the money . . . for the information . . ."

Rakestraw made it a practice to pay a standard fee of twenty dollars to his spies when they came to him with information of this sort, but he was in no mood to give Paul a cent today.

"I'll tell you what," Kurt said at last. "You haven't given us anything of any use yet, but if you want to come along with us and help us track this bunch down, I'll pay you two dollars a head for every one we kill or capture. And I'll pay you ten dollars a head for every one that you shoot personally."

Paul seemed to squirm. "Well, sir, I ain't no soldier, as you know yourself . . ." he stammered. "And this old rifle of mine, well, I dropped it last week and I think maybe the firing pin . . . I been meaning to have it fixed . . ."

"This might be a real good time for you to get out of my sight, you cowardly little bastard!" Kurt warned him. "And on the way home if you don't have anything better to do, you might spend some of the time thinking about how lucky you are to be going back with only empty pockets to show for the sloppy job you made of this!"

Quickly gauging Rakestraw's angry mood, Isaac Paul took the suggestion to heart and headed to where his horse was tied. By the time he had mounted up and started down the trail leading back to Independence, most of Rakestraw's men were also in the saddle, ready to begin the pursuit of the fleeing bushwhackers.

Rubbing his empty stomach with his free hand, Isaac Paul continued to curse his ill luck as he followed the meandering trail back toward Independence. It wasn't his fault, he reasoned, that the bushwhackers had taken off when they did. What was he supposed to do? Ride into their camp and try to talk them into staying on another day? That damned Federal captain might call him a coward, but where would he be without men like Paul who were willing to bring him information for a fee? And wasn't twenty dollars a small enough price to pay a man for risking his neck spying on the likes of George Todd and Bill Anderson?

Paul thought that his luck might have changed when he saw the wallet lying in the dust at the edge of the trail. This was the same route the soldiers had taken earlier to reach the cave, and it seemed like a stroke of poetic justice that must have caused one of them to lose his wallet along the way. He stopped his horse beside the find and grinned in anticipation when he spotted the corner of a greenback peeking out of the folding wallet. He stepped to the ground and reached down to pick it up.

"Hello, Isaac," a voice said casually from the brush a few feet away. Paul straightened up in alarm and suddenly found himself looking down the barrel of a rifle. "I thought that might be just the right sort of bait to get you stopped and out of the saddle," Jason Hartman said.

For an instant Paul was too stunned to

speak, but finally he asked, "What are you doing here, Hartman?"

"Well, for the past hour or more I've just been standing right here waiting for you," Jason replied calmly.

"What made you think I'd be coming past?"

"I saw you earlier riding in the other direction with those soldiers, and I figured you'd try to get out of the area as quick as you could after you led them to the cave. So I just stopped here and waited."

Jason's casual tone confused Paul, but somehow it seemed to stir more fear in him than if his captor had been bitter and hateful. Except for the gun he held leveled at Paul's chest, Jason's attitude was almost friendly.

"They're right behind me," Paul muttered hurriedly. "When they saw that the caves were empty they decided to head on back to Kansas City, and they're only about a quarter mile back right now."

"I doubt that," Jason said. "But even if it's true, it doesn't make any difference. This matter between us won't take but a minute."

"Please, Hartman," Paul muttered, realizing with sickening clarity what his captor had in mind for him. "I didn't shoot your old man. Remember, it wasn't me that pulled the trigger. And as for this business today, hell, I knew your boys and the others would already be gone by the time the soldiers got there. I just figured it was a good trick to make a few dollars. That's all."

"Don't beg, Isaac, because it's not going to make any difference," Jason told him. "Believe me, I take no pleasure in killing. I believe it's against God's commandments. But I also believe that there are certain wicked people who have abused the gift of life, and I'm certain that you are such a man. The world will be a better place after you're gone from it, Isaac."

"But you can't just —" Paul sobbed frantically.

"Yes I can," Jason said, squeezing the trigger even as he spoke.

The scouts reported back about every half hour, bringing Kurt Rakestraw the word that they were steadily gaining on their prey. It was a little unsettling to him to think that they might so easily overtake and kill these men, and he kept First Sergeant Andrews constantly busy checking on the outriders and making sure that every man in the company was fully alert to any sudden dangers.

By early afternoon, they had passed into

432

an area that, until recently, had been the exclusive domain of the bushwhackers. Early in the war the Union forces stationed nearby had learned how hazardous it could be to ride into the brushy hills to the south and east of Independence. Whole companies had been cut to ribbons there in '62 and '63, when Quantrill's band was at full strength and his men were still driven by the conviction that they could force their enemies from the state.

Things were different now, of course. Current intelligence placed the strength of the surviving bushwhacker bands at perhaps a third of their former numbers, and those who remained were discouraged, disillusioned, and hardly in any condition to mount the sort of resistance they once had. For these reasons alone Kurt Rakestraw decided to push on even when his company plunged into unknown territory and his scouts began reporting that the countryside ahead was about as rugged and impenetrable as any they had ever seen. In numerous places his outriders were forced to pull in and ride along with the main group because the brush on either side of the column was simply too thick to pass through, but each time they fanned out again as soon as possible to guard the vulnerable flanks of the company.

A ripple of excitement and tension raced through the main column when the first few shots sounded a short distance ahead. The Union soldiers, veterans all, automatically began to check the loads in their rifles and scan the brush on either side of them, alert for any unexpected dangers. Kurt Rakestraw quickly ordered additional men out on the flanks, and then he continued to lead the main column forward, though at a more cautious pace.

The firing was sporadic, indicating that his scouts had been confronted by only a few of the enemy, and moments later a lone rider came galloping back to confirm that fact.

"They caught us with our pants down, sir," the breathless rider admitted, "and we lost two men in the first volley. But it looks like there are only half a dozen of them at most. My guess is the worst of their wounded have stayed behind to buy some time for the rest of them to get away."

"What's the lay of the land where they are?" Rakestraw asked hurriedly.

"They picked a good spot," the scout reported. "They're scattered out on both sides of the trail at a spot where the hills rise steep in both places. It's not going to be an easy job to circle around them, but we'll lose a lot of men if we decide to charge them straight on. They've got a good field of fire in front and plenty of rocks to use for cover."

Judging by the facts that were presented to him, Rakestraw decided that a charge was out of the question. He wasn't willing to sacrifice the lives it would take to rout these fugitives from their positions. That left him with only one alternative.

The first sergeant had been nearby when the scout made his report, and Kurt turned to him now to issue the necessary orders.

"I want you to send about fifty men straight up the trail to keep these fellows pinned down where they are," Kurt instructed. "But tell them no heroics. Their orders are to say behind the best cover they can find and to keep up a steady fire. Then break the remainder of the men up into two groups of twenty-five men each. One will turn left and try to gain the high ground to the west of the bushwhackers, the other will swing around to the right and try to get behind them.

"Tell the leader of the second group," he continued, "that if he sees any sign that some of the bushwhackers have pushed on to the south, he is to pursue them with all possible haste. If this is a plan to delay us so that some of them can escape, I want to have at least part of the company continuing the pursuit while the rest of us pause to clean this pocket of resistance out."

Andrews acknowledged each order with a nod, agreeing that it was the wisest plan of action given their situation. Then, when Rakestraw was finished, he said, "With your permission, sir, I'll lead the group to the right."

"Fine, Sergeant," Kurt agreed. "But in case we stay separated for the rest of the day, I want you to get those men out of here before dark. I don't care if you're in sight of the enemy when the time comes, give up the chase and get out of these hills while you still have daylight to do it with."

"Yes, sir," the sergeant said, tossing Rakestraw a quick salute before turning his horse aside.

After considering the matter for a moment, Kurt decided to remain on the trail with the main body of his troops. After the two smaller groups Andrews had designated split away on their separate missions, Kurt began to lead the remainder of his unit cautiously forward toward the sound of gunfire ahead.

Finally, when they had proceeded a few

hundred yards farther, Kurt ordered his half of the men to dismount and move ahead on foot, knowing that they could not find any adequate cover for themselves otherwise. The rest of the men remained on horseback to guard their back trail and to serve as reserves in case the fighting became more heated than expected.

When Kurt reached a spot where he could survey the enemy position, he saw that the rebels had, indeed, chosen well. They were scattered out amidst a tangle of granite which had, sometime in the past, sheared off a steep rock face above them. The trail had become so narrowed by the rubble that two horses abreast could not have passed through it, which made the prospect of a frontal assault extremely dangerous.

The bushwhackers were firing only occasionally now, partly to conserve their ammunition, no doubt, but also because of the heavy fire Rakestraw's men were beginning to throw in their direction. They changed their positions frequently, scrambling among the rocks like lizards, popping up now and then at unpredictable spots to toss off a shot and to ensure that none of their opponents were slipping in toward them.

It would be a waiting game now, Kurt knew, until the groups he had sent around to the sides reached the objectives he had set for them. But once the men he had sent to the left reached the high ground above this bottleneck in the trail, the scattered bushwhackers in the rocks ahead would be easy targets.

At first Kurt was merely confused when he began to hear the crack of gunfire on the hillside to the left. It was too soon for the men on that side to be in a position to fire. Then his confusion turned to alarm when yet another series of shots sounded out straight behind them down the trail.

Something was going terribly wrong, Kurt realized. Somehow, despite all his precautions, he had been drawn into a bushwhacker ambush, but during those first few moments, it was impossible to determine the scope or dimensions of the disaster.

When the first few rifle shots sounded from the rocky heights above him, Kurt began to realize that his men were just as exposed and vulnerable to gunfire from that direction as the bushwhackers he was after would have been if his men had been able to gain the high ground.

"Pull back!" he called out to his troops, some of whom were already falling victim to the deadly fire from above. There didn't seem to be that many riflemen up there, but their aim was true and their targets were many. Firing blindly toward the heights as they ran, his men began to scramble back down the trail, helping their fallen companions when they could as they struggled desperately to flee the hailstorm of bullets. At one point, when Kurt stopped to help a wounded man to his feet, he felt a searing pain low in the middle of his back, but there was no time to stop and examine the wound. He found that he was still able to stagger on, so he did so, dragging the wounded man along.

When at last the survivors reached the spot where they had left their horses, they found themselves immediately entangled in yet another desperate skirmish. As many as three or four dozen bushwhackers had attacked the group of men that Rakestraw had left behind on the trail, bloodying them severely and slaughtering scores of horses before finally withdrawing to regroup and reload. By the time they attacked again, most of Rakestraw's men had been able to seek some scant cover and repel the charge, but their numbers were dwindling rapidly and by this time practically all of their horses had either been killed or scattered.

From the west, through the entangling brush that covered the steep hillside, Kurt continued to hear the steady rattle of gunfire. The men he had sent in that direction seemed to have been caught off guard just as he had, and he knew that it was senseless to hope that any of them could come to his aid at this point.

"Men, we've got no place to run so we'll hold the ground we've got," Kurt shouted to the troops around him during a brief lull in the shooting. "We've known all along the kind of men we were up against, and we all knew that someday it could come to this. But I know there's not a coward among you, and the time has come to make them pay in blood for every foot of this trail they try to take away from us."

The third and final charge by the bushwhackers lacked the ferocity and determination of the previous two, and Rakestraw's men easily held their ground. It was obvious that the attackers had also suffered heavy losses, and now that the Union troops were dug in and waiting, any further direct attacks would be costly and pointless.

Most of the shooting had stopped by the time First Sergeant Andrews reached the scene with his small detachment of men. They alone had remained untouched by the ambush, and the first sergeant quickly dispersed them on all sides of their bloodied comrades.

Kurt Rakestraw tried to rise to his feet when he saw the first sergeant riding toward him, but the movement caused sharp spears of pain to rip throughout his body, and a wave of dizziness overpowered him. Unable to even raise his arms to break his fall, he toppled forward limply across the rock he had been using for cover. Strong hands lifted him, but already his senses were beginning to dull and he realized that consciousness was slipping away from him. He tried to speak, to instruct Andrews to get the surviving men to safety as quickly as possible, but his tongue felt thick and numb and the sounds that issued from his throat were gutteral and unintelligible.

"The captain's hit!" he heard a voice call out, as if from a great distance away. The vague shape that loomed above him was quickly being swallowed up in the growing darkness. "Henderson! Get over here and see what you can do for him!"

From somewhere deep in the recesses of Kurt's mind a woman's face appeared, her features finely formed and delicate, sur- rounded by flowing blonde hair which seemed to shimmer like finely spun gold. He felt as if he could almost feel her soft fingers on his face, and the smile on her lips gave him an immediate feeling of peace and happiness. It was remarkable, he thought. How could she possibly have found him way out here?

Daniel Hartman crouched in the brush no more than a dozen yards from the nearest Union soldier, dabbing with his sleeve at the gash on the side of his head which he had suffered when his injured horse pitched him out of the saddle. He felt safe enough despite his close proximity to the enemy, knowing that at this point the Federals weren't likely to go out searching for anybody. After the beating they had just taken, their only thought would be to get back to a safer area as quickly as they possibly could.

It had been a brilliant ambush, one of George Todd's best, Daniel thought, and if there had been time to round up additional men and supplies, they could have completely annihilated the Coloradans. As it turned out, though, most of the bushwhackers had been left with empty guns after the third charge, and by then their numbers had been reduced so much that there was no alternative but to withdraw and scatter.

But they had made their point, and Daniel was filled with a sense of pride to realize that even now they could still whip the best that the Federals could throw at them. And yet he also felt a sense of sadness in knowing that this fight had probably doomed whatever hopes he and his brother might have had for a parole before the war's end. When Jason Hartman had come to Wyatt's Cave in the early morning hours to warn them, he had told his sons about his conversation with Mollie, and he had also told them who would be leading the enemy troops who were coming after them.

This was Kurt Rakestraw's outfit, and after such a resounding defeat, he wasn't likely to look favorably on the idea of a parole for any of the bushwhackers — even those related to the woman he loved.

Daniel became more alert when he heard the sound of footsteps on the loose gravel of the nearby trail. A few minutes earlier he had heard an enemy soldier stop somewhere in the vicinity, and now it seemed that another was coming to join him.

"Andrews says to come on back," Daniel heard one of the men tell the other. "We're pulling out. They've made litters for the worst of the wounded, and the rest will ride on what horses they could round up. But it looks like those of us who are still in one piece will be walking back."

"What about the dead?" the other man

asked. "Are we going to just leave them here?"

"For the time being I don't guess we've got any choice. Maybe we can come back for them tomorrow after we've got some reinforcements and some more horses."

"Well the captain better figure out something," the second man grumbled. "None of us is willing to let our friends just lie here and rot!"

"The captain?" the first man exclaimed. "Haven't you heard yet? The captain's dead! He caught one in the back and he bled to death just a little while ago."

"Damn!" his companion exclaimed. "He was the best officer I've ever been under. Damn!"

The voices of the two men began to fade as they walked away to rejoin their unit.

Damn is right! Daniel thought as he considered his Aunt Mollie and the impact this news would have on her. It would be a long time before any of them would be able to convince her that she hadn't murdered the man she loved as surely as if she had held the gun and fired the bullet that killed him.

Chapter Eighteen

May, 1865

Jason called out before he reached the camp so his sons would not be alarmed when they heard him approaching. He held a cloth sack of food slung over his left shoulder, and in his right hand he carried a rifle.

John and Daniel were sitting beside their tiny campfire, idly feeding it twigs and leaves so it would not die out completely. They had little to say when their father laid his burden on the ground and sat down to join them.

The camp was located only about two miles from Jason's farm, but it was situated deep in a secluded patch of woods which even the local residents seldom entered. The brothers had been staying there for more than two weeks now, figuring that since no place was truly safe for them anymore, they might as well be as close to their family as was practical under the circumstances.

"There's more news," Jason told them. "The papers are saying that Quantrill's been killed over in Kentucky."

"So that's where he got off to," John said. "He wouldn't tell anybody what his plans were before he left. That's why hardly anybody agreed to go with him. Most figured he'd slipped a cog and was headed off to do something crazy."

"Well, I guess they were right," Jason said. "The article said that before he died he told the authorities he had planned to make his way to Washington to kill Lincoln."

"It's a little late for that, I guess," Daniel commented wryly. "That fellow Booth beat him to the punch by more than a month." Then, turning to his father, he asked, "Did the paper say anything about Frank James? He went along, you know. He left with Quantrill."

"It mentioned the names of several others who were killed or captured, but Frank's wasn't among them. Maybe that means he's all right."

"Maybe," Daniel said without enthusiasm. For nearly six months now, ever since the battle with Rakestraw's Coloradans, the Hartman brothers had been almost constantly on the run. Occasionally they joined up with others of their kind for a few days, or perhaps a week at a time, but most often it was just the two of them. George Todd was dead now, killed in October near Independence a mere two days after his last big triumph. And two weeks after that Bloody Bill Anderson had met his end, cut down in a Union ambush in the south part of Ray County. It was said that his head had been chopped off and hung on a pole, where it remained for days before somebody finally had the courage and decency to take it down and bury it.

Even the war itself had ended for most of the combatants by now. Lee had surrendered at Appomattox more than a month ago, and during the ensuing weeks practically every Confederate commander from the Carolinas to Texas had followed suit, surrendering their colors and disbanding their troops.

But in official circles, the debate continued about how to deal with the remaining scattered bands of rebels and bushwhackers, especially in Missouri. Many wanted to simply continue the no-quarter policy and hunt them down to the last man, but others maintained that they, like everyone else, should be given the chance to return to a peaceful life now that the great rebellion was ended.

John and Daniel both wanted desperately to turn themselves in and go home, but their former comrades who had done so had met with mixed results. Some had been killed outright by the angry military units they surrendered to, and others had been imprisoned and held for trial on various criminal charges.

In fact, a number of former bushwhackers who remained at large had become little more than common criminals while hiding behind a facade of continuing the rebellion. They wandered the less populous areas of the state, taking what they wanted and killing whom they choose to kill, as they always had. Arch Clement, who now bore the nickname of "The Butcher of Centralia," led such a band, but neither John nor Daniel had any desire to join him. They had fought to the end, as they had always vowed to do, but now that the end was here, they only wanted to live in peace like everyone else.

"I'm going to Kansas City tomorrow," Jason announced to his sons. "I got a letter from your Aunt Mollie, and she's finally got me an appointment to see the adjutant general of the Western Military District. I'm going to ask him to personally write out a safe conduct so the two of you can go to

Kansas City and turn yourselves in. And if he won't do it, I'll try somebody else."

"Do you really think it will do any good, Daddy?" John asked. "Do you think it will keep us alive long enough to be paroled?"

"It's worth a try, son," Jason said. "You can't just keep on living out here like this, like wild animals in the woods. Your mother and I want you with us. We want you home again."

John looked at his brother, and the two of them seemed to debate the issue without ever speaking a word. Then finally Daniel nodded his head, and John turned to his father, saying, "All right then, we'll try it. Whatever happens, it couldn't be much worse than this."

Leaving the sack of food on the ground, Jason rose to leave. "I'll tell your mother to send Ben or Cassie out with another sack of grub in another day or two," he told them. "You two take care of yourselves until I get back. And have faith, boys. Have faith that it will finally all turn out right."

Daniel pitched a few more twigs on the fire as Jason turned and walked into the darkness. Not speaking, the two brothers sat gazing into the flames as the sound of their father's footsteps faded into the distance.

ABOUT THE AUTHOR

Over the past thirty-five years **Greg Hunt** has published over twenty Western, frontier, and historical novels. A lifelong writer, he has also worked over the decades as a newspaper reporter, photographer and editor, a technical and freelance writer, a tech project manager, and a marketing analyst. Greg served in Vietnam as an intelligence agent and Vietnamese linguist with the 101st Airborne Division and 23rd Infantry Division.

"Writing fiction has always been my true obsession," said Greg. "I tried to give it up a couple of times when things got rough, but it always kept its grip on me until I finally realized that I could never not be a writer."

Greg currently lives in the Memphis area with his wife of twenty-six years, Vernice.